M000217139

Aventurine and the Reckoning

Aventurine and the Reckoning

AN AVENTURINE MORROW THRILLER

Anne Britting Oleson

Encircle Publications
Farmington, Maine U.S.A.

Encircle editor: Cynthia Brackett-Vincent
Cover design: Deirdre Wait
Cover images © Getty Images

Published by:

Encircle Publications
PO Box 187
Farmington, ME 04938

info@encirclepub.com
http://encirclepub.com

For my friend of long standing,
Karen Girvan,
1958–2019

A woman who loved books and adventure,
and who is deserving of far more than
this little book about adventure.

Aventurine and the Reckoning

AN AVENTURINE MORROW THRILLER

Part I

Paul

Sometimes I think:
always look over your shoulder.
Then I forget.

—*Aventurine Morrow*

One

"Take Paul with you," Micheline suggested. She lit a cigarette. She had only recently begun smoking again, after quitting once Paul was born.

It was late. Maybe early. We'd both had far too much to drink.

Outside the windows, the light was that nebulous silver halfway between night and day: the time when trees were ghosts and everything else masqueraded as something it was not—or perhaps was revealed as what it truly was. Unnerved, I dragged my eyes away from the windows and flicked on another light. I watched the smoke from Mick's cigarette curl up toward the high ceiling of the kitchen in her enormous house, the house that was far too big for her, that echoed far too much. I had not realized just how much loss could echo. I splayed my fingers on the cold granite work top between us, shifting on my barstool.

Micheline turned her head, her cap of golden hair the first thing I saw in her reflection in the French doors leading to the veranda. Despite the wavering half-light, it was way too dark out there, as though dawn would never come. Hell, the entire world was too damned dark.

"I don't know what to do with him. About him. Everything I say is just wrong." She took a long drag on her cigarette, playing with the package on the table between us. L&M long lights. With filters,

1

as though that made any kind of difference. When she looked up at me through the smoke, her eyes were shadowed. "Maybe he'll talk to you." Her tone was desperate, the sound of a woman, a mother, who had one last card in the hole and was now drawing it out.

I waved her suggestion, like the smoke from her cigarette, away.

"He's always been close to you," she pressed. Beyond that strong hint of anxiety lay a hint of—jealousy?—in her voice, and it occurred to me just how hard this was for her to say. She reached out a hand to grasp my forearm. "Please, Aventurine."

My sister looked haggard, fine lines between her brows and around her mouth, bruisy bags beneath her eyes. To be fair, she'd looked this way for months now, since the news of the flotsam of the *Màquina de los Vientos* had reached us. I wondered if I looked haggard, too; we *were* identical twins, after all. But Shep had not been my husband.

Paul was haggard, too, his hair longer than I was used to, and unkempt. He was uncommunicative when we checked in at the kiosk at Terminal E. He fumbled with his passport, swore, tried to slot it into the machine again. Until that morning, I had not seen him in months—not since the memorial service, after which he'd dropped everything and taken off cross-country to help deliver a college friend to a new job in Spokane. When I'd leaned in for the hug before we'd boarded the shuttle to Logan, he had seemed distant, stiff: someone who had forgotten what closeness we'd always shared—what closeness even *was*.

I felt his confusion, his pain, his *differentness*, like a switchblade between my ribs. He'd always been quirky, a spacial thinker, empathetic: he was the one to come home with stories of elderly dogs surrendered to the shelter, knowing his parents could never resist him at his most tragic, knowing those elderly dogs would live out their days under his care. I'd make my flying visits to Waterboro every summer or on holidays and meet a new member of Paul's menagerie. I loved this kid as though he were my own, recognizing so much of me in him. He wasn't my own, though, I had to remind myself sternly. He was Micheline's and Shep's child.

Now he was a fatherless child. I bit back the impatience I felt whenever I had to travel with anyone, because this trip was special, and, as Micheline so desperately hoped, might be just the thing to bring Paul back to himself.

Take him with you, Micheline had said, that night, months ago now, when we'd gotten so drunk. She had never asked that of me before, in all the years I'd been free-lancing. But we had never been in this situation before. That night she had held my gaze, her face my mirror, while to my right, our twin reflection had wavered and broken up in the early morning window. *Please.* Her voice had cracked.

Paul and I cleared security with hours of waiting ahead.

"Hungry?"

Paul shrugged, brushing his hair from his eyes. "Yeah."

Directly ahead were the fast food joints. Along with the signs overhead. *London 3260 miles.* I steered him away from those, to the left, down toward the restaurant closest to our gate.

"We'll sit," I said decisively. "Have a real meal."

"They're going to feed us on the plane, aren't they?"

I slewed him a glance. "Airplane food, Paul. Airplane food. Only the dessert is good, and that's because it's made almost entirely of sugar."

It had always been a neurotic move of mine, to go to this particular restaurant and have their overpriced fish and chips before I flew to the U.K., mainly because it gave me a baseline for the specialty: no fish and chips in the U.K. would ever fall this low. Even the overpriced bit didn't bother me, because each time I'd flown to Heathrow, it had been on assignment or spec. Research. Thus, tax-deductible.

Paul ordered a beer and a burger from the waitress in starched black and white. He had downed the lager by the time the food arrived, and ordered another.

"Jet lag's going to be a bitch," I reminded him.

"I just want to go to sleep," he said. He slowed down, however, and the second beer lasted as long as the hamburger and fries did. I just drank water, knowing I'd get dehydrated, knowing nerves would keep me running to the ladies' room anyway. I was not a good flyer; I had no idea whether Paul was.

The fish was doughy and undercooked. The fries were okay. Paul finished his and reached across for mine. He'd always done that. I'd always let him. At least that much hadn't changed.

As we taxied down the night runway punctuated with its varicolored lights, I noticed Paul, from the corner of my eye, surreptitiously patting down his pockets: shirt, pants, jacket. My initial fear was *passport*—had he misplaced it already? Years of traveling, and I still checked mine obsessively.

"Front pocket of your backpack?" Mine, I knew, was in my cross-body bag, tucked down by my side, but I reached in and touched it anyway. A talisman.

The plane was picking up speed on the darkened runway, the engine's roar building, the tiny guide lights beside us a blur.

"Gum," he said, indicating his ears.

Mine were popping already.

Stupid, I know, but I had a tiny package of gummy bears in the bag, and I fished them out. Gummy bears had been Paul's favorite as a kid, and I'd always been well-stocked on my visits—*don't tell your mother*, I'd whisper, and he'd nod conspiratorially. He'd then save out the orange ones—my favorite—and sneak them back to me.

Now I handed them over. Haribo, the best kind. Paul stared at the package in his palm for a moment, and then, suddenly, he laughed. The first time he'd laughed since we'd met up outside the bus station this morning. The sound was rusty, as from disuse: this might have been the first time he had laughed in a year.

Two

In the cemetery on the Fox Hill Road, up beyond the house we lived in as kids, under the whispering boughs of the giant white pine, a tall monument cut of some reddish stone leans drunkenly, thrown off by the roots snaking beneath it.

Sacred to the memory of Captain Eleazar J. Wheeler, it reads on the flat surface below where the stone tapers to a spire. *Lost at sea, February 18, 1846.*

I had often wondered about the nature of an empty grave, of the family who, having no body to bury, erects a monument to their heartbreak. Did they visit the stone in their grief? Because they could not bring themselves to visit the sea, the monstrous depths which had taken their father, brother, son. It must have ached somewhere, like the phantom pain of an amputation. After February 18, 1846, Eleazar Wheeler became an itch his family could not scratch.

We had grown up near that stone and that cemetery, Micheline and I. Unconcerned then with ghosts, we had played among the stones, climbed the pine, thrown cones at one another while shrieking with laughter. Ghouls, both of us, playing our games among the dead. Karma had caught up to us at last.

• •

I learned of Shep's plan from a phone call while I was finishing up a story in Juneau, a follow-up to the book of several years previous.

"I never thought he was serious," Micheline repeated, probably for the fifth or tenth time. "I always thought it was a kind of pipe dream." She was keeping her voice low, no doubt because Shep was somewhere in the house, somewhere near, and she didn't want to be overheard. Her words ended on the tiniest quaver.

His wanting to sail the *Màquina* around the world single-handed was news to me. "This doesn't sound like the Shep we know and love," I agreed. He had frequently plotted and sailed long trips with friends, sometimes including a teen-aged Paul, though in the previous couple of seasons, he had navigated port-to-port up and down the East Coast solo.

He had bought the larger sailboat, the *Màquina de los Vientos*, replacing a smaller boat he'd given to Paul, upon his early retirement from Osterman Brothers, where he'd accrued his *nth* million as a director. It had suited him, taking us out on day sails whenever I visited, his face reddened by sun above his open-necked shirt. Shep liked playing the captain, and Paul adored playing first mate. I'd never seen my brother-in-law happier than when he was hauling away on the sheets and guys. Even so, he was a careful sailor, cautious about winds and waves and possible weather. The same caution that had enabled him to last so long in the investment world played out on the *Màquina*.

"He's charted it out," Micheline said. "I've seen the charts spread out all over his desk in the study. He's researching provisions. He's ordered a better radio and navigation equipment."

This did indeed sound serious.

"He wants to leave from Southampton in the United Kingdom."

That had, for some reason, sounded ominous to me. "Southampton?"

"His grandparents were from Southampton."

I hadn't known that, but that was not what was nagging at me.

There was something buried in my memory, something unsavory I knew about Southampton, but which I couldn't bring to the surface. I had finished our conversation and slipped the phone into my pocket, still anxious without really knowing why. It wasn't until I got back to my own computer that I looked it up: the *Titanic* had sailed from Southampton on April 10, 1915.

Tonight Paul and I flew through the dark sky, several miles above the North Atlantic. Even though the blind was down, Paul had opted to take the middle instead of the window seat. He hadn't told me why, but I could well imagine that his relationship with the ocean was not a comfortable one. The *Màquina de los Vientos* had lost all radio contact somewhere near Bermuda, on the last leg of the Atlantic crossing. The weather had been fine, with fair winds and no storms on the horizon, Shep having chosen to make the journey well before hurricane season began. There had been no distress call over the radio. No one had heard from Shep after that last radio message. A merchant vessel had come across a field of debris a day or two later: a cooler, some buoys, a life jacket with the name of the boat stenciled on it. The life raft had not been found.

Three

The plan was to spend a few days in London, my favorite city, before we headed up to York on the train, then eventually back down to Southampton, visiting the boatyard and the music festival. Paul had never been to London—my sister and her husband had preferred the Mediterranean, where the sea was blue and the sun was warm. But when I asked my nephew what he'd like to see in this, the largest city in Europe, he only shrugged.

I'd persuaded, by means of a small coin, the desk clerk at the hotel near King's Cross to let us into our rooms early, mostly so we could dump our cases and I could wash my face. I opted to change out of my jeans and into a skirt, too, my clothes feeling grubby on my skin after the flight. After that I slipped down the corridor and knocked on Paul's door.

When he finally answered, he was rubbing sleep from his eyes, and rubbing licks into his already shaggy hair. He looked heartbreakingly young.

"You shouldn't have gone to sleep," I admonished. "You'll be all turned around. You've always got to stay up until your regular bedtime. You know that."

"I'm not twelve," he shot back. "You know that."

He'd always had a quick verbal volley, but today his words were tinged with something I didn't recognize. Some sort of unfocused

9

anger. I recoiled slightly and bit my lip. "Sorry." Over his shoulder I could see the contents of his suitcase strewn over the bed, the chair, onto the carpet. "Get your coat. We'll walk. If you see anything you want to look at, we'll stop."

Paul fell into step beside me after locking the door. Once outside, it was only a matter of a few steps along the park to the Euston Road, the King's Cross St. Pancras tube stop further down. We took the Underground to Victoria and climbed up out of the station into the watery sunshine, and, taking our bearings from the tower of Big Ben, headed toward Westminster. We could visit the things Paul had heard of, read of, I reasoned. We threaded our way through the jostling crowds, past a group taking selfies with the oversized Winston Churchill. The wind coming up off the river was fitful and gusty, and my hair, longer than I was used to, tumbled around my face; I shoved it impatiently back. We turned back and maneuvered through the throngs, past the carts touting flags and bags and T-shirts, between suited men and women with tight expressions, on their way to do government business. At the far end of the bridge, the Eye spun its lazy circle against the blue sky patched with clouds. Beside me, Paul had his hands stuffed into his pockets and his shoulders hunched.

"I used to stand out here and recite Wordsworth's 'Composed Upon Westminster Bridge' to myself," I told him, trying to instill in him some sense of the magic. It was rough going. "'Earth has not any thing to show more fair,' and all that. I thought I was pretty hot stuff—and then I found out the sonnet is on the wall inside the Eye entrance. It felt sort of cheapened after that."

"Why? Because the masses have the same taste as you?" The words could have been sharper; it sounded as though Paul were trying to reclaim his old laughing sarcastic self, and not quite making it.

We walked in silence for a few moments. I wracked my brain, trying to remember the other thirteen lines of the Wordsworth sonnet; my memory was a bit spotty, and somehow that made me sad. *Dull would he be of soul.* I felt dull, and sluggish. "Breakfast?" I asked at last. My stomach was growling. The hard cob and bitter coffee on the plane had been hours ago. "Or do you want to wait?" When I glanced over my shoulder, back at Big Ben, the clock in its shrouded tower read nearly eleven.

Paul only shrugged.

Near the center of the bridge we stopped and leaned against the parapet, looking eastward. Below us one of the river tour boats was loading, the passengers all in brightly colored windbreakers, jockeying for seats on the upper deck. I saw the waving umbrella of their tour guide. The river was ruffled by the wind, white tips on dirty green waves. The silence between us was not companionable, but rather heavy, laden with the darkness pressing down on my nephew. He almost pulsed with it; I could almost smell it on him. The darkness that was the loss of his father. I'm not certain what Micheline had in mind when she had begged me to take him on this research trip. To get him away, from their home, from the life which Shep formerly shared? The trip with his college roommate to Spokane—if that hadn't helped, how would a stretch being hauled about the U.K. with his old aunt?

He's always been close to you, Aventurine. I imagined Micheline's pained, anxious eyes, so much like my own.

"Here's the plan," I said at last. "I've got to head on up to York on Thursday, to begin interviewing Genevieve Smithson on Friday. You're welcome to come, or stay. It's your vacation, after all. I'm the one who has to work."

Despite the weakness of the morning sunlight, Paul dropped his sunglasses onto his nose and looked along the river toward the next bridge, and the one beyond that. "I don't want to spoil your trip," he said, his voice hard to hear above the traffic behind us. "I don't know why you agreed to bring me. I don't know why Mom asked you to."

My turn to shrug. "Your mother loves you," I offered helplessly. The wind was cold on my cheeks.

He made a wry face, then nodded, once. "I know."

I took a deep breath, dove right in. "She's worried about how your father's death has affected you."

Paul jerked back as though he'd been slapped. Then he adjusted the sunglasses again, and turned away toward Big Ben, as though imperative he find out the time. Still under repair, the clock face was surrounded by scaffolding, the chimes silenced. I remained still, but I could sense his uneven breathing.

I had to say it. "Have you thought about talking to someone?"

His breathing became more labored, as though he were trying to control his emotions, his response. Having jabbed at him with words like so many needles, I gave him as much privacy as I could, my eyes on the river. The tour boat, now fully loaded, was easing away from the pier slowly, its wake oily. I could hear a voice over a loudspeaker, though the words were indistinguishable.

Someone bumped into me, apologized, moved on. I glanced around. The sunlight was growing stronger. Another tour group, led by a woman waving a furled pink umbrella over her head, surged past. Beyond them, a man in a dark jacket turned away and wandered toward the south bank. I took a second look. There was something familiar about the set of his shoulders, the way he walked. Then he was lost in the crowd and I shook my head. Imagining things.

"I've thought about it," Paul said. His tone had a finality to it, and I decided it was best to drop the subject for the time being. I'd ask Micheline the next time we spoke.

Ships, towers, domes, theatres, and temples lie/ Open unto the fields, and to the sky. "Let's walk," I suggested again. My head hurt. "I could use something to drink." Coffee. Tea. London ale. By this point I didn't even care.

• •

We ended up dodging our way through the crowds lined up for a spin on the Eye, then threading along the Queen's Walk past street performers, skateboarders, and the likes as we searched for a drink that would suit. At a cart, Paul settled for a lemonade, while a bit further along I plumped for a cup of black coffee to keep me from flagging. Then we continued to walk. The clouds thinned, then disappeared altogether. We passed a pair of buskers doing a passable job on "Hey Jude," and Paul tossed a pound into their open case. We did not stop. He seemed driven, and I had steps to make up on my Fitbit anyway. The coffee warmed me inside, but did nothing for the headache.

Once past Waterloo Bridge, the crowds lessened slightly. I was starting to feel the difference in our ages—Paul plowed along as though the hounds of hell were following, and my shins ached. Too soon my coffee was empty, and I found a trash can to dump the cup. We passed the National Theatre, went under the Blackfriars railway bridge just as a train rumbled through. Ahead, the Globe Theater—the flag flew over the thatch. When I asked if Paul wanted to stop and take a look, he shook his head.

"Too crowded."

London as a whole was too crowded, but I said nothing.

Eventually we made it as far as Southwark Cathedral, and I insisted we stop and visit the Refectory. Not because I was particularly hungry, but because I was tired and jet-lagged. I handed my nephew some cash, and slipped off through the soothing dimness to the ladies'.

When I'd returned, he'd brought a laden tray to a table overlooking the garden. He'd purchased an Americano for himself, and a latté for me; he'd also chosen scones with jam and cream for both of us. I settled in, facing the courtyard; aside from a couple at the far side of the room bent over a guidebook, we had the coffee shop to ourselves. All sounds, appropriately, were muted.

"Sorry," he said, ducking his head to his coffee. He had spread clotted cream over his scone, then jam.

"You're a Philistine," I told him, indicating my own scone, slathered in the proper order: jam, then cream on top. "And that's the only thing you have to apologize to me for."

The corner of Paul's mouth quirked. I sighed, watching him eat his scone gingerly, leaning forward over his plate in an attempt to keep the crumbs from cascading down his shirtfront. He had a bit of his father in his face, with Shep's wide forehead, and green eyes. Other than that, Paul was definitely a member of our family, his nose and cheeks inherited from Micheline's and my genes. His wavy blond hair, usually cut short, was a bit shaggy and unkempt now, but it was definitely ours. Both Micheline and I had to keep our hair cut severely, to obviate its bushiness. He had grown from a handsome boy to a handsome man, had Paul; he had the best of the genetic material from both sides of his family.

I leaned back in my wooden chair, studying the beams of the ceiling high overhead. I wished I could help him. I hoped that his grief over his father's death should eventually work to a balance with his former good temper. His sense of humor. His wryly sarcastic self. This new withdrawn Paul was shocking to me. I looked over at his handsome face quickly, and then, fearing he'd sense my anxiety, turned my gaze upward again.

The Refectory was filling up. A family with three small excited children entered, and took a table close by; the high childish voices echoed as they first laughed, then began to bicker. By mutual silent agreement—we still understood each other that much, anyway—Paul and I finished up our coffees and scones, brought our tray back to the counter, and headed into the cathedral proper. I wanted to show Paul the Shakespeare window, and the miraculous carving of the reclining Will, hanging out before the relief of the cathedral itself. The nature of the place dictated that the cathedral would be much more quiet than the tea room. Maybe it was Paul's demeanor, or jet lag, but I suddenly felt the need for more quiet. *Too many people.* I was generally fairly sociable, but right now I knew how he felt.

The glowing Shakespeare window, casting prisms at our feet, was just as glorious as I remembered, though I hadn't been in to look at it in years. Despite the sign at the entrance asking one pound for a photo permit, Paul slid his cell phone out of his pocket and surreptitiously took a picture.

"You're breaking the rules," I stage-whispered.

He raised an eyebrow. "Like you never have."

"I'm a totally morally upright person," I said, feigning shock.

From somewhere I heard the echo of a short laugh. I glanced around, but there was no one anywhere near us. The sounds amidst the stonework carried strangely.

"Don't lie in a cathedral," Paul said. "Even God is laughing at you."

I flipped him off.

He snapped a picture.

In that moment I so wanted to throw my arms around him, to grab onto that glimmer of my old Paul, and to hold on with everything I had. How I loved that kid.

Four

For dinner Wednesday evening we walked southeast, down into Farringdon and toward Smithfield. The sun threw long shadows, the tops of roofs glowing, the streets below dimming. Pigeons strutted everywhere, plucking at bits of jetsam in the gutters. Every now and again Paul would cluck to the birds at our feet, but they made no answer, save to protest among themselves as they scattered before us.

I was feeling my way along the alternately busy and leafy roads as though tracing a finger on the map in my mind, trying to remember the route. I hadn't been down here since a dinner I'd had with Mick and Shep several years ago, at the end of my research journey with Mobius, the subject of my fourth book. I led Paul past the Farringdon underground station. He looked up at The Castle hopefully, but the crowds there were spilling out noisily onto the corner. The air smelled of cigarettes and hops. A panda car, siren wailing, muscled its way past. We walked on, Paul with his hands jammed in his pockets, shoulders hunched, as if he were mindful of the Smithfield fires of Bloody Mary—though I was fairly certain he had no idea where we were, either geographically or historically.

There had been a time when Paul looked up while we walked, at the sky, at the trees, at the rooftops. His child's face had been burnished with wonder, such that I always found my chest constricting with love and gratitude. He was so like what I wanted to be then, so breathless about the world and what it showed him. Now, though, his eyes remained steadfastly on the pavement, as though he could not bear to find happiness in anything. I knew, with a fleeting bitterness, that there had been a time when I'd too walked with eyes downcast, hands stuffed in pockets: right after Neil's betrayal. But—that had been years ago. It had taken me a while to discover interest in the world again; I prayed fervently that Paul would make that discovery for himself soon.

We turned onto Charterhouse Street, and then after a few minutes, bore left where the road split, into the spur allowing foot and fire access only. I recognized the archways fronting the building next door to the pub immediately.

"Here," I said. I pulled the door open and held it for Paul.

After conferring at the bar, we found ourselves a booth near the back, cut off from almost all of the other diners by an ornately carved wooden screen. The interior was exactly as I remembered, and I was suddenly awash in recollections. That evening, Gio had left me outside on the sidewalk, and I'd gone in alone to find my sister and her husband. *No, not this time,* he'd said when I invited him to join us. It had been early in our now-long-over relationship, and he had kissed me there, in the rain-slicked street, for the first time, our fingers sliding away from the other's as in some scene in a film. I'd realized later that Gio, the most self-conscious person I'd ever met, had most likely rehearsed that scene many times in his mind before playing it.

"What is it?" Paul asked now, looking up from his menu.

"What is what?"

"You laughed. To yourself."

Hard to explain about a former lover to your nephew, so I just shook my head. "I came here once with your mom and dad," I said instead. I glanced around our enclosed space, the gleaming wood, the embroidered pillows on the bench cushions. It *was* very much as I remembered from that night. The menu seemed familiar as well, bearing few changes. I considered the offerings. "I had the bangers and mash then. I think maybe the lamb shank tonight?"

Paul made a face. "I'll try the bangers, then." He looked up, and just as quickly dropped his eyes again to the menu. "What did Mum and—Dad—have that time? Do you remember?"

I didn't remember, but I hesitated to say so. Paul was searching for something, threads from his father's past to pull out and use to mend the torn memories he carried about with him. "Oh," I said, closing the menu and setting it aside, "your father had the bangers and mash then, too. He could never resist them." Shep had loved a good fry-up, that much I knew, so the lie might not have been a lie at all. And if it made Paul feel better, I was all for it. I was all for anything that made him feel better.

They had been here, in London, for only a couple of days. Shep's retirement was looming, and he had come to the London office to hand off some clients and accounts to others, and to tie up some loose ends. Micheline had come along for the ride, as it were. I, exhausted from a year following Mobius around the countryside, from festival to festival, concert venue to concert venue, would be heading home shortly to recoup. Paul was just entering his sophomore year of college that fall, and so had not joined them.

"I wish I had gone," Paul murmured now, as the waitress set our pints before us. She took the menus and our orders, then swished away. I looked out after her into the rest of the dining room, where the tables were filling, the noise growing louder, but the books still stood silently on the shelves above the doorway, overlooking us all. "I wish I had."

"You couldn't have known," I said. Helpless. None of us could have known how little time we had left with Shep. The dinner here had been one of the last times I'd been out with both of them. As always, we three had laughed most of the evening. That was one of the best things about being with my sister and her husband: how much we laughed. Sarcasm in every word. Intelligent fencing. I missed that; since Shep's death, Micheline had been too emotionally exhausted to laugh, except in bitter despair. "I didn't know then how special that dinner would turn out to be."

Paul looked up impatiently. "Not that. Not their trip."

"Then what—" Realization struck me, and I bit back further words. Uncomfortable, I lifted my pint of Guinness to my lips.

"*That* what."

Paul too picked up his stout, took a drink, wiped his upper lip with the back of his hand. The silence between us, as it had been for the past thirty-six hours, was too heavy to lift, even for both of us together. But—we weren't together, Paul and I. There was a disconnect between us that had never been there before. It was too painful to bear. I pressed a furtive hand to my chest, in an attempt to alleviate the ache within.

Maybe coming to this pub was a mistake. I had remembered how I liked the interior, how I liked the dinner; but in some deep part of me, I had shoved away the sadness I should have known I would feel at the absence of my brother-in-law. Which was nothing compared to the grief my sister and my nephew were feeling.

Micheline's call had come in the middle of the night. I had, for once, been home, tucked away in my fourth-floor apartment in Back Bay, safe in the knowledge that the most recent set of galleys had been returned to my editor at the publishing house. The phone was on the charger, and the ring jarred my sleep. I knew then, before I pushed the icon to answer, that it would be bad news: no one ever called in the middle of the night except with bad news. At the same time, I knew it would be Mick, and I could feel her distress through the distance, through the night, through the darkness. *My sister needed me.* We had always been this way, she and I, linked in our emotional extremity.

19

"Shep's missing, Avi," Mick said, without preamble. She wasn't crying, but her voice shook.

"Mick—"

"The *Màquina* is missing."

I remember falling back onto the bed, me legs unable to support me. With a free hand I tried to find the switch on the lamp on the bedside table, thinking irrationally that it would be easier to understand what my sister was saying with the light on. I knocked over a glass of water, a pile of books, and a bottle of nail polish before the lamp blazed up.

"Stop," I said, part to myself, part to her. I jammed the ball of my hand into my eye, trying to make sense of what I was hearing. "Stop, stop, stop. I don't understand. What are you saying, Mick? *What are you saying?*"

A deep breath from the other end of the connection.

"I've just had a call, Aventurine." There was the sound of riffling papers. "A Chief Warrant Officer Something? Oh, damn it, I can't find where I wrote this down." A stifled sob.

"*What's happened?*"

"He said—he said—a merchant vessel found things—floating—"

My mind immediately flashed to the worst thing I could imagine. Shep. Floating. His white face to the sky, his eyes open to nothing.

"No—"

"Not Shep. Not Shep." Her strangled words might have been echoing my thoughts. "But pieces. Of the boat. A life jacket. A water cooler."

"But how could they know? There's a lot of crap floating in the sea." I still couldn't formulate a rational thought. In my mind's eye I saw the swirl of the Pacific trash island, which I'd investigated when writing the Alaska article. "Tons of crap."

I could feel Mick's impatience flare up. "It's all stenciled, Aventurine. All of it. Somebody found debris near where the *Màquina* made last contact. And the things—say *Màquina* on them. It's Shep's boat."

"The lifeboat?"

"No sign of it."

I closed my eyes, shook my head. None of it made sense to me, but I felt my sister's need, just as I'd felt her need throughout our childhood, up to when she and Shep were married, and when Paul was born. "Paul." The word was out before I realized.

Another hiccup. "He doesn't know yet, Avi. He's not here. He's off with friends for a few days." Finally, Micheline broke down, her sobs heart-rending over the phone. "He doesn't know yet. And how can I tell him? Oh, God, how can I tell Paul?"

"I'm coming, Mick. I'm leaving now."

"Aventurine—"

"I'll be there in two hours, Micheline."

I didn't even bother to pack.

"I should have gone then," Paul repeated, his voice low, his eyes on the plate the waitress had left before him: sausages and gravy mounded over mashed potatoes. "With Dad."

Fork in hand, I sucked in a breath. I wanted to leap over the table and crush Paul to my chest, hold him there, rock him. A foolish thought: he was no longer a child, but a young man, taller than I, broad of shoulder, though it was hard to tell when he was so slumped with grief. And guilt? I set the silver gently on the table once again and forced myself to lean back, bringing my hands together to clasp them tightly in my lap.

"I might have been able to do something."

I licked my lips, watching him in the dim lighting. His eyes were sunk deep into his face.

"I might have been able to save him."

This, then. *This.*

I knew that this conversation would be delicate. If I were to tread wrong here, there was no telling what harm I might cause.

"Your father wanted to solo," I said slowly, choosing my words with care. "He'd worked toward it for years." How do you tell a kid his father didn't want him to come? Without making it sound like a rejection? But Shep had not wanted anyone to come on this voyage. That was the entire point.

"He would have taken me if I'd asked." That stubborn jut of chin. Just like his father's. I bit my lip. "If I'd pushed it."

"By why on earth would you have?" My dinner, on the table before me, was beautifully presented, but suddenly I had no appetite to eat anything. My stomach was roiling. I tasted bile. "Why? Your father was an accomplished sailor. A grown man. He knew what he was doing. He didn't need someone to look after him."

The glance Paul slivered in my direction cut. "Apparently, he did."

Because the boat had foundered. Because Shep had disappeared. I had to take a mental step back. Beneath the table, my hands were twisted together so tightly they hurt. "But, Paul," I protested, "you can't know you could have made any difference. Like I said, Shep was an accomplished sailor. Whatever happened out there, happened *despite* who he was, not *because* of it. You can't be sure you could have done anything to save him—you can't be sure you could have been any help at all."

Paul's face might have been carved from granite. "I could have tried. I could have *died* trying. For him, I would have."

I shook my head. "And where would that have left your mother?" My voice was sharper than I'd intended, and I forced myself to slow my breathing, to try to regain some semblance of calm. I was grateful for the enclosure in which we sat, grateful that we weren't drawing attention to ourselves by having this painful discussion out there, in the open dining room, where conversation ebbed and flowed.

"Don't kid yourself. She would have died for him, too. You know that. She would have died in his place if she could just have figured out how." The anger and ache in his voice was violent and raw. He turned his face away, to stare, unseeing, at the woodwork. His Adam's apple moved in his throat.

"But she had to let him do this, Paul." I suddenly realized that there were warm tears coursing down my cheeks. I scrubbed them away with my heavy napkin. "She knew him. Knew what he loved. Knew enough to let him do what he needed to do." I sighed, and tried to catch his eye, but he looked steadfastly away. "She knew she had to let him go, even though she didn't want to, even though she hated the idea of his sailing solo across the ocean. But she knew him and loved him and had to let him do it."

"It was a gamble that didn't pay off," he muttered bitterly.

"It didn't."

"For any of us."

Paul lifted his pint and downed it. I pushed my plate away.

Five

I didn't think of the strange laughter in the cathedral, nor the strange man on the bridge, again until we were on the 9:06 train from King's Cross to York on Thursday morning. Paul and I had spent a couple of days visiting the National Gallery, and both Tates; my attention span was much more limited than his, and while I spent the time wandering from gallery to gallery, he settled in front of whatever painting caught his eye, and sketched in the small notebook he always carried with him. In that, at least, he remained consistent. I much preferred the afternoons we'd spent walking, such as Tuesday on Hampstead Heath, stopping in to visit the Rembrandts at Kenwood House before continuing on to the Spaniards Inn for a pint.

I had dozed off soon after we'd pulled out of the station, and now the slowing of the train jolted me awake. It was just as well, for I had been dreaming sequences filled with paranoia, and I found I was sweating. Always there had been someone just around the corner, always a voice too far away to be intelligible—but always there was something that hinted at an undefined danger. When, slightly panicked, I looked out the window at the unfamiliar countryside, I could see nothing untoward, and could remember nothing specific of my dreams to cause this anxiety. I wiped my damp palms surreptitiously on the legs of my jeans.

The retreating figure on the bridge. The laughter in the cathedral. I stared out the window at the rainy Cambridgeshire countryside—or had we passed into Lincolnshire? The dreams, I realized, must have harkened back to those two things. But why should those two occurrences have stuck with me? London, one of the largest cities in Europe, was full of people, many millions I did not know, and who had no interest in me whatsoever. To think that out of all those millions, a random person, back-to, with a familiar walk, might be someone I had met before: it made no sense. The prickling on my neck was mere foolishness. *By the pricking of my thumbs.* I cursed William Shakespeare and shook myself mentally. I had to stop being idiotic.

Across the banquette, Paul was watching me. He plucked one of his earbuds out. "Someone walking over your grave?" he asked.

I shrugged. Maybe. I didn't know. He wound his earbud back in, returned his attention to his phone. I looked back out into the damp fields slipping by. As the rainy countryside snicked past numbingly, I focused on Paul's reflection in the glass. His eyes closed after awhile, the gentle rhythmic rocking of the train, or the music from his earbuds, lulling him to sleep. His face smoothed out, like a face underwater. I could see all of his ages: Paul as a teenager, as a nine-year-old, as a toddler. Until I had first held him at the hospital, shortly after his birth, I had not realized how deeply I would become invested in his life, in his future—eagerly awaiting details of his growth from Shep and Micheline, eagerly awaiting his voice when he was old enough to call or Skype himself.

I sighed, and opened up my iPad, where the screensaver was a picture of the three of them from a couple of years ago: my sister, her late husband, and Paul. I sighed again, and clicked through to my notes about Genevieve Smithson, trying to concentrate.

There were two rooms reserved for us at the guest house on Fulford

Road, both on the second floor. One was at the front, overlooking the street, while the other had a window that opened above a rear garden complete with the romantic remnants of a ruined stone wall. When I offered to let Paul choose, he demurred, so I plumped for the front room. I knew, after all this time, which he really wanted, though he was far too polite to say. As much as I loved ruinous things, he loved them more.

"Meet me down there." I gestured to his window and the garden below, where the formal beds were in riotous bloom, roses of pink and red edging the path to the double archway in the medieval wall at the far end. Tables and chairs were scattered about on the terrace; only one table was occupied, by a couple in hiking boots and gaiters, leaning over a map, foreshortened by height and distance.

"Give me a couple of minutes."

I went to my own room to scrub my face; for some reason, train journeys made me feel grubby, as though I'd spent the miles in a coal tender, or stoking a steam engine. I changed my clothes, then wandered, shoe in hand, to peel aside the curtain at the window. Below here, on this side of the house, the street was as lazy as it had been when we'd arrived from the station in the taxi. An elderly man in a cap and blue cardigan shuffled along the pavement, and I watched him until he disappeared at the corner, wondering what his story was. How old? I estimated his age in the seventies, though I could have been either really high or really low. So many things aged a person: tragedy, disease. My thoughts flitted to Shep and away again.

Genevieve Smithson. She had been a teenager during World War II, and here she was, in her 90s, finally agreeing to tell her story. Finally agreeing to tell it *to me*. I felt the familiar flutter of excitement beneath my breastbone, the one that told me I might be onto something fantastic. When she'd first reached out to me after the publication of *Night Watch*, suggesting we talk, I had immediately pitched the story to the big glossies. My number one choice had jumped at it, as I knew they would; they'd offered a pretty chunk of change as well, and a fairly flexible deadline. Still, I had my eyes on a bigger prize: what if Genevieve Smithson's story could be the genesis of my next book?

She had been a spy. At sixteen, lying about her age, dropped behind the lines in France. Now, almost eighty years later. A woman who had remained reclusive and secretive for her entire adult life. I thought back over my notes, the skeletal material I had been able to glean from research before setting out. *It's time to tell the story,* she'd said when we had first spoken on the telephone. *I've heard quite a bit about you. You're the one to do it.*

I smirked to myself. Deprecatingly. She would have heard a lot more about me, and possibly a lot earlier, had my burgeoning career in investigative journalism not veered so crazily, almost into oblivion, at the get-go. Nevertheless—and I drew myself up, straightened my spine—I had persevered. The most recent three books had not only established my ability to tell a well-researched story over several hundred pages, but had cemented my earnings. I *was* the one to tell this story. I took a deep breath, trying to regulate my excitement, but it was no use. This was going to be big.

I put a hand out to the windowsill to steady myself as I pulled on my shoe. A movement below caught my eye. Just another pedestrian, this one a man in a dark jacket, walking briskly along the pavement on the other side of the street. Just another pedestrian. Then I looked again. Foreshortened, back to. Shoulders thrown back as though he owned the world. Dark hair maybe just a little too long, as though the conventions didn't apply to him.

I knew the walk. I knew the shoulders.

It was the man from Westminster Bridge.

And he still looked familiar. Because he was. What the hell?

Except it couldn't be. And he couldn't be.

The excitement changed to raging anxiety, as though my brain had flipped a switch.

Paul was already waiting when I made my way out onto the terrace. He'd drawn up a chair at a small table as far from the two ramblers as possible—they were still poring over their ordinance map—after he had collected a couple of pints at the bar. He slid one across to me.

"I got you the brownest thing they had that wasn't a stout," he said.

The boy knew me well, even when he didn't know himself.

The breeze wafted the scent of the roses along the path to us. I'd brought out a light cardigan, and now I shrugged my way into it. Despite the sunny afternoon, I felt chilled, but then I realized, the feeling had very little to do with the weather. I took an enormous draw from my pint.

"What?" Paul asked.

I slewed my eyes to him and away again. "What, what?"

He shook his head. "I don't know. You look a little—strange. Spooked. Haunted." Paul seemed to cringe from that idea. He dipped his head quickly to sip his beer. "I don't know. Your eyes look really wide."

"Maybe I'm stoned."

His laugh was a single short bark. "Really. No. You're a morally upright person. We've already established that." He took another drink. His pint, a reddish beer, was half gone. "What happened up there?"

I think this might have been the longest conversational gambit he'd made since we'd met up, and something made me want to prolong it, to get him away from his moroseness. I made a face, sipped my beer. It was very strong, but a brown, not a stout. "I was looking out the window and I thought I saw someone I recognized."

Paul's eyebrows drew together. "Here? In York?"

"Here. In this street."

"Do you know anybody in York? Apart from the lady you're going to interview tomorrow, I mean."

I shrugged, frowning in return. "I don't even know *her.* We've just talked on the phone. I don't think I know anyone who lives around here. I mean, I have a couple of friends in the U.K., but they're in London, and in North Cornwall, or riding around in a tour bus."

"They could have moved up here. They could have a gig up here," Paul suggested. He set his pint glass back on the table. I picked it up and slid a coaster under it. "Or they could be visiting."

The beer tasted sour on top of my anxiety, which hadn't abated much. I took another drink anyway, and grimaced. "Possible. Incredibly coincidental, though." I paused, thought back over the past couple of days. "Especially since—" Did I want to tell him this part? He'd probably just think I was overreacting. Hallucinating. He didn't know the backstory. I had never told him; Micheline and Shep had had no reason to.

"What?"

I closed my eyes, tried to envision Westminster Bridge. "I thought I saw the same person in London. Back to, both times, so of course I could be imagining the entire thing. I probably am." But my words were weak, and didn't even come close to convincing me.

"So—who was it?"

That was where I stumbled.

I dropped my face into my hands. I hadn't seen him in almost twenty-five years. I had not intended to see him ever again. I had vowed back then to get over him, to move on with my life, to repair the ravages he had caused with his calculated cruelty. I'd done a pretty good job, all things considered.

At the same time, I could still remember, viscerally, the way he looked, the way he walked, the way he smelled, that small dimple in his left cheek, the way his brows drew together when he laughed, which was often. I could remember everything about him after all this time, and suddenly I was an archaeologist, digging up all the painful history and sifting it for gold. Of course there was only dross.

I could remember my twenty-four-year-old self, picking up the newspaper from my desk, opening it, and seeing the announcement of his National Press Award. I could remember the way he betrayed me, searingly, a pain like nothing I'd felt before or since. I could feel that pain right now.

"Avi," Paul said, and there was a surprised urgency in his voice. "Avi, are you okay?"

I wasn't okay. I gulped in a breath, and another.

"Avi?"

I lifted my eyes, groped for my pint glass, knocked it over. The remainder of the brown beer went everywhere.

It was the jolt I needed. Instinctively, Paul leapt back away from the table, knocking over his chair. The beer splashed my shoes, but not much else, as it sought its level on the terrace, running along the mortared spaces between the stones. The couple across the way looked up from their ordinance maps and then quickly away, probably embarrassed to see what they thought was some middle-aged woman in her cups.

"I'll get something to wipe this up," I gasped.

"No, I'll get it." Paul was on his feet, heading inside, but not before throwing me a puzzled look over his shoulder.

"Let's walk," Paul said, once we had mopped up the beer with the cloths the bartender had given us.

It had been our pattern for the past few days: have a pint, skirt around an uncomfortable conversational topic, go for a walk. A hard and fast walk. Good thing I was a rambler by inclination, because Paul walked like a man possessed by demons. Which, after a fashion, he was.

We passed out of the sweet-scented garden through the archway at its foot, turning, then turning again when we came to the Fishergate. The pavement, as the afternoon advanced, was still mostly empty, and we could walk side-by-side—we'd grown accustomed to each other, and had adjusted our strides over the past few days. Paul kept his hands stuffed deep in his pockets, the attitude to which I'd also grown accustomed; every once in a while, he glanced over. Concerned. Calculating. Curious.

"It's not like you to be spooked by stuff," he said at last, glancing away from me, at the grimy window of a newsagent's. I saw the flash of our reflection as we passed, a tall handsome young man out for a walk with his middle-aged aunt. I saw no one else in the street, save a young woman walking purposely with a push-chair. I tried to take deep breaths, tried to calm myself. It was nothing, nothing, I had not seen anyone I knew, my imagination was overreacting. We were in York. In the U.K. We were not in New York, and Neil was not here.

Neil.

The name had washed up as if on a tide. I had shied away from it for more than two decades now. I stumbled on a rough spot of pavement, and Paul caught my arm. It was as though, if I banished the name, I could rid myself of the man. Now it was back. Perhaps he was, too. My neck prickled, and I glanced around. Other than the woman and the baby, there was no one else nearby.

"Fear of the name equals fear of the thing," I muttered.

Paul raised his eyebrow. "It's not like you to paraphrase J. K. Rowling, either."

He was right. On both counts.

"Let's go to the Minster," I said. "Exorcise some ghosts."

"Always a good plan."

• •

We cut through Fishergate Bar, and after a bit, reached Lead Mill Lane. Just beyond that was the gate into a burial ground, shaded by trees; a path meandered around the perimeter. By silent agreement, we slipped inside, and followed the worn track around to the back where a squat stone held pride of place. It seemed lonesome, save for the fact that it was well-tended, and obviously well-visited.

"I thought we were exorcising ghosts," Paul said, leaning forward to trace the carving with a long finger, "not communing with them. Who is this guy?"

"You don't know the legend of Dick Turpin?" I don't know why I did: probably my childhood fascination with the romantic exaggerations of the British ilk.

"Or John Palmer. Or is that only on Thursdays?"

I shook my head. "Foolish boy. Dick Turpin was a highwayman. Stuff of legends, especially long after he was hanged. Books written about him, movies made about him."

"Anti-hero sort of stuff? Misunderstood? Stole from the rich and gave to the poor?"

"Pretty much. Though I doubt he was really much more than criminal, stealing from anybody and giving to himself." Holding onto this thought, I drew my little notebook and a pen from my bag and made a note to myself, to further research Dick Turpin. There might be something there I could use in building a world around Genevieve Smithson's story. What was the York she grew up in, before she lied about her age and joined forces with the SOE? How much did it matter to her story? The answer was, of course, that I would not know until we had talked. I wrote a few more scribbled notes to myself and tucked the notebook away again, next to the little digital recorder.

When we turned, a tall thin woman, with her hands clasped on the knob of a walking stick, was watching us from under the brim of a sunhat resembling a pith helmet. She nodded, her face a map of wrinkles, as we passed.

"Don't be dismissing our Dick," she said, with the smallest hint of a smile. Her eyes were hidden behind dark lenses. "His ghost still rides Black Bess here, it's said." Then she continued on.

We were barely in time to shell out almost seventeen pounds apiece to climb up into the tower of the Minster, and fortunate that the pack of hardy souls already in line in the echoing dimness was not large, so there was room for us. I followed Paul up the stairs, winding around and around, careful not to look down, steadying myself with a fierce grip on the rail; I knew from experience that returning from the top was going to be a nightmare for me. I was not good at heights, had never been; I had been ascending to the tops of things for years—towers, bridges, observation decks—hoping that I'd become acclimatized. I never had. My stomach still clenched up, and my palms, on the cold metal rail, were sweaty and slick.

However, the view was amazing. The city sprawled out below us, the rivers Ouse and Foss angling by on either side as best they could, joining together at a point between us and our guest house. The wall, too, visible in places, pretended to protect us from whatever lay on the other side; at this late date, though, that was really only more city. I clutched a guide, trying to match what I was seeing to its reference point on the page. Somewhere across the river and beyond the wall, Scarcroft Road and Genevieve Smithson, my appointment for tomorrow, lay. I put my hand on the cool stone and leaned forward—not *too* far—to look in her direction. Despite the anxiety of earlier this afternoon, my excitement was growing again. I couldn't wait until tomorrow: I couldn't wait to meet this woman who could be my next book.

Part II:

Genevieve

Sometimes I think: I was
a particularly blood-thirsty child,
who believed herself to be invincible.
Sometimes I think: I was just a child.
Sometimes I think: I was never a child.

—Genevieve Smithson

Six

I still remember the first man I killed.

By that, I mean I remember viscerally: a full body sensation, as though it were happening now, in real time. It's one thing to do the crash course with the SOE, one thing to look into the eyes of the instructor—they all had such flat *eyes—they knew most of us operatives would be dead within six months—and say yes, I was prepared to kill. But remember, none of us had ever killed, as far as we knew, before we were inserted.*

Her intensity frightened me, and I was immediately aware of the disconnect. This elderly woman—back straight in the high-backed library chair, dark eyes brilliant and incisive, but skin tanned, wrinkled—speaking so matter-of-factly of the violence her age-spotted hands had done. We sat facing each other in a dim and musty room, surrounded by books; my phone, set on record, sat next to my digital recorder on the table between us, while I took notes of her words, her looks, her surroundings.

When I had knocked on the blue door of her row house an hour earlier, I had expected to be allowed in by a housekeeper, or secretary. I was surprised, then—and couldn't hide it—when the door was opened by someone who could only be Genevieve Smithson herself. The woman from Dick Turpin's grave.

"There are ghosts," she said now, her eyes narrowing as she assessed me, "and there are ghosts. I'd rather thought that was you yesterday." But she hadn't let on then, and she gave no explanation now, as she allowed me entrance, then snicked a series of locks into place.

No stick today, though several stood at the ready in a tall vase in the hall at the foot of the stairway. Genevieve Smithson turned sharply on her heel and walked away, down the carpeted hallway. I was obviously meant to follow. I turned for a moment to count the locks, of which there were several; the street noise was muffled now, leaving only the echoing tick of a parlor clock from the room to my left. I followed her, my footsteps deadened: the hall runner beneath my feet was thick, and, I thought, expensive.

She stood in the library with her hand on the back of a chair, from which she shooed a tabby cat, and indicated I should take the seat across the table. Tea had been laid. "I'm glad you're punctual. I'd have served you cold tea otherwise."

Her tone implied that it was a test. Possibly one in a series. At least I had passed the first hurdle. We sat, chit-chatted in the way people do before they get down to real business, about the weather, my journey from the U.S. and from London, but I felt instinctively that she was impatient to get to the interview, and that this socializing was an act. She would have had to have been good at acting, working in espionage; she would have to be fluent in French, too.

"*Continuez-vous à pratiquer votre français?*" I asked, a test of my own.

"*Si vous voulez jouer à des jeux, je suis bien meilleur,*" she replied, lifting her teacup to take a drink.

I immediately felt foolish, which was no doubt her intention. I had, in my career, interviewed celebrities, criminals, heads of state. I prided myself on having developed an urbane, unshakeable front. There was absolutely no reason why, with that experience,

38

a semi-reclusive woman of over ninety should cause me such discomposure. Perhaps it was the constant evaluation in her sharp eyes as she rested her chin between thumb and forefinger. Watching. Waiting. There was an aloofness to her that both challenged me to break it down, and made me despair that I ever would.

She had, after all, rebuffed all other reporters who would have told her story—until she had chosen me. She was the one who had made the initial contact, the one who had arranged our preliminary interview schedule.

I sat back in my chair, a momentary surrender. With a smile that did not reach her eyes, she cut a slice of cake with an ornate silver server, plated it, and handed it across. I felt as though I was being given a reward for following unspoken orders.

"Apple cake," she said. "I made it myself this morning." Indeed, it was still warm.

"Forbidden fruit," I replied.

"Perhaps that's why it's always been my favorite." Genevieve's voice was arch. "Shall we begin?"

In my initial interviews with subjects, I'd fallen into a pattern over the years: let them begin to tell their stories in their own way, then ask questions to probe further, or to get at material they hadn't brought up. After looking at my phone and recorder in mild distaste, Genevieve began. She spoke clearly and distinctly, as though she'd assessed her audience and material and decided upon her presentation accordingly. Something told me that she would be one of those subjects who tried to control the interview, tried to control the story—but it was my job to wrest that control away.

A sentry, no more than a boy, but I didn't know that until he lay, gently gurgling his lifeblood away, on the ground before us. Not much older than I was. I wondered fleetingly whether he, too, had lied about his age to join this great adventure, the war. The moment we met was the moment when it became far more than a game for both of us.

It was like being blooded after the fox hunt, save for the fact that I took him from behind, reaching around to plunge my knife into his throat, as I'd been taught. The only blood was on my hand, and I quickly wiped that off on the tail of his coat. I remember thinking of the line from Macbeth—*you know the one. "Who would have thought the old man to have so much blood in him?" But I had neither the time nor the inclination to fall into insanity like Lady Macbeth. Pierre and I merely dragged the boy out of the path, and moved on. I kept thinking, though, about what a beautiful night it was, the sky above black velvet and spangled with stars, the sounds of far-off nightbirds in the sighing trees. And beyond all that: me. Genevieve. The angel of death, if you will. It was heady, that power.*

She talked on for nearly three hours, and I let her. Her anecdotes were gripping, always balancing on the edge of danger and cruelty, if they didn't involve *obvious* danger and cruelty. How Commander Smith had beaten her down and built her up again over those few months of intensive training at the base in the Highlands. How she had hated every minute of it, butting heads and losing, but how it had also filled her with a sense of exhilaration.

"Smith?" I asked.

She looked at me with that crafty expression. "Come now. Surely you didn't think he'd give us his real name."

"But—Smithson?"

The expression broadened into a wider smile, as though at a joke. "Surely you didn't think I'd give you mine." She laughed, but it was not a pleasant laugh. I didn't think she was capable of a pleasant laugh. "I haven't used my real name since 1943. It's better that way. Sometimes I don't think I remember the name I was born with. Sometimes I think of those years before I was recruited, and I really can't imagine I *lived* before then. I was born the day I realized that Smith was my parent. My father *and* mother. The only parent I really needed."

Abruptly, at the muted sound of the clock from the next room, she pushed herself to her feet. "Come," she said. "I'm an old woman, and my joints stiffen up if I allow myself to remain sedentary. Let's walk."

The command was so like Paul's that I almost laughed. The tension was lifted as suddenly as it had fallen, when I had begun listening to Genevieve's recollections. I checked the battery life on both my phone and the recorder before turning them off and tucking them into my bag. I closed my notebook and put that away as well. I wanted to speak more, to listen more; refraining from asking questions was becoming progressively more difficult. Genevieve's material was, so far, all that I could have dreamed, and more. Her telling was gripping, and I could already feel the framework of the story coming into view, a skeleton before I draped it in its skin. I didn't want to stop, but I knew that pushing my subject too hard, too early, could easily backfire.

She was already out in the hall, pulling on a light jacket from the hall closet, settling the hat on her iron-gray hair, selecting a stick from the giant vase by the door. "Take one of these," she ordered, waving a hand. "You'll want it."

I didn't agree, but I didn't argue. I selected a blackthorn stick from the collection, and followed her outside. She locked the door behind us with a set of keys she had plucked from a hook near the door, and then slipped the ring into her pocket; there were, as I'd noticed earlier, several locks.

"I trust no one," she said, rechecking the locks. She looked over at me from under the familiar hat. "It has kept me alive all these years." Then she led the way to the street.

Seven

Genevieve set a brisk pace, neither looking left nor right. I prided myself on being a fairly strong walker, but I was hard pressed to keep pace with her, despite the difference in our ages. Over the light traffic I could hear the snick of her stick on the pavement as she used it more to set her tempo than as any support. After a few moments, when we turned onto Upper Price Street, I realized that my own stick was rapping out the same cadence.

She obviously didn't need the walking stick; her back was straight, her step so purposeful that it was difficult to credit her age. I found myself wondering about it, how she punctuated her walking with the sound. Something she'd obviously picked up since her sojourn behind enemy lines in France, where she would have had to learn to move silently. The story of her first kill still enthralled me and frightened me, and I shivered. What must it have been like, as a mere teenager, to sneak up on the enemy, to swiftly reach around, pull his jaw upward, to stab surgically, to eliminate him without a sound?

That had been her first, and she remembered it vividly. I looked over at her profile, the hawk-like nose, the determined mouth. No doubt there were others. Probably several others. She had been behind the lines until the liberation, and she had survived, where so many others had not. Commander Smith, whoever he had been, had let her know that she was a tool for use in the great machine, and that she was unlikely to last after doing her part for a couple of months. Instead, she had outlasted the enemy, the war, and most likely, Commander Smith himself.

I was crossing the A1036 with a murderer.

But—in the service of one's country, was one really a murderer? Or was one a patriot?

We passed through Victor Gate, and after a few moments, found ourselves accessing the wall at Skeldergate and Baile Hill. I followed Genevieve into a small tower and up the stone stairs to the top; I tried not to appear winded when she waited for me to complete my ascent.

"I walk the walls every day," she said, tapping the toe of a hiking boot on the stone. "Keeps me young. Helps me pretend I'm in control here."

"You're not?"

She turned and walked again; we were going clockwise.

"I'm an old woman," she tossed over her shoulder, ironically.

Sixteen in 1943. Yes, she was an old woman. But she did not walk like one, and age had not softened her in the least.

"The world is not kind to old women," she said. I fell back behind her to let a couple pass going the other direction. Then I pulled back abreast. "Especially old women with no children, no husband, no living relatives."

"You have your home."

"For as long as I can hold onto it," she said, still with the ironic note in her voice. "My general practitioner, and anyone else in any position of petty power, keep urging me to give up my home, to move into some sort of assisted living facility. As though I can't take care of myself." If she could have spat over the wall onto her general practitioner and those in petty power, she would have: her contemptuous expression made that clear.

She had not slowed her pace. My thighs were burning, and I

did my best to hide my discomfort. I thought of the dim library, the high-backed chair, the tabby cat winding around her legs, tail aloft. Hers was a home formed around her personality. Genevieve, I knew, would not leave that easily, not without a fight—and I did not envy the fool who attempted to move her.

"Fortunately," she said, and we moved aside again for another group of three laughing young people, "fortunately I have enough money set by to live on, enough to have a char in twice a week. I have my books, and I have these walls." She ran a hand over the pitted stone surface to her left. Then she looked up at the sky, where clouds scudded past. The breeze was picking up. "When I die, I hope it's in my own bed, just suddenly done and done, just as my husband did."

Husband.

This was the first time she had mentioned his existence. I tried to imagine this sharp, hard woman in love. I tried to imagine her softening to someone's caress.

Obviously, I was now supposed to start digging about her husband.

Again I had the sudden sense that she was playing me, information-wise. A bit here, so I could run with it, a bit more, and then she would set the hook and reel me in, leisurely, knowing that I would be unable to escape. Genevieve was enjoying herself. I made a mental note: who were her friends? With whom did she spend time? Did she play them in conversation as she was playing me?

Had she been like this at sixteen? Was it part of her attraction to the agent who recruited her, or to Commander Smith who had trained her? I imagined of a clash of wills, those men, this girl; sure, she had lied about her age, but I wondered whether they had known that she lied, whether she knew that they knew—and whether any of them had cared.

We paused at a place where the walk became a wide circle, and looked back toward the aged bailey. That ancient manmade hill was green with grass and populated by trees, the tops of which swayed in the breeze. I clutched my walking stick, tapping it on the runic stone map set at my feet. Clifford's Tower and Baile Hill were incised on either side of the wavy lines representing the river.

"My husband," Genevieve said, her expression softening, "liked to tell people this particular place was named after me."

She cocked her head, waiting. I obliged. "And its name is?"

Was that—almost—a smile? "Bitchdaughter Corner."

Genevieve pointed out Victoria Bar as we came to it, and I took a quick picture, knowing I wouldn't remember later where we were. I needed a map, and cursed my own stupidity for not picking one up yesterday in preparation—but then again, I had had no way of knowing I'd be forced-marching the walls today. Just a getting-to-know-you interview, I'd thought complacently, not an endurance test. Even now, Genevieve was pulling away, her stick clacking imperatively on the stone, and I had to hurry to catch up.

"If you want pictures, we can stop at Micklegate Bar," she offered, sweets to a cranky child. "You can go down into the street, if you like." She cast me a glance, her lips twisting slightly in distaste. "We'll skip the museum, as they call it. The Henry VII Experience. A bit too touristy-ghoulish for my taste. All fake heads on spikes and such."

I almost laughed.

We approached Micklegate Bar, with its ornate towers, the tiny statues perched atop them. Here again, Genevieve stopped, leaned back against the parapet, gazing upward at the figures. I looked down at the traffic passing through to gate. There was a stone staircase for access to the street. The wall walk skirted the gates, and, I suppose, the fake heads on pikes.

She was still looking upwards. "Who are those people?" I asked, squinting at the figures silhouetted against the milky blue sky. They looked like loiterers, oddly out of place atop crenellations too delicate for the tower they crowned. "What's their story?"

"A disguise," Genevieve said wryly. "Those are relatively modern replacements for the statues that replaced the spikes for the real traitors' heads."

It all came back to those damned heads. I shivered—the breeze was still steady, scudding a few more clouds overhead—but Genevieve seemed perfectly comfortable.

"And you, Aventurine Morrow?" she demanded. "What's your story?"

It was an odd question. A surprise. What *was* my story, and what part of it did she mean?

"The boy you were with yesterday, who wanted to exorcise ghosts. Your son?"

I shot her a quick look. Her face was impassive, gave nothing away.

"No. My nephew."

Her look at me was not fleeting, but deliberate, a study of my features. "Then I'm mistaken. He looks very much like you. Very much."

I couldn't hold her gaze. "My sister's son. My twin sister's."

She had noted my reaction, and I had the sense that she was filing it away as a curiosity, something to be taken out and examined later, when she could give it the kind of attention she thought it deserved. Despite myself, I flushed hotly. I clenched my hands around the knob of the blackthorn stick, but then saw her making note of that, as well.

"His father recently died." I stopped myself from speaking further. Maybe she would decide my awkward response could be attributed to a family grief at my brother-in-law's death.

"Ah," was all she said. I still felt less than comfortable. I wasn't used to being asked questions; I was the one who did the interviews. "And the other man with you two?"

It took me a moment to realize what she had asked. Frowning, I turned toward her. "Pardon?"

"The other man. In the churchyard, at Dick Turpin's grave."

I had not noticed another man. "No, we're here together, just the two of us," I told her. "Paul and I. No one else."

"No? Dark hair, grey at the temples, dark jacket, sunglasses?"

My neck was prickling. "No. No one was with us."

She shrugged. "Again, my mistake. Come to think of it, he did stay some distance away from the both of you. On the far side of the loop, near the fence. By the trees."

There was a long pause. I ran back over her words, listened again for her tone. Genevieve was trying to tell me something. She had not made a mistake, I suddenly knew; she was intentionally misconstruing what she had seen, to let me *know* what she had seen.

Before I had a chance to say anything further, Genevieve straightened. "And here he is."

I jerked my head up, my chest suddenly tight.

She eyed me. "Your nephew, I believe."

Paul had clambered up the steps from the street. Eschewing the rail, he had his hands, as always, curled into the pockets of his denim jacket.

"He looks very like you," Genevieve repeated, her voice low.

Paul seemed not to have heard her. "Fancy meeting you here," he said, though there was something automatic to his tone, as though his voice were on auto-pilot. He paused, looking between us. I wondered, with Genevieve's revelation, whether I looked *stoned* again to him. "Am I—interrupting?"

"No, no," Genevieve said. She held out her hand. "Genevieve Smithson. You are the nephew."

He shook the proffered hand, nodding. "Paul. Paul Genthner." He looked to me.

"We were taking a break. Taking a walk," I said. "I'm surprised to see you, too."

He shrugged, hands back in his pockets. "Stepped out there for a pint," he said, jerking his chin toward the street below, and the pub just along it. "I've made it nearly all the way around."

Genevieve nodded approvingly. "It's good exercise."

"Mrs. Smithson tells me she makes the circuit every day."

"Keeps me occupied in my old age."

"It's a fair walk," Paul said. "I've been out for a while."

Again Genevieve nodded. "Two hours, give or take, if you don't stop."

"Two hours every day?" He could not disguise his surprise, assessing her upright figure.

She cocked her head. "And what else have I to do at my age, young man?"

If I hadn't known better—even this early into our acquaintance—I would have thought she was teasing Paul. But I could see that the slight grin didn't quite reach her eyes. She was playing a part again, though for the life of me I couldn't be sure why.

"Have you had lunch?" Paul asked.

"Not yet." I looked at my watch at almost the same moment a bell nearby chimed the hour. Two o'clock. I hadn't even thought about lunch, full of tea and apple cake as I had been when we'd set out. "What do you think?" I asked Genevieve. "Are you hungry?"

For a moment she looked calculating. She was used to walking the wall, taking her two hours per day. Something told me it was a straightforward march, without stopping for tea, lunch, a pub— probably not even a pit stop at a toilet. However, now, she nodded. "I'd like to move on a bit first, if you don't mind. Come along with us," she invited Paul.

It was more a command than an invitation; somewhere along

the line, Genevieve had obviously acquired the habit of expecting to be obeyed. Paul fell in and we continued on. There were more people on the wall now, as we headed along to a point where the walk made a sharp turn to the right, back toward the river. Again I wished I'd picked up a map.

"Tofts Tower," Genevieve said, naming the corner as though counting off the beads on a rosary. She tapped her stick on another brass marker at her feet. "Take a picture of that for your aunt," she instructed Paul, who pulled out his phone and did as he was bidden, surprisingly without question.

From there we quick-marched single file, with no opportunity for conversation. That was fine with me, bringing up the rear, because it gave me a chance to think about what Genevieve had told me. Outside confirmation that all I'd been anxious about over the past couple of days was *not* imagination, *not* hallucination. Someone was following us, or at least arranging to be where we were. The worst part about it was that I had that niggling fear that I knew who that someone was—the last person I would ever want to see, ever again.

The very last person.

My hand went to my bag, slung across my body. The zip was still closed. I patted the side, feeling the lumps that were my digital recorder and my phone, the flat rectangular-ness of my notebook. The three were still there. I kept my hand on my bag as we walked, clutched the walking stick tighter with the other. *You'll need this,* Genevieve had said, and I had thought she meant because of the length of the walk, but now I wondered if the suggestion was part of her disguised warning. Perhaps I'd need a weapon? But now I was just being paranoid.

I wouldn't use it, I didn't think, on our stalker, if he made an appearance. Unlike Genevieve, I had not killed my first man at sixteen, nor had I killed any subsequently. I didn't think I had it in me, that sort—any sort—of physical violence. Just anxiety. Just anger. Fury. I could taste the rage at the back of my throat even now, rising, transforming from age-old remembrance to present reality. I looked around, behind us on the wall, wondering if we were being followed today.

And why?

I hadn't seen him in years. Years. What did he want with us—with me—now? Because, I had to admit to myself, it could be no one else.

No one other than Neil Barrett.

When I caught up to them where they had paused, waiting for me, Paul was framing yet another picture of another brass marker. The old railway station was inside the wall here, and a signal box outside. I leaned on the parapet to look over, and Genevieve joined me, standing with both hands on the stick. A lip of stone jutted out below us, and the scrub trees grew nearly to the box. I could not see the ground.

"A person could hide there for a long time," I said. "Never be found." I glanced around again. Maybe he was here somewhere. Maybe I was spooked.

She peered at me, her eyes narrowed. "Oh, you'd be found eventually," she assured me. "It might take awhile—but we *are* in the city. And no one ever stays hidden for long, no matter how hard he might try."

Eight

It was masterful, the way Genevieve Smithson got Paul to talk.

We stopped into a pub before we got around to the Minster, choosing a place just inside Bootham Bar heading into High Petergate. We were too late for the lunch crowd, and only a few stragglers, or perhaps early drinkers, remained. We ordered at the bar and made our way outside into the beer garden in the back. Perhaps it was the anxiety Genevieve had revived in me, but I looked around furtively. A pair of elderly men sat at a table off to the side, pints between them, playing cards. Otherwise, we were alone.

Paul had ordered fish and chips, and Genevieve laughed. "Order that in a restaurant, young man, and everyone will know you're not from around here. You get your cod and chips at a chippy, the greasier the better. And you don't use silverware."

"But I'm not from around here," Paul protested, almost grinning back at her. "Though I suppose I could be persuaded to let you take me to your favorite greasy takeaway."

Genevieve grimaced. "Thank you, no." She stirred sugar into her tea, then set her spoon aside. *I don't drink*, she'd said, when Paul had asked her what beer she'd recommend. *I like to keep a clear head*. She probably didn't eat at greasy chippies, either, because she liked to keep clear arteries. Well, she *was* in her nineties, after all. She had learned the secret to a long life.

Snarkiness aside, I filed this information away to ask about later: had she ever drank? When one had to fade into the background, especially when everyone else was partaking—how did she manage that? The keeping of a clear head, however: that made perfect sense. Except—and I shot her a quick glance—the war had been over for decades. Yet I had observed that parts of her training were still ingrained; this might just be one more holdover from that time. Or was there some other reason for it?

Now Paul was telling her about our waiting for news of Shep after radio contact had been lost.

"Near Bermuda," she mused. "What time of year? Not hurricane season."

Paul shook his head, took a sip from his pint, then set it aside. He picked up a chip and stared at it without seeing it. "No. Dad sailed earlier than that. Early May, so he'd be across before the season started." He coughed. "He'd done so much research for this: years, I think, before he'd retired and finally decided to take the plunge. Talked to so many people who'd done it. Sailed that route with friends. He was fairly confident that he could do it solo. And excited."

He fell silent, picking at his lunch. His face had that pinched look again, the look that made him appear so young. *I should have gone.* I felt the familiar crush in my chest at his unhappiness. I remembered what it had felt like to have him climb into my lap when he was small, and wished, illogically, that he would do that again. Though, at twenty-three and taller than me now by several inches, he would *never* do that again.

"How long did you have to wait?" Genevieve's voice was low. Curious, but kind. She lifted her tea cup and took a sip, watching over the rim. She had to be the most watchful person I had ever met—and I had met, over the years, many, many people.

Paul shrugged. "I don't even know. So long. Not long. Days. A merchant vessel found some debris, and then there was just—nothing." He downed the remainder of his pint, as though hoping it would give him courage. "A life jacket. Some boards, a cooler. A bunch of stuff labeled as from the *Máquina*."

"They gathered what they could, radioed it in." I wanted to reach out and put a hand on his arm, but I didn't.

"And they never found—him?"

I caught a breath. Genevieve had almost said *his body.* Had it been someone who looked less crushed, less vulnerable than Paul, she might have. I was grateful for her forbearance. And yet—it was not kindness that caused her to refrain from the word, but rather a quick psychological read: what approach would glean her further information.

It didn't seem to have the desired effect now, however, as Paul didn't answer. He looked away, over the buildings at the far end of the beer garden, toward the tower of the Minster, where we had been only yesterday afternoon. I probably had looked down into this garden when I was making my circuit of the platform, but hadn't really seen it, not understanding much of what I had been looking at. I wondered now if someone up there was looking down at us. And not seeing us.

Or maybe they were.

I shivered.

That was really stupid. We were far too far away. No one up there would be able to make us out, even if he were looking for us specifically. Even with binoculars, and that bit of imagination was really stretching things.

Neil Barrett.

No. I would not think about him. I jerked my attention back to the uncomfortable conversation between my nephew and Genevieve.

"There had been a storm," Paul told her now. His words were hurrying, tumbling over themselves, as though he'd bottled them up for so long—which he had—that they were now escaping under pressure. "Not a hurricane, though. But the weather service and radar showed a storm in the area where Dad had last made radio contact, and there were reports from other ships in the vicinity of high winds and waves. The weird thing, though, was that there was no record of any distress call from the *Máquina* that night. Nothing. Regular radio contact, then nothing. Whatever happened to Dad—happened fast."

His voice trailed off.

"How awful for you, though, and your mother. The waiting."

When Paul spoke again, he'd changed tack. "The last day I spent with him was the day of my graduation from college. He flew out the next day."

"Out?"

"Here. To the U.K. He'd overwintered the *Máquina* in a yard in Southampton. He'd sailed it over the previous fall with some friends. I didn't go: I was starting my senior year." There was a great weight in his words again: he hadn't gone, he should have gone. But how could any of us have known?

Abruptly now Paul stood, picking up his empty glass. Wordlessly, he waved a hand in the general direction of both our drinks, and when we demurred, he headed inside to the bar.

"A tragedy," Genevieve murmured. She poured the last of the tea from the yellow pot into her cup and looked into the swirling brown as though reading the future—or the past. "He's so young."

I wondered what *young* meant to her. I wondered if she'd ever been young.

"He had his own sailboat, Paul did, from the time he was a young teen," I told her. "Shep taught him. Shep sailed the *Falcon* that fall, once he'd delivered the *Máquina* to Southampton. Before it was put up for the winter, too." I looked back over my shoulder into the dimness of the bar. "Paul sold it after Shep disappeared."

"A tragedy," Genevieve repeated. Her gaze up toward the rooftops was speculative. "Young people have it so hard nowadays—because they don't experience the kind of difficulties that make them tough, make them able to bow and not break."

"Like you did."

She slewed me a glance. "Like I did. I was in a war, Aventurine. I saw death. I *caused* death. That makes a person hard. Perhaps for her entire life." She sighed. "I might have been an entirely different woman, had I not chosen the life path I did at such an early age. But circumstances dictated much of that choice."

"People come back from wars and resume their lives," I protested.

"People come back from wars and suffer from PTSD. Shell-shock. People choose never to speak of their experiences again, and bottle them all up inside. People die by suicide. And some people go home, marry their sweethearts, and start a family. Some of those live happily ever after. Some of those abuse their spouses and children." She turned to look me full in the face. "Everyone must deal with the tragedy of war in his or her own way. But don't kid yourself. Everyone who lives through it is changed in some way."

I fished my phone out of my bag, switched on the recorder, and set it on the table between us. Again, she eyed it with something akin to disdain.

"How did the war change you?"

She laughed, an impatient sound. "It made me unable to trust anyone, it made me unwilling to love anyone, it made me find most people, and most of life in peacetime, exceedingly boring."

"And yet—here you are. More than seventy years later." It was a question disguised as an observation.

She smiled at me, pityingly, and with the glint in her eyes that made me understand that there was so much more I didn't know.

"Because I've been useful. There are wars, Aventurine, and there are wars. I've been fighting in different, secret ones for much of those seventy years."

I drew in a breath. "MI5? MI6?"

The smile was arch. "If I told you, as they say, I'd have to kill you."

Nine

I met Neil Barrett in the journalism program at NYU. Even back then we all knew he skated close to the proverbial edge. Rumors abounded about his work, his sources. I lost track of him after graduation; while I opted for the grad school program, Neil went straight out into the world to find and report his stories.

Then I was out, too, finding a position with the *Post* almost immediately, as I'd interned there, and had found a mentor in the editor. I loved the opportunity to pitch a story at the weekly meeting, to hash it out, to begin the process of research and interviews. At first it was mostly fluff—the meaty stuff was handed out to writers with more experience, more contacts. Eventually my name started to appear in tiny print at the end of several higher-profile pieces, as in, *Aventurine Morrow also contributed to this article.*

Neil was back, and he eased his way into my circle slowly: he appeared at some parties I attended, nodding from across the room. Then came the night Micheline, her newly minted fiancé Shep, and I were at a bar in Soho, and Neil struck up a conversation, buying a round, charming my sister, joshing with Shep. We compared notes. He was free-lancing, stringing for some of the bigger papers; *more freedom,* he'd said, and he liked it.

Just like that, he was part of our group. It seemed only natural that he and I should pair up; we dated, we fell into bed with one another. There was something exhilarating about being able to come home and talk about the work with someone who understood what I was doing, someone who was interested in the ins and outs of any given story, and I fancied myself in love. Sometimes we would lie in bed in my two-room-and-a-bath walk-up and stare at the lights playing across the ceiling from the street below, brainstorming what kind of pieces the journals who bought his stories would want next, or how I could get some information, or score an interview with some big name. Neil was a riot those nights, doing impersonations until we convulsed with laughter before coming together in wild abandoned sex.

Then came my break. The Malvern story. I'd got a lead which piqued my interest while working on an entirely different article, and the murk just kept getting deeper the more closely I looked at it. David, my editor, at first was hesitant, but slowly grew more excited as I lay information and interviews before him. It became apparent that I was investigating a story of massive extortion and fraud, and that there was evidence—provided and corroborated by trusted sources and poorly hidden documentation—that indicated that several prominent businessmen and members of Congress were involved.

I worked feverishly on that investigation, the first big story David had allowed me to run with as the lead. I filled notebook after notebook, mini-cassette after mini-cassette, with notes and interviews and meticulous documentation. I worked all hours, whenever and wherever the leads would take me. I carried my drafts from home to the newsroom and back, all on computer disks carefully backed up and labeled. I had just completed a full first draft that one afternoon, preparatory to presenting it to David at our meeting in the morning, and was elated: the end was in sight, publication of the story that would make my reputation was on the horizon. It seemed appropriate to come home to Neil, cooking a celebratory dinner of scallops in wine.

The nausea hit me suddenly, midway through the meal. The sweats broke out first, along my hairline and under my arms. I shivered uncontrollably, and when I looked across the table at Neil, his face swam in and out of focus.

"What is it?" he asked, laying aside his knife and fork. "Aventurine?"

His voice seemed to come from a place incredibly far away. I clapped my hand to my mouth and staggered toward the bathroom, desperate to make it in time. Dropping to my knees, I vomited until there was nothing left, until I felt as though my guts were turning inside out. I leaned my forehead against the cold porcelain.

"Avi?" Neil was at my side, holding a cool cloth to the back of my neck. He reached over to flush the toilet.

I let him help me to bed, where he sat with me until I dozed off.

When I awoke in the weak morning light, his side of the bed was empty, the pillow smooth. I wandered unsteadily out to the kitchen, headachy as though hungover, and found last night's dirty dishes and half-eaten dinner still on the table, a rotten fishy smell on the stale air.

There was no sign of Neil.

When my head was clear enough to check, I found there was no sign of my story—no notes, no disks, no drafts—either. Weeks, months of work. Gone.

I avoided David in the newsroom for three days. Three days searching fruitlessly for my material. Even the back-up disks were gone. Then came the morning that David threw a rival newspaper on my desk on the way by, uttering a single word before he slammed into his office: *Scooped.*

The byline was Neil's.

Ten

As I was leaving Genevieve's that evening shortly before seven, my phone pinged with a text from Paul. *Chippy. 1 Lawrence.* There was a link to Google Maps. I clicked through. On the other side of the river, around the wall, about a half-mile from the guest house.

It was cooling off as the evening drew on, but at this point in high summer, the light wouldn't fade for another couple of hours. I found Paul seated at a scarred outdoor table, huddled between the shopfront and the road, before a paper plate piled high with cod and chips. He was apparently taking Genevieve at face value. Even from a distance I could read the frown that had become his characteristic expression over the past year. He stared at the screen in his hands.

"He's obsessive," Micheline had said the night she'd asked me to take Paul on this research trip. "He keeps trying to retrace his father's steps." Perhaps, I realized now, Paul's obsessive researching was akin to mine: trying to get to the *why* of any given situation, so we could understand it, accept it, and move on. The idea of this common trait was both oddly comforting and unnerving.

He looked up. I waved, and his expression softened and closed down as he set his phone aside. "Hungry?" he asked as I approached. He indicated his plate. "This is tons better than at that place in the airport. Better than the pub at that gate. Can I get you some?"

"What, no beer?"

He shrugged. "Just a takeaway, not a pub. There's a bunch of places on the way back to the guest house if we need to stop."

When he made a move to stand, I put a hand on his shoulder, bony under his denim jacket, and pushed him gently back into his seat. "I'll get mine. You stay." I was still jazzed by the afternoon's conversation with Genevieve, and I didn't think I could settle. Inside at the counter I pawed through my bag for my wallet, touching my notebook, my phone, my recorder as though they were talismans. All still there, all still accounted for. While I waited for the counterman to pull my battered fish and a hefty amount of fries from the grease, I thought of the person Genevieve had seen the previous afternoon at Dick Turpin's grave, and who she had assumed made a third to our party.

Or didn't.

I glanced over my shoulder at the window. Aside from Paul's head, bowed once again over his phone, I saw no one else, other than anonymous pedestrians passing briskly, made oblivious by their own concerns.

Genevieve had been warning me. There *was* someone following us, and I knew who it was. How it could be? And why? Those were questions that bore further investigation, but right now, I didn't have the time, nor the concentration, for that. I patted my notes and my recorder again when replacing my wallet, then zipped the bag and did the flip-over latch as well. I knew what Neil had wanted last time—I knew that oh, so well. Something told me that following us now was not because, after twenty-five or so years, he had suddenly discovered an undying love for my person. Neil only had undying love for one, and that was himself.

I smiled at the counterman as I took my paper plate, heavy and hot. Then, when I rejoined my nephew, I opted to draw a chair around to sit beside him, rather than across from him. Genevieve had warned me, because I had been obtuse and unobservant. I would not turn my back to the street again.

I was never captured, though I came very close on a number of occasions.

Commander Smith had warned us, before we were inserted. "Be on your guard, even in your sleep. It will be the difference between—" *and he had smiled in that grim flat way he had "—remaining alive for six days, and remaining alive for six weeks." The way he spoke, though, made it clear: no one remained alive for six weeks.*

"Capture," he had said another time, "means torture, and then, when they've squeezed you like a sponge, it means death. You would be wise to kill yourself before you let them take you alive."

So there was to be no light at the end of the tunnel for us. There was, in fact, no end of the tunnel. We were trained, sent forth to find out what we could, to hit the targets we were assigned, and to die.

But I was sixteen, and I didn't believe in death. In that way, I was invincible.

"How did you manage to join so young?" I had asked as our afternoon wore on. "Surely there were papers which had to be examined when you joined the F.A.N.Y. Documents."

Genevieve had sipped her tea, raising her eyebrows. When she spoke, it was with that arch tone I'd quickly become so familiar with. "I had an older sister who died in the Spanish flu epidemic, well before I was born. It was a simple thing to adopt her name, her birthday. Besides. It was war. It was all hands on deck. Let's just say that Colonel Buckmaster had no time for those sorts of details, as long as you stacked up well against his other tests. Physical, psychological—you know."

Genevieve must have been one hell of a sixteen-year-old. "And you stacked up well," I prodded.

She laughed shortly, as though I'd failed at recognizing the obvious. "I'm still alive, Aventurine," she reminded me gently.

I felt a fool, as no doubt she had intended.

"What was your sister's name?" I asked after a moment, curiosity winning over meekness.

"Mary."

Mary. A plain name for someone who had died before her sister had been born, but who had served her country, and the Allies, well, even in death.

"Did you have trouble keeping your names straight?"

Again the arch look. "Don't be silly. Commander Smith gave me a new name after training, and that's the only one I've needed since."

Eleven

*O*h, *I had a husband. I was married.*

It wasn't until I was in my middle fifties, of course. There was no need to marry earlier, to legitimize any children I had no desire to have. And as I told you before, war changes people—or at least makes them much more of what they were previously. Magnifies them, if you will. In any case, that's what it did to me. War made me unable, or at least unwilling, to trust anyone—and that, you must realize, makes marriage difficult. Maybe impossible. Unless—the person you marry is so like you, in personality, in psychological makeup, and in experience. Then, even though you don't trust, it's possible to—love.

It's possible, too, to be asked by that person to do the impossible, and to do it.

I hadn't really thought about what she had meant until after I'd played the recording over to myself. Public records I'd dug out from the GRO indicated that Genevieve had married Charles Ingraham in 1979, when she was in her fifties, and they had remained married for twenty-two years, until he died of complications related to Alzheimer's disease. Twenty-two years, almost as long as Micheline and Shep had been married. A fair length of time, I thought, shying away from my own track record, which was non-existent.

Of course, there was the difference between Genevieve and me: she might not have trusted Charles Ingraham, but she had admitted to loving him. After Neil, I trusted no one, and outside of family, I loved no one, either.

Micheline called as I was going through my notes, leaning against the headboard, duvet covering my knees.

"What's wrong?" she demanded as soon as I picked up. Not unusual. We had always received strange emotional waves from each other, no matter how far I traveled away from her. Not telepathy—we had never shared thoughts. This was something far more visceral, far more difficult to explain. There were times I felt my sister in my blood, as I'm sure she felt me in hers. "Is it Paul? Is he okay?"

"Still gloomy," I said, drawing a breath. "Not much better, but definitely not worse. He's been talking about Shep a little." Mostly to an elderly woman he'd only just met, but I didn't bother to say that.

"Then it's you," Micheline said. I heard the concern in her voice. No one had ever spoken to me with the concern my twin had for me. "What's going on?"

I never considered not answering. "Neil," I said.

A long pause. Even over the distance I could hear her breathing pick up, become rougher, angrier. "No, Aventurine," she ground. "*Not* Neil. Don't you even consider it. Don't you *ever* go back there."

"I'm not," I said quickly. "You *know* I'm not. But I think he's here, Mick."

"In York?"

"I thought I saw someone who looked like him, in London. Then I thought I saw him again here, a couple of days later."

"*Thought.*"

"Yes."

"But you're not sure." Then a rush of words. "Aventurine, when was the last time you saw him? Not in years, right? Please tell me you haven't seen Neil in years."

Absolutely not. "Not in person since that party. The one just before Paul was born."

She knew what party I meant. She knew that was the last time we'd traded places in public, she wearing my accustomed blue, while I wore her usual green. Because we'd both wanted to go see our friends off, and, as things stood, we couldn't both go without some sort of subterfuge.

I could hear Micheline's breathing slowing again, as though she was making an effort to calm herself. "Do you know where he's been? I mean, he *did* practically drop off the face of the earth, not long after he stole your prize."

"He couldn't hold another job, it seemed."

"Because he didn't have your work to steal," Micheline agreed darkly. I heard the snick of a match; she was lighting a cigarette. "But you don't know where he's been."

I'd lost track of him twenty-odd years ago, and, bearing my scars, made no effort to find out what had happened to him. Far be it from me to wish death upon anyone, but I skirted pretty close. "No idea."

"And you haven't seen the face on this guy," Micheline reminded me. "The one who might or might not be Neil." She made a sound like a clearing of a phlegmy throat. "God, just saying his name makes me want to vomit."

"No. I haven't seen this guy fully. Just glimpses."

"So it might *not* be him." She had gone into logical and reassuring mode. "Of all the gin joints in all the world, as Rick would say—"

"It's improbable," I agreed. "Unlikely. Damn near close to impossible. I know." I swallowed. "But Micheline. Genevieve saw him, too."

Again the long pause. Then, "Whoa. Whoa, whoa, whoa. Back

this manure cart up a minute. Genevieve Smithson. Your interview subject. The cagey World War II espionage agent. She *knows* Neil?"

My turn to backtrack. "See, she asked me about the third person who was wandering around York with me and Paul the first afternoon we were here. She saw someone following us, and either assumed he was with us, or was trying to warn me by telling what she saw."

"Which one do you think?"

"I think the second. I think she knew he wasn't with us, but didn't want to alarm us if there was nothing to it. She seemed pretty certain. But—"

"So again, you don't really *know*."

I reached to the bedside stand for my glass of water, and took a drink. I felt the anxiety building up again. The tension headache prickled. I *didn't* really know. But at the same time, I *did*.

"Mick," I said, and my voice cracked. "I don't like it."

"Avi," she answered, using my nickname as I had used hers, the way we had always done when we felt and spoke with intensity. "Do your job. Do it well. And be careful."

Twelve

*M*y mother was French. My brothers and I—we learned, from the time we could talk. We conversed. When I first replied to that advertisement I saw in the magazine at the newsstand, contacting the MEW as instructed, and received the invitation to report to the Inter Services Bureau, I simply determined to speak French to the interviewer, who I later learned was Selwyn Jepson. That apparently was what the service was hoping for: native French speakers, or as close as possible. Et j'aurais facilement pu être français. He and I had two more interviews, before SOE work was even mentioned—but I wasn't stupid: I'd guessed early on what I was getting into, and it was exactly what I'd wanted.

Preliminary was simple enough, and my French got quite the workout there—my mother would have been pleased, had she any clue what I was up to. I was impatient at preliminary. I never let on, of course, because impatience was not seen as a virtue in espionage. Eventually my cohort and I were sent along to Arisaig, where the real training began, in weapons, in explosives, in getting around without being seen nor heard. It was hard work, but in an odd sort of way, I enjoyed it—maybe too much. From there, to parachute training, then to finishing school at Beaulieu, and I was ready to be dropped into France with my circuit.

"You weren't frightened?"

We were atop the wall again, circling the city clockwise. My inclination was counterclockwise, always—widdershins. However, I was right-handed; and as far as I could tell, Genevieve led with her left. It was early afternoon, with bright sun and no wind, and there were more people walking the wall than on the previous day. We would not be meeting Paul, however: he had announced, early that morning, his intention of visiting Haworth for the day.

Anne, Charlotte, or Emily? I had asked him before we split up.

He'd only skewed a glance toward me. *Branwell.*

I'd duly reported to Genevieve at nine. Hell, I'd almost run to Genevieve's house, I was so excited to get back to her and her story. After the previous evening's sorting through my notes, I'd made a list of further questions I wanted to ask, to get the talk flowing again. Of course, I smirked at my own confidence as interviewer: it was fairly obvious that Genevieve, expert at interrogation that she was, would only be telling me the things she wished me to know, in the order she wished me to know them. Still, I'd been at this job a long time. I was a fairly competent interviewer by now. Part of my excitement was at meeting Genevieve head on, and getting at parts of the story she might not wish, at first, to give to me.

Again, tea, and this morning, crumpets and strawberry jam with our talk. Now, the daily constitutional, with my cross-body bag held tightly to my side, and the borrowed walking stick in my hand. I was growing accustomed to the heft of the stick, the feel of the smooth knob in my palm, the click of brass cap against stone.

"You weren't frightened?" I asked again, when I had a chance to draw abreast.

She barely skimmed a look in my direction.

"Of course I was frightened. Anyone who wasn't frightened at the prospect of being parachuted behind enemy lines, with an uncertain future—perhaps no future at all—would be an idiot, wouldn't you agree?" She sighed. "But that, I've decided, is what courage is, if you choose to believe in the concept. Being as frightened as hell, but knowing that you have to do something anyway, and so simply—doing it."

"And what did your family think?" I knew that in the early meetings with Jepson and his ilk, potential agents were asked about their families, their backgrounds, anything that might make them a weak link or a potential liability.

She turned her head slightly, her thousand-mile gaze resting momentarily on something out there that didn't exist anymore. "My father died shortly after I was born; my only sister, as I've told you, died in the flu pandemic in 1919. My mother, I've always thought, collapsed under that weight. My brothers enlisted as soon as they could, the youngest, like me, lying about his age. Not one of the three made it off the battlefield and back home. There was really no one to care, no one who remembered me as a child—was I ever really a child? So I was reborn, code-named Genevieve, and I just kept on, as that person. Even after the war, it became my life."

There was a defiance in her words, but behind them, a resignation. This rebirth was as much a sorrow as a regeneration. I felt the sadness, but did not remark upon it, for somehow I felt any sympathy would be met with scorn and distaste. I would leave that probe for a later time, when she trusted me more. Or, I corrected myself, when she distrusted me less.

"After?" I asked instead.

"After. I remained useful to the government—that's the euphemism we always use: *I work for the government*—over the years. As Genevieve, I've worked off and on for—certain centers of activities; when I was younger, I traveled, though for the past twenty years or so, it's just been easier to direct *traffic* from the comfort of my own library."

The library she had welcomed me into over the past days, with tea and apple cake.

"Traffic?"

Genevieve shrugged slightly. "You don't *have* to be on the ground to coordinate an effort. In this day of internet activity, you don't have to be on the ground to coordinate information. The circuits of the SOE are a thing of the past, Aventurine. Dinosaurs."

There was so much I didn't know, despite the masses of preliminary research I had done before coming to the first interview. In fact, the more I researched and interviewed, the more I found I needed to research. It was both exhausting and exhilarating. Breathtaking, even.

Not for the first time did I wonder why Genevieve had chosen me for her project. But that was no longer all that important. I only knew I had to gather as much from her as I could: she was, after all, in her mid-nineties. As indomitable as she seemed, she would not live forever.

Paul was restless when he returned from Haworth, his leg jiggling under the table as he sat, as though he were revving up to take off again. After an afternoon spent going through a box of faded photographs with Genevieve, listening as she told the stories of each one, the agents—most long dead—and the locations, I felt uneasy as well. Haunted by the restless ghosts of people I didn't know, who had been dead for decades.

"Didn't Genevieve force-march you around the wall enough today?" Paul asked. He frowned, as though the question were an effort. He did not meet my eyes.

"Didn't the Brontës force-march you up to Top Withins?" I countered.

Our mutual restlessness sent us out toward the Shambles all the same, late though it was; it was almost as though we couldn't just sit together, spending the evening talking. There was still plenty of daylight, though some of the shops were buttoned up for the night, and the daytime crowds had thinned out. I bought some chocolate

and a new pen in a shop by the alleged birthplace of Guy Fawkes; Paul opted for a touristy T-shirt and a small book, which appeared, from the briefest glance I caught of the cover, to be about World War II. Genevieve was getting to him, perhaps as much as she was getting to me.

The streets were narrow, the building fronts overhanging the cobbles, shutting out the remains of the fading evening sun. As we ambled along, lights began to go on along the alley, strings of pearls glimmering above our path.

"Hungry?"

Paul shrugged. I felt his eyes on me, but when I turned my head, his glance slid away. I felt vaguely uncomfortable with his response—with his entire demeanor. I had thought that, over the past several days, Paul had begun to come out of his dark place, talking a bit more, allowing the sunlight in, just a little. Now I was uncertain. He seemed withdrawn again. Wary. Testy, even, as though my company grated.

Up ahead, the brilliantly lit window of an Italian restaurant, broken up into its tiny panes. I slowed to look at the menu posted by the door. Much mention of seafood, of mushrooms, and of garlic; my heart and taste buds were captivated.

"Here?" I asked. Again the shrug. I pretended I read that as assent, and opened the door.

There was a tiny table in the corner, recently abandoned by other diners; after a few minutes for clearing and resetting, Paul and I were shown to our seats. The ceiling was low and criss-crossed by black beams, the room humming with low conversation, the lighting atmospheric. I ordered a gin and tonic, while Paul asked for a dark beer, then subsided again into silence. He studied the menu intently, not looking across at me, not making any small talk.

"How was Haworth?"

He didn't lift his eyes. "Good."

71

"Did you actually get out to Top Withins?"

He shook his head. "Just the museum."

The waiter came, took our dinner orders, left us.

Paul took a long drink from his pint, then wiped his upper lip with a finger.

I waited, but there was nothing else forthcoming.

I watched the waiters weave between the tables, carrying drinks, plates. Outside the window, the night drew in.

"Are you all right?" I asked finally.

Paul's eyes flicked up at me, and then away again. "Fine." His voice was terse. He lifted his glass again. Then he caught the waiter's eye and indicated his near-empty pint.

I bit my lip. I think I might have taken one or two sips from my gin; I wondered, not for the first time, about Paul's drinking habits. Did he drink too much? I hadn't noticed him drunk on this trip, but I couldn't help but worry. Especially with his dark mood. Depression and drinking, in my experience, never mixed well. I drew in a breath, reminded again of the depths of his unhappiness. Yet, this evening there was a sharp edge to it.

I tried again. "Did something happen today?"

I could almost see the hackles rise. Paul's expression was hard, and at the same time, wary. "Why? What would have happened?"

"You tell me."

Our food arrived, on white plates like islands. Paul had chosen the sea bass, while I plumped for chicken and mushrooms in wine and cream sauce. The waiter sailed away.

"Nothing happened." Paul picked up his fork, but paused with it in midair. "I saw the painting. I saw the little books. I saw the graveyard. I saw some stuff about their father, Patrick, who was an absolute shit, and I don't wonder Branwell was screwed up."

His outburst was so venomous, and so unexpected, that I drew back in surprise, dropping my fork on the floor. Without any indication on my part, the waiter flitted by and left another on the table, retrieving the other before disappearing. This seemed as good a time as any to take a drink from my gin.

"What—" I took another quick sip. "What brought this on?"

Something told me it wasn't really about Patrick Brontë, but damned if I knew what the outburst was about. Patrick Brontë was a shit who lived. Shep, who died, was *what?*

"Nothing." His gaze slid away again, and he poked his fork into his fish. "Just tired."

For the rest of the dinner Paul managed to have his mouth full when I spoke, so was only able to nod. He was silent, too, on the walk back to the guest house.

Thirteen

One of the things our parachute instructor would do on our practice jumps at Ringway, once we'd graduated from the tower, would be to send me first—me, the only woman in our training group. This wasn't a problem, because I found early on that I enjoyed the exhilaration of flight, no matter how brief. The reason I got dropped first, though, was not because of my eagerness: it was because the instructor knew well that the men in the belly of the plane wouldn't back out if it meant being shamed by me.

I was dropped in October from a Lysander, on a clear cold night with a hazy moon, along with our radio operator, whose code name was Pierre. We'd had a cramped flight, low under the German radar. The circuit had been established earlier in the year—Magician, it was called, and I liked that, even though we were replacing a radio operator who had been captured in a raid, and a courier who had been killed. That had meant a relocation of the circuit base into the forest several miles away from the designated drop field, so after disentangling ourselves from our parachutes, Pierre and I joined our Maquis landing party in a brisk march into hiding.

"Je parie que vous pourriez y arriver en volant, *Madame Hawk*," one of the Frenchmen said, edging uncomfortably close, and laying a hand on my arm in the dark beneath the trees. His breath smelled of brandy.

"C'est mieux que de ramper lá-bas, maître ver," *I hissed, and the next thing he knew he was on the ground. There was much subdued laughter from his companions, then silence for the rest of our withdrawal to the camp.*

After that, no one used my alias. I was always Lady Hawk.

"Take these," Genevieve said as I was leaving that afternoon. We had to call it quits earlier than usual, because of an appointment she had with her GP, which, she informed me with impatience, she was definitely not looking forward to. Now she waved an imperious hand at the box she'd brought out a few days previously. "There's a print shop over on Walmsgate that can scan these for you, so you can examine them all at your leisure. It might take them a few days, depending on their backlog. Just bring the box back when you're done." For a moment she looked mischievous. "I might need to will them to the National Archives or some such thing, after you've published this book."

"After I make you famous?"

"Of course."

The box was unwieldy, and we agreed that it would not be feasible for me to walk all the way to Walmsgate carrying it. Thus she waited with me just inside her door, holding her walking stick, until the taxi arrived; we parted on the pavement, and just before she closed the door behind me, she leaned forward and murmured, her lips barely moving, "He's across the street." Then she locked and double-checked the door before she moved off briskly along the road.

As the cab pulled away from the curb, I craned my neck to look back out of the rear window. I saw Genevieve's resolute figure on the pavement, bending to pat a corgi on a lead. Just beyond her, that now familiar figure in its dark jacket, head covered by a dark fedora, walking away. My skin prickled. I clutched the box all the more tightly, not releasing my grip until the cab had crossed the river and threaded itself through the streets to the print shop. I handed the driver some notes, and looked both ways—suspicious, paranoid—as I darted from taxi to doorway without waiting for change.

The road was nearly empty. I was safe, but sweaty and shaky.

When I got back to the guest house, there was no sign of Paul. I texted him about meeting for supper, but by seven he had not replied. He was twenty-three, I told myself. An adult. By now he knew more about getting around in York than I did. Still, I didn't like it.

I took myself out to supper at the Light Horseman, then returned to my room to examine my day's notes and prepare for tomorrow.

Fourteen

Stealthily we crept through the underbrush toward our target, a railway bridge over a low-flowing river. We each carried a pack with explosives, detonators, and the like, homemade as we'd been taught in guerrilla training, but effective. My first objective since joining the circuit. I was sweating under my black clothes, the grease blacking my face making my skin itch, but I could taste the excitement. More than I could ever say. I had never felt more alive.

The moon was barely a sliver, low in the sky, slipping in and out of clouds. Up ahead, the road, infrequently patrolled, which we would have to cross to reach the railroad embankment. We gathered in the ditch, awaiting the all clear, but when Pierre stupidly cracked a twig underfoot, we all heard the tell-tale click and shuffle of a bolt sliding back.

I slid to the left, circled. The soldier loomed as he swung his gun barrel around, taking a step or two closer to our hiding place. His eyes glittered beneath his helmet.

I unsheathed the knife strapped to my thigh.

He swept the barrel to the side.

It was all I needed. I leapt up behind him and plunged my blade into his throat, as I'd learned in training. With a gurgle, he collapsed, almost in slow motion, his body rolling slightly down the incline, head lower than his feet. In the dim light, his expression was of surprise, the look he'd wear for all eternity. I wiped the knife on my pant leg, and slipped it back into the sheath. Wiped my hand on his coat.

Where there had been one, there would be more. I jerked my head, indicating the others should follow. We dashed silently across the road while the moon hung blanketed by clouds.

Within fifteen minutes, the explosives were placed, the timers set. We faded off into the night, back to base, though more than anything, I wanted to see the destruction of our first objective: the explosion, the blaze. But it wasn't wise to wait around.

In the morning I stopped by Paul's room and knocked with no result. I had called before my shower, but had been shunted straight to voice mail. For all I knew, he could have stayed out all night. I wondered for a moment about the night life in York—were there clubs? Dancing? Of course there were. There was certainly drinking. And hell, Paul was a good-looking young man: there were certainly women in York. Men, too, for that matter.

I couldn't help but worry, though, and after I'd had my full English—without beans; I really hated the beans—I stopped by his room once more on the way to my own and knocked again. This time I heard movement inside, so I waited. The door scraped open, and Paul's bleary eyes looked out at me, blinking, squinting against the light. There were bruisy circles beneath his eyes, and deep lines etched between his brows.

"You don't look well."

He was shirtless, though he wore jeans. His feet were bare, his hair standing nearly straight up. He looked feverish and smelled terrible and sour. Behind him, the room was still in darkness, the drapes drawn against any sun that might be so insensitive as to shine this morning.

"Bender?"

I meant the question to be teasing, but Paul stiffened. He never

used to be that sensitive—back when he was a teenager, he had once called me, rather than his parents, to rescue him from a pit party when he found himself incapacitated. That boy had retreated far away, however, and I had no idea how to find him right now.

"Sorry," I said. "Do you need anything? Tylenol?"

He coughed, still holding the door partially closed. "Got some. I'm going to sleep in this morning."

I half-laughed. "I should think so. But what about breakfast?"

For a moment he looked as though he wanted to vomit. His Adam's apple worked. "No breakfast." He sighed. "Avi, I'll go out for something later. Maybe you could just go to work and let me sleep this off."

He sounded abrupt, desperate for me to go. For the barest moment I felt hurt. I took a deep breath, tried to let it go.

"Okay. Call me later. If you need me I'll come back."

"I won't."

He shut the door, and I stared at it dumbly. He had never spoken to me like that before. Slowly I turned and went back to my room to collect my things.

"Something's bothering you," Genevieve said as she poured the tea and served the cake: a blueberry lemon pound cake this time. Still the delicate china, the heavy silverware with the scrollwork on the handles, which I imagined would work as weaponry should the occasion warrant. "Let's get it out of the way so we can get back to work." Her voice was matter-of-fact, but not unkind.

I sipped my tea, too hot, burned my tongue. I hardly cared.

"Paul," I said.

For a moment Genevieve said nothing, only blew on her own tea before taking a small sip. She tipped her head then, not looking at me. "He's a troubled boy," she murmured. Curious, as though considering a specimen of some sort.

"Hardly a boy," I protested. "He's twenty-three. He's been of age for five years now."

She lifted her fine eyebrows. "I'm ninety-four. To me, at twenty-three, he's a boy. But we won't argue the point. He's still troubled."

"He is."

"His father?"

I sighed. "I was thinking he was coming out of it with me. We had one good conversation in London. He certainly had a lot to say to *you* about his father, more than I've heard him speak about Shep since he disappeared."

"But?"

"But. Paul was so odd when he came back from Haworth." I struggled to find the description. "Monosyllabic. Morose. Didn't want to tell me about it, which would have been unusual before his father's death. We used to talk about everything, Paul and I. He always wanted to share new discoveries, new ideas. But I don't know anymore what unusual *is* with Paul."

"Did something happen in Haworth?"

Nothing had happened in Haworth since the Brontës had died out. But I didn't say that. "I don't know. He didn't say. He *wouldn't* say. He provided no details of anything he saw, anyplace he went—something he used to be really eager to do. He has always been a person with a fascination for details."

"Such as you have always been."

I didn't answer that one.

I loved pound cake; I loved lemon and blueberries. Even on its plate of sprigged flowers, this slice of cake looked unappealing. I set it aside. "It was as though the entire sensory experience of Haworth had been erased from his mind. Or had simply never registered."

Genevieve leaned back in her chair, took another sip of tea. Her brow was furrowed. "But *what* exactly erased it?"

"You don't think it's just time alone, thinking over Shep's death?"

She shrugged her strong shoulders. "It might very well be. Grief comes in waves, some of them very high." Genevieve sighed, then refocused. "Perhaps he is having a relapse, if you will, into the depths of that grief. I can't say—I'm not a psychologist, by any means."

"But you don't think that's it."

Now Genevieve turned her gaze back on me, frowning. "There's quite a bit of strangeness in your world right now, Aventurine. I can see all sorts of disparate pieces, but I can't quite see the pattern. So I'm not yet in any position to make a judgment."

I sighed, set aside the tea. I fiddled with my notepad, my phone, my digital recorder. Nothing was quite right. I was used to being able to concentrate on work, to bringing a single-mindedness to it which cut through all the dross. But now? I fought to find myself, the purposeful researcher and writer. It had always come easiest, I realized suddenly, when I had not had any personal demands, and could be wholly professional. This trouble with Paul, with Micheline, with *Shep*, damn him, was side-tracking me in ways I didn't like at all. I wouldn't even consider the anxiety Neil's apparent reappearance was causing me. There was a reason why I had remained single and unattached all these years.

"Come," Genevieve said now, setting her own cup and saucer on the tray and getting to her feet. Once again I was struck by her height, by the fact that, even at her advanced age, she did not stoop. Her spine must be, obviously, made of steel. "Let's go look at my uniform."

"Uniform?"

"F. A. N. Y.," she said. "I still fit into it." There was a touch of vanity to her words. I followed her into the hallway and to the stairs.

Fifteen

Aventurine is a green stone from the quartz family, sometimes called the "Stone of Opportunity." It's supposed to bring luck, and perhaps that's why I ended up with the name. Our parents had been married for close to sixteen years before I was born. I was, they thought, their lucky child.

They didn't realize, however, that I was not the only one, but there were two of us; even the obstetrician claimed to be surprised by my twin's appearance, some twelve minutes after mine. He had not heard a second fetal heartbeat—but I always attributed that to our being so closely aligned, even in the womb.

Thus, our parents had no second name chosen for the baby I'd argue was their luckiest child. Born with the umbilical cord wrapped around her neck, she needed to be resuscitated and stabilized. My father, a man who died far too early, firmly believed that my mother walked on air, and named my sister after her: Micheline, for Michelle. Thus the two of us matched, not just genetically, but in terms of naming. And thus we all, father, mother and me, had spent the remainder of my childhood, and the remainder of my parents' lives, feeling as though we had to protect Micheline. The surprise sister. The underdog. I'd have done absolutely anything for her.

• •

So it was while I was at my lowest, after the personal and professional havoc that Neil had wreaked on me, that Micheline and Shep came to me with their suggestion. Plan? Plea? At that point, it hardly mattered. The connection between my twin and me *had* always been such that I would do anything for her; and at that point, my self-esteem was so low that all I really needed was to be—*needed.*

"We want a child," Micheline said, sitting across from me, holding her husband's hand. Actually, Shep was holding hers, clutching so tightly his knuckles showed white; he was obviously uncomfortable with this conversation, but he was there, and something in me appreciated that, without knowing yet what they were asking. I remembered everything about that moment, as if it had been distilled. As I watched, Mick put her other hand over his. He might have been shaking. Micheline, however, was confident, with that absolute assurance that I would agree to whatever she requested.

There was a pause, which I filled with suppositions. Adoption? I considered and discarded each. My brain was still sluggish after the shock and betrayal from Neil. I knew that, since the tumors, which had dictated a total hysterectomy when we were in college, it had been Micheline's great grief that she would be unable to bear children. She would not even be able to provide the eggs for artificial insemination, for a surrogate.

I caught the slightest glimmer of where this was going. My eyes shot to her face, the mirror image of mine.

"If you would be an egg donor—"

Again the pause.

We were identical twins, Micheline and I. Created with and from the same DNA. If I donated an egg, it would be identical to those Micheline no longer had.

"If I agreed—"

The rest of the question, unspoken, hung suspended between us. Shep was studying their intertwined hands. Micheline held my gaze, and I could feel the force of her wanting. I could feel her pulling at the bond that held us, forever tied together.

"Would you be our surrogate?"

Fast on the shock of the suggestion came the realization that it made perfect sense. It was easy to agree, for so many reasons. Because she was my sister, the person I loved more than anyone in the world. Because I knew that she and Shep would be the best possible parents. Because I needed to be needed, needed to be successful at something.

Even the plan to keep the elaborate plot concealed was easy, as long as, in the last trimester of our pregnancy, Micheline and I were never seen in the same place at the same time. Ours was a secret that we'd kept for twenty-three years. We were both, Micheline and I, simultaneously, Paul's mother and aunt; though Shep, without question, was his son's father.

Paul didn't know. At first that had been cause for anxiety. However, somewhere along the line, keeping that secret had ceased to bother me. Now, with Shep's death—I truly missed my brother-in-law, and couldn't think of him without a sharp pang—and Paul's reaction, I felt even more strongly that I should support Micheline's decision.

As for the complexities of switching a child at birth? Made ever so much more simple by our identical twin-ness. And money. Because money has always solved a great number of problems, and even then, Shep had so much of it.

"I've been reading about you," Genevieve said, as she placed the hanger on the bed and unzipped the protective cover. Inside lay her uniform, olive drab, breast pockets on either side. There were decorations ranged on it, which I did not quite understand; she stepped aside as I snapped a quick picture of them with my cell phone, then moved in closer to photograph each bar and medal separately.

"Reading *about* me?" Most people read my articles in *The New Yorker* or *The Atlantic,* or bought my books and read those instead. I wasn't exactly wildly well-known, not Stephen-King-known, though judging from sales, I was reasonably well-read. I hadn't led an interesting life, unlike my subjects; if anything, I lived vicariously through them. "I don't know what you mean."

She ran a finger over the ribbons and bars, frowning. Then she turned to take down a hatbox from the wardrobe shelf, from which she drew a uniform cap covered in protective tissue; this she slid off and set aside. She rubbed at some invisible dust on the insignia at the front of the hat, a circle around crossed bars. "Oh, of course I've read your books. Obviously, I wanted someone who could write well, someone who could tell my story with a bit of flair."

"The flair with which you lived it?"

That familiar ironic half-smile. "More. I've read all the articles as well, just to see what your personality and character and obsessions are. To see if we were, as they say, *simpatico.*"

I laughed ruefully at that. "I'm hardly a mafia don here."

She quirked an eyebrow. "But I might be. You don't know."

Genevieve was right. We had been working together for nearly a week now, long days of interviews and going through documents and photographs together. Still, knowing Genevieve was like peeling the layers of an onion. The deeper I went, the more I discovered I didn't know. She was an enigma. Of course she was. She had spent most of her life as an operative. *Keeping* secrets, not telling them, was her specialty. And her greatest pleasure, I was coming to realize: she wallowed in it.

"But—you've been reading up on me," I prodded, trying to steer the conversation. "Why? And more to the point, what on earth did you find out?"

As always, the shrug was non-committal. "You've got a pretty extensive entry on Wikipedia."

I took a picture of the cap and its insignia. I indicated that she should put it on for a photo, but Genevieve declined. "You can't fool me," I countered. "That entry is primarily concerned with my publications. My publicist created that."

"You *are* rather quiet on social media," Genevieve continued, much as though I hadn't interrupted. "The Facebook and Instagram accounts are public, and, I think, maintained by that same publicist?"

"What on earth do you know about Facebook and Instagram? You're ninety-four years old, as you keep pointing out to me." I watched her thin lips turn up slightly in amusement, and held out a hand. "No. Don't tell me. Never mind that I even said that."

She shook her head. "I've also kept telling you that I've been an agent for most of my life. One has to keep up with the times, don't you agree?"

It took me a moment to recover my equilibrium, imagining as I was Genevieve scrolling through Facebook on her iPhone, reading about the twenty-five times a rude customer got the best karma smackdown, or some such thing. At least she wasn't likely to be fooled by bots or Russian influence farmers. She was probably reporting on them to MI5. What she said, too, made sense, about keeping a finger on the informational pulse, as that was now primarily electronic. Suddenly I caught myself wondering whether there was an SOE Facebook page, and I couldn't contain my laugh.

"What is it?" she demanded.

I told her.

This time I swear her blue eyes, narrowed in the wrinkles of her face, twinkled. "And how do you know there isn't?"

"Because," I shot back, "it would be a very small group, your having outlived nearly all of them."

"Oh, but it would be a terribly interesting group, wouldn't it?"

Genevieve had an incisive wit, one had to admit. She was also a skilled conversationalist, practicing the kinds of rhetorical thrusts and parries that elicited more of a response than her counterpart had intended or perhaps even realized. I recognized this, as I had worked hard to hone the same skills in myself. Her gambit, here in the upstairs storage room, was obvious. But was it deceptively obvious? She might be playing a double game. Or she might want me to think she was, which would amount, almost, to the same thing. Trying to untangle the possibilities made my head hurt.

"What kinds of things did you discover about me?" I asked again. "And are we *simpatico?*"

"Never been married. No family, save a twin sister, a now late brother-in-law, and a nephew. Rumored to have had a secret fling several years ago with the singer Gio Constantine."

I slowed my breathing. Harmless stuff. Well, I repeated to myself, I *was* harmless. I was the medium, not the message.

"Rising star in investigative journalism straight out of college, momentarily stymied when your first story was scooped by a competitor."

Genevieve stepped to the window, drew the heavy curtain aside, and examined the street below.

"In the course of my research, I also read that competitor's scoop. It was very thorough, well-researched, but with some curious— though only occasional—lapses in the quality of the writing."

There was another pause. Genevieve let the curtain fall back into place, then took the cap from my hands. She returned it to its box, tucking the tissue around it as though tucking a baby into bed.

"It was almost as though two people had written it, one, shall we say, more talented in the ways of language than the other."

Now she lifted the box easily onto the upper shelf of the wardrobe, her back to me. Her ram-rod stiff, unyielding back. This woman, who had the will to defeat everything, from the Germans to osteoporosis. I waited, watching her, as always realizing how much she knew and how little she revealed. The anxiety was back, as it always was eventually.

How I wanted to be like this woman. I had thought I was beyond hero worship, but obviously not.

"When I compared the article, byline Neil Barrett, to some of your published work over the years, it became fairly obvious who had written the bulk of it. Obvious that it wasn't a case of a story being scooped, but rather a case of a story being stolen wholesale."

When I tried to speak, my mouth was dry. "It was—" I had to stop, to lick my lips, which felt stiff and cracked. "It was a long time ago." My palms, though, were damp with sweat. "Almost twenty-five years."

Genevieve zipped up the wardrobe bag over the uniform, then hung that up again, closing the wardrobe doors on it with a hollow thunk.

"Yes," she said, and turned the full blaze of her gaze on me. "And now he's back, isn't he? Neil?"

When I didn't answer, she shook her head, and passed me on the way out the door and to the stairs.

"More tea," she called over her shoulder. Dumbly, I followed her down.

Sixteen

I'd never liked school. I liked learning, but learning according to my own interest, and in my own time. Much of the work in the classrooms of my school was rote, and memorization has always come easily to me. I'd do my school work, and then be punished for doing nothing, when I was only waiting for the next assignment. Leaving school was probably the best thing I ever did for myself. And my ability to memorize quickly and easily aided me when I volunteered. So much to remember: code name, transmission codes, details of my new identity, contacts.

No, I was never captured. We lost Pierre six weeks after we were dropped in, when his aerial was discovered during a transmission. Magician had to relocate. Our new radio operator, Honoré, who was dropped nine days later, was a New Zealander who had lived outside of Paris and done God knows what before the war, most of it probably unsavory. He had a bit of a crush on me, but I adhered religiously to Colonel Buckmaster's strictures against personal relationships in the circuit. There were other people who didn't, of course, and perhaps no one could blame them, looking for comfort when there was no guarantee of a future. As far as I could figure, however, and especially after we'd heard that Pierre had been shot at the Gestapo prison in Paris, no one could be trusted. No one. We were all on our own, even in our circuits. Some circuits were betrayed by members who were not careful about those with whom they drank; one circuit, Spindle, was betrayed when a member had an entire uncoded list of their contacts stolen from him on a train. I knew I'd never betray our people—I'd swallow the pill in my lipstick case before I'd let the Gestapo torture anything out of me—but I did not have the same faith in anyone else.

Genevieve had not figured out the triangle of Paul's secret and complicated parentage, so I had that much to be grateful for. I washed my face with the coldest water I could bear in her downstairs lavatory, then stared at my white cheeks in the mirror. I looked as shocked as I felt. Which was very shocked. Every detail she had brought forward was true and correct: though an untrained eye would not have seen it, I knew the differences in the quality of small sections of the Malvern story. I knew the material I had drafted before it had disappeared from my apartment. I could even tell where the editor of the paper that had printed the story with Neil's byline had smoothed the writing. I was still appalled that the selection panel handing out the prizes that year had not seemed to take those uneven spaces into consideration when awarding Neil the prize for my story—even beyond the fact that Neil had received a National Press Award for investigative reporting for *my story*.

And now he's back, isn't he?

Genevieve had gone to the upstairs window, had lifted aside the curtain, had looked down into the street. Was he there now? Neil? She had seen him the other day, when I'd climbed into the cab with my box of research treasures. He was here. He was following me.

Why?

The answer, I was afraid, was fairly obvious, once I'd broken down and accepted his return. He'd struck gold stealing a story from me at the beginning of our careers. Having mined that lode, and having been sporadically employed since—the stories he produced and flogged to the papers hadn't garnered nearly as much attention as the Malvern story, and none had come close to earning such accolades—he was in need of another rich vein. Whether he had followed Paul and me from the States to London, or had stumbled upon us that first day on Westminster Bridge—whether he had known about my project with Genevieve Smithson beforehand, or realized when he'd overheard Paul and me discussing it that this could be something good—he was here now. Shadowing us. Shadowing *me*. Because he didn't want me, he wanted my story. He'd never really wanted *me*.

I splashed more cold water onto my face and used the hand towel hanging on the hook nearby to wipe it off again. Then I took a deep breath before returning to the sitting room and Genevieve's knowing gaze.

"We're supposed to be talking about you," I said, pushing the tabby cat aside more abruptly than I'd intended, resulting in a hiss and a swipe from its paw. I ignored it and resumed my accustomed seat. I held out my hands for the tea cup and saucer Genevieve handed across to me. Suddenly, I needed its warmth. "We've spent all morning talking about me."

"I'm sorry," she said. She did not sound it. "It's arrogant of me, you probably think. To be investigating your life behind your back." She poured tea for herself. "I told you I wanted to find out whether we would be a good fit—I didn't want to lay out the sordid details of my entire life to someone who wouldn't understand, who wouldn't be sympathetic."

"Sordid?"

I was becoming used to the way she tipped her head to the side, as though considering the relative merits of continuing this conversation, or relationship, or anything else. "I haven't exactly been Little Miss Mary Sunshine." She paused, seeming to find the appellation amusing. "I thought I'd made that fairly obvious. I've told you that I've killed people. Other people, other human beings."

"It was war."

She nodded. "Most of the time."

I flinched. She didn't.

"Let's walk," she said.

Outside, it was grey and looked as though it would rain; I might have felt a few spatters against my face as we stepped out into Scarcroft Road. Once again Genevieve had handed off one of her walking sticks from the vase in the front hallway. I was becoming more adept at keeping pace with her, after the past several days, which, when I thought about it, was probably symbolic. My thighs no longer burned at this pace, either. I was beginning to understand how Genevieve had made it to ninety-four, as this level of daily exercise had to be good for her, since I could feel the difference in myself.

"It's one of the things I think about frequently," she said as we came to Skeldergate and mounted the wall at Baile Hill. Again we turned to the left, to circle the city clockwise. *Deisul,* we'd say if we were witches; and maybe we were. Below us, umbrellas were sprouting in the streets like a riot of varicolored flowers. The falling of rain was becoming more regular, though not yet heavy. "My husband."

There had been a studio picture of him in the box I'd taken to the print shop; he had been a dashingly handsome man, rather in the Clark Gable style. The scans were to be ready for collection later this afternoon.

"Charles," I prodded.

"Charles." Had her voice grown soft?

"Tell me about him."

We paused at a point where the ground fell away from the base of the wall below us, tumbling downward toward a row of houses, and a building which had obviously originally been a church and was now something else. A community center? The sign was too far away to read. The birds here seemed louder, in a cacophonous protest against the rain, perhaps; fleetingly I wondered about the kinds of birds I was hearing, as I was that ignorant of birdsong. This stretch of wall seemed oddly deserted, for all its being in the middle of the city, in the middle of the day, in the middle of the summer.

"He was a New Zealander," she said, and her lips quirked.

"Did he have a bit of a crush on you?"

"You're quick."

"We're *simpatico*."

Genevieve took a deep breath, looking out over the wall. If one were having a flight of fancy, she might have been looking for her husband, or the memory of him, but her eyes did not have a dreamy, faraway expression to them. She was too much *here*, too much constantly aware of her surroundings. Even in the midst of remembering, she was cautious.

"Yes," she said, and there was a curious mix of laughter and sadness in her voice. "It was Honoré, from the circuit, though we didn't marry for more than thirty years after we'd first met. Oh, we'd crossed paths several times after the war and in the years after. We'd slept together upon occasion, as well. He was an amazing lover, Honoré."

"His crush didn't die?"

"Oh, no."

"So he finally convinced you?"

Now she turned her eyes on me. "I allowed myself to be convinced, at a time when it suited me. There's a difference, Aventurine, and you need to understand that."

Her voice carried strength and decisiveness. In all things, including, apparently, sexuality, and emotional attachment, Genevieve made her own decisions.

"But you married him."

"We had a shared history. We understood each other and the world we lived in and, in fact, helped to create. That's attractive. Comfortable, even."

"You have never allowed yourself to be comfortable. Don't give me that."

"Perhaps comfort means something different to me than it does to you."

Abruptly she turned and headed off, and, surprised, it took me a moment to catch up to her.

She threw one impatient glance at me and forged on, throwing her words over her shoulder. "He was handsome, Charles Ingraham. Charming. And brilliant. His capacity for memorization was enormous, greater than mine, and I'm definitely no slouch, even at my advanced age. It was so hard for him when the Alzheimer's started to erode his mind. Forgetfulness was foreign to him. Being unable to draw upon his vast knowledge when he wanted. Losing those neural pathways. He knew, after consulting all his medical experts, that the disease would only progress, and would steal everything that was valuable to him about his memory, his reason. His life."

It sounded horrible. To be a man who valued the life of his mind, who saw his ability to be useful in terms of his mental capacity, and who had that stripped from him, slowly, layer by layer—it must have been absolutely untenable.

"Charles trusted me to do what was best for him at the end."

She kept walking. I stumbled to a stop, watching that ram-rod stiff back. Knowing what she had intended I should know.

Twenty-two years of marriage.

Nearly an entire lifetime spent together, in one capacity or another, as agents, as lovers, as husband and wife.

I've killed people.

• •

I ran to catch up.

"I miss him," she said to me, as though I had not faltered. Up ahead, a faraway view of the Minster. She had her eye on it, a challenging look, though I knew from our conversations of the past week that she held no belief in God. "It was difficult for me to do what he asked of me, but I understood that he couldn't bear to live the way he was degenerating. It was the right thing to do. And I don't regret it for a moment."

The only sign of possible distress, I realized, was in her hand, the one clutching the knob of the blackthorn walking stick. Stiff, tense, white-knuckled. The hand of a woman who had killed her first man at sixteen, and perhaps her last some fifty-odd years later.

"He was a good man, Honoré," she said, almost to herself. "He'd managed to survive the chaos of war, the dangers of being a wireless operator behind enemy lines, and years of 'working for the government,' only to have his own body betray him at the end. I'd say that was unfair, if life wasn't equally unfair to everyone, in some measure."

"You loved him," I protested. I hadn't meant it as a protest, but I was having trouble controlling my voice.

"Of course I loved him, Aventurine. Don't be obtuse. It's only because I loved him that I was able to do what he asked."

We came down off the wall at Barker Tower and crossed the bridge, then cut through the museum gardens, which I had learned we had to do, as this stretch was one where the wall had been destroyed ages ago. Genevieve, in all our excursions save the first, had made it a point to march briskly onward, crossing the road at the Theatre Royal to regain the wall at Bootham Bar. *I* had always made it a point to allow her to lead the way, both in daily conversation and in daily constitutional. I hardly noticed the traffic, as I was still in shock from her revelations. She could have chosen to climb up onto and then climb down from the wall at every possible access point, and I would have followed her without question or comment.

"A pint," she said now, looking up at the signs above the storefronts. We passed through the gate, stopping at the pub we'd gone to with Paul that first day. "I've upset you."

I didn't know whether a pint would be the best remedy, but didn't have the voice to argue.

The rain was picking up, a cold and unfriendly drizzle. In the dimness of the pub she led us to, after we'd stepped in and shook ourselves off, we found Paul again. He looked up as we approached, his face a pale moon; his expression immediately grew wary, as though a shutter had dropped down. He stood, though, when he saw my companion; even in his depression, his manners were too well imprinted.

I smiled. "Of all the gin joints in all the world—"

"—You had to walk into mine." But Paul's response was automatic; there wasn't even the ghost of a smirk behind the words.

Genevieve pulled out a chair with the tip of her stick, and settled herself into it, with the air of a woman who had made a guess and had found it to be correct. I looked at her sharply, but her expression gave nothing away. "Would you get me a pot of tea?" she asked me.

"I'll get it," Paul said.

"Something dark for me." I dug out a note, but he simply nodded and turned toward the bar. I sighed and sat.

"He knows what you like?" Genevieve examined the plate at Paul's place, where a pile of gravy mash was crowned by partially eaten bangers. It appeared as though Paul had been pushing his food around on his plate again, unable to force himself to eat.

"After this week, he should."

She nodded. "He's hungover today?"

"I think so." I couldn't keep the concern from my voice. "I told you he was out all night, didn't I?"

Genevieve didn't have time to answer before Paul was back, and setting the tea and beer before us. He took his own seat, picked up his fork, and pushed the mash around the plate some more.

"I heard," Genevieve said, holding her teacup in both hands before her, "that you'd spent the other day in Haworth. I haven't been to visit the Brontës in quite some time." When Paul only nodded but did not speak, she went on as though she hadn't noticed. "Patrick, of course, is the one I've always wondered about. The psychology of a man who, whether intentionally or not, attempted to stunt his children. Only succeeded with Branwell, however: the girls were made of sterner stuff."

Next to me, I felt Paul stiffen. He set his fork down and picked up his pint.

"It makes one wonder, doesn't it? About how those children would have turned out had they lost their father and not their mother. Anne, Charlotte, and Emily had to have drawn their innate steel from someone, and I sincerely doubt it was from Patrick."

Genevieve's calm, intelligent voice threaded its way through the ambient noise of the pub, and Paul, listening to the even flow of her undemanding conversation, seemed slowly to relax. I drank my pint, learning more than I'd ever thought I'd hear about Genevieve's contempt for the Brontë characters, except, perhaps, Heathcliff, which I guess shouldn't have surprised me.

"His motivations were suspect, of course," she told Paul, leaning forward, "but his goal was clearly defined, and remained a constant until his death. That focus I always find attractive in a human." She finished her tea and set the cup aside. Then she sighed, lifting her sleeve to look at her watch, which she wore with the face inside her wrist. She gathered her stick as she got to her feet. "I don't mean to rush or anything, but I'd like to finish my circuit of the wall before the rain becomes torrential."

"Don't they close the walls in bad weather?" I objected.

She cast me yet another scathing look, then reached into her coat pocket and drew out her ring, jingling the keys in her palm. Then wordlessly, she replaced them.

I should have known.

She hadn't cared about the rain earlier, or ever, for all I knew; this *was* the woman who walked the wall even on the iciest days of winter, when they were officially closed to traffic. Now, of course, I knew how.

I'd finished my pint as well, and both Paul and I stood. The prospect of a downpour was not particularly attractive to me, but I would be damned if a woman twice my age was going to show me up. I knew exactly how those male agents in the belly of the transport planes felt.

However, Genevieve waved an imperative hand at me. "You, Aventurine, need to go to the print shop and collect the scans. I think at some point after that—dinnertime, perhaps?—you should bring the box back to the house, and I can lock it up." That settled, she turned. "And you, Paul—I think you should accompany me on the wall." When it looked as though he might bridle at being so peremptorily ordered about, her voice changed. "Just to see me safely home. I *am* an old woman, after all.

I almost laughed. Sly, manipulative bitch.

It wasn't until I was paying for the copying at the print shop that I realized that same sly, manipulative bitch had manipulated me right out of any conversation she was planning to have with my nephew.

Seventeen

In one of his more lucid moments, as the disease had crept up on him, Charles had written me a letter, detailing what he expected of me. It was to be simple: a pillow held to the face while he slept.

"I trust you, Genevieve," he wrote, his handwriting—which had always been so incisive on the page—already beginning to wobble and fail, "to know when the time is right to end my life. More than that, I trust you to do this final duty for me, as an act of love. For I do love you, Genevieve, and wish to die before I forget you and what you have meant to me for nearly sixty years."

And so, as my final act of love, I held that pillow to his face one night in the summer until his struggles were done, and he was still. Then I sat beside him on the edge of the bed and held a match to the final letter he had written to me, until it was no more than ash in the glass on the bedside table. Finally I kissed Charles—Honoré—on his forehead, smoothed a hand over his disheveled hair, and let myself out to walk the wall in the moonlight. Somewhere between Harlot Hill Tower and New Tower, the Minster over my left shoulder, I shook the ash out over the parapet, then hurled the glass after it.

I've walked the wall every day since that one night. Every day.

As instructed, I arrived by taxi at Scarcross Road at six, bearing the box of photographs and documents; I had spent the afternoon zealously uploading the scans to my Dropbox account in case something untoward should happen to my thumb drives that held the digitized versions.

The rain had tapered off. Genevieve opened the door at my knock. "I'll take that," she said, reaching for the box.

I held tight. "I'll bring it through. Remember—you *are* an old woman, after all."

"When it suits me," she agreed pleasantly. There was no apology forthcoming; I hadn't really expected one. She latched the door after me, lock after careful lock. "Leave it on that table then—" she indicated the one at the foot of the stairs next to the umbrella stand—"and come through to the kitchen. Your nephew is putting the finishing touches on the sauce."

We passed by the door to the dining room, and I saw that the table was laid for three, the chandelier above it sparking fire on the deep red curtains and carpet. Our last evening together before Paul and I were to journey to Southampton, and it would appear that it was to be a bit on the formal side. I looked down at my sweater and slacks, and wondered whether I was underdressed. At least I had combed my hair and pinned it behind my ears before I'd left the guest house.

In the kitchen, Paul was indeed gently stirring the contents of a saucepan with a whisk. A three-ringed binder cookbook lay open on the worktop beside him. He sported a long white apron over his T-shirt and jeans, and as he stirred, his face seemed more relaxed than I'd seen in ages. His jaw tightened when he looked up at my greeting, and I wondered, not for the first time since his return from Haworth, what I might have done to elicit his—what? Anger? Disappointment? Mistrust? I couldn't read him; I had no idea.

"We're having a Sunday roast, despite it not being Sunday," Genevieve announced. She filled a cut-glass pitcher with water, and handed it to me. "When you're retired, any day can be Sunday. Or every day. Bring that through to the table, will you?"

I did as I was bidden. Between the three of us we brought through the plated roast, the sauce, the potatoes, carrots, and candied parsnips.

"I thought you did just the plain old meat and two veg?" I asked.

Genevieve settled at the head of the table, indicating that Paul and I should take the chairs to either side of her, across from one another. My nephew seemed perfectly amenable to her direction; not for the first time, I tried to imagine their conversation of the afternoon, and failed. However, it was fairly obvious that Paul seemed more than comfortable in her company. They were, to use her word, *simpatico*. I couldn't help but feel a bit jealous. Of both of them.

"We do," she said pointedly, "whatever I damned well please." Leaning across, she lit the candles on the table between us.

Paul snorted into his water glass.

I snapped out my napkin—gold damask which had been folded into something that might have resembled a crown—and positioned in the middle of my plate; I lay it across my lap.

"Normally I'd have the butler serve, but he's off for the evening." Genevieve offered me the serving dish, and I helped myself to our Sunday carvery. "Hand your aunt the Yorkshire pudding," she directed Paul. "I have taught Paul the correct way to make a good Yorkshire pudding, but I have sworn him to secrecy, so you had best not attempt to have it from him."

"Are you saying I've been making them wrong all my life?"

She only raised her eyebrows.

The beef was delicious and tender, juicy and perfectly seasoned. I had always considered myself a dab hand at making popovers, but this dinner definitely surpassed my abilities with a roast. It was all I could do to keep myself from licking the plate once I'd eaten everything.

"I'd offer you more, but we have a flan for afters. Also made by Paul."

I looked across the sparkling table at my nephew, surprised. As far as I knew, Paul had never expressed an interest in cooking; he had never worked in a restaurant in either his high school or college years. "You?"

His raised eyebrows were eerily reminiscent of Genevieve's. He was apparently learning more than cooking from her. Again the flicker of jealousy. He stood, collected our plates, and carried them out to the kitchen. I could hear him moving about out there, clinking dishes, opening and closing what I assumed to be the drawer where the servers reposed.

"You taught him to make a flan?"

Genevieve shrugged. "It seemed something to do to keep him occupied. He needed time to busy his hands while he organized his mind."

"And did he tell you what's been bothering him since Haworth?"

She shook her head. "I didn't ask. I thought he might tell me, a relative stranger, but he's still playing his cards close to his chest, as the gamblers say. So we just cooked. And that was enough." She cast me a warning glance, but I didn't need it; I could hear Paul's return from the kitchen.

He set the dessert plates before us. The flan was a creamy pale yellow, a darker brown caramel smoothing the top. At the side of the plate, Paul had scattered a couple of pale pink rose petals.

"My God, Paul, this is gorgeous." I refilled our water goblets.

He nodded. "Thanks." His voice was flat.

"I like the petals," Genevieve said. "Maybe you and I should learn how to candy them—that might be a nice edible garnish."

Paul nodded again. He was frowning slightly, his head tipped. I could almost see the wheels turning in his head: he used to look like that all the time as a child.

The first spoonful of flan melted across my tongue.

"This turned out well," Genevieve said. This, from her, was a major compliment. I hoped my nephew was sensitive enough to nuance to realize this. "I don't think I've ever made one better, in all the years of my attempts."

"Thanks." There was a flush crawling up from Paul's collar. I needn't have worried—he was obviously pleased. When he spoke the word to her, his voice was *not* flat.

"This is not a new recipe, then?" Another spoonful for me. I could have probably eaten my serving, theirs, and whatever was left in the kitchen.

"One of my mother's," Genevieve said.

She had not said much about her mother, her childhood. I made a mental note to probe further when we resumed our interviews, once Paul had returned home.

"She taught you how to cook?" I thought of the cakes we'd had with tea each day before our walk out onto the wall. Each different, each delicious. I had suspected, despite Genevieve's claim to have baked them, that the cakes had come from a bakery—had even searched Google to see whether there was one nearby—but now I was thinking perhaps I was wrong. Very wrong. I felt suitably chastised.

"She was a brilliant cook, my mother." Genevieve wiped her lip with her damask napkin. "I don't know much about her parents—she didn't talk about them, and I have a suspicion that they died in the Great War—so I couldn't tell you where she learned. But she seemed somehow—more *whole* when she was cooking. As though there was one thing in her life over which she had control." She took another delicate spoonful of the flan.

Control. It was an interesting idea. Genevieve's entire life, as it was slowly unfolding in her telling, was about control: she held on to the disparate strands of her existence with the proverbial iron fist, unwilling to release anything to chance. She had learned that, I suspected, well before she turned sixteen—or twenty-four, as her papers suggested. Hell, she even controlled her own age. In that, she had wrested control from her mother, who, it would seem, felt she had no control at all.

Except when she cooked.

"Everything she made had a slight *flair* to it. *Elan.* We were not well-off, and we scraped quite a bit; but there was always a garden plot behind whatever terrible flat we were living in. Herbs in pots on windowsills. Freshness when she could; flavor when she couldn't."

"And you? Do you have a garden plot?"

"Good heavens, no." Genevieve's tone was appalled. "I haven't the time nor the inclination to tend a garden. And why should I, when there's a perfectly good grocer at my disposal?" Her dessert finished, she set her spoon aside and lifted her water goblet from the gold tablecloth. "For most of my professional life, you have to understand, I really had no way of knowing whether I'd be around to care for a garden anyway. I might have been away on business, and it would be a pity for all my vegetables to wither and die when I was in Moscow or Nicaragua or some equally faraway place."

Moscow. Nicaragua. I made another mental note, thinking to ask for dates, places. This working for the government in her later adult years was proving to be a veritable mine of interesting details.

"But the cooking."

"I obviously didn't have much opportunity as a young woman. I did find that I made note of flavors while in France—visiting restaurants or cafés while cycling around the countryside in my work as a courier was a perk. And after growing up with my mother and her herbs, I knew what I was tasting, and could remember, and reproduce it later. It was then that I began to understand what made my mother so meticulous in her cooking."

"But you two were using a cookbook." I looked from her to Paul and back.

"*I* was using a cookbook," Paul corrected. "I didn't know what I was doing."

Genevieve sighed. "I wrote down some of Charles's favorites early on in our marriage, so he could make them for himself when he wanted."

"And did he?"

She shook her head ruefully. "No. He claimed nothing tasted the same when he made it. He once accused me of leaving out a secret ingredient—you know, as people are rumored to do—in order to make him dependent upon me." For a brief moment her expression softened. "A lie, of course. I never left a thing out of those recipes. Charles was simply too lazy to do for himself when I was away. I know for a fact he always took himself out for meals. I caught him at it a number of times."

"*Caught* him at it?" She made it sound as though it were some sort of illicit affair, Charles and restaurant food.

"Heavens, yes. I always knew what that man was up to, even when I was elsewhere, even when *he* was elsewhere. As I'm sure he knew exactly what I was doing as well." She laughed shortly. "He was never unfaithful to me, though he was always unfaithful to those recipes and this kitchen. In some respects, he was an incredibly predictable man."

Paul pushed his empty plate away. He was looking at her steadily, a burning intensity in his dark eyes. "And he was the love of your life."

Genevieve tipped her head to look at him kindly. "Yes," she said briskly. "Oh, yes." She touched Paul's hand with two fingers. "For my entire life, just about. Those things do happen, my dear boy. Those things certainly do happen, even if you believe you're too hard and unyielding for them. Charles was the love of my life, and I miss him every day."

I stared down at my hands.

As we were leaving, well after our places were cleared and the dishes washed, Genevieve paused in the entryway with her hand on one of the Yale locks.

"One last thing, Paul," she said, looking at the box I'd left on the hall table. "Do you think you might run that upstairs for me? Second floor, first door at the landing."

"Third floor," I said, *sotto voce.*

Genevieve shook her head. "Americans."

Paul hefted the box and headed up, his footsteps pounding. Genevieve watched him, holding up an admonishing hand to prevent my speaking until he had turned the corner at that landing and started up toward the top floor. "Light switch at the head of the stairs," she called.

"A clever ploy to get him out of the way?" I asked, keeping my voice low.

Her expression grew suddenly solemn. "Yes. I think—you need to be careful of him." Her tone was grim. "He *is* behaving strangely, more strangely than when we first met. I agree with you that something *must* have happened in Haworth. He learned something, or he heard something—or he realized something that he didn't know he knew." She blew out a breath. "You need to watch him carefully."

Then Paul was back downstairs, and he and I began the walk back to the guest house through the lamplit streets, the warm evening breeze at our backs

Part III:

Southampton

The pen you wield in your long-fingered hand
Magic words and spells at your command
And I pretend that love—is for me alone

— *"Love Language,"* Gio Constantine

Eighteen

On Thursday, two weeks after we'd come north to York, Paul and I took the train back down south, to Southampton, for the music festival, and for the visit to the last port of call for Shep. I had no idea what Paul thought he would find at the boatyard, especially after all this time, but it was possible that seeing the last place his father had set foot on dry land would provide a sort of closure for him. I could only hope so. Something in me desperately needed Paul to return to the boy I knew and loved.

After the festival, he'd fly home, and I'd return to York for a second round of interviews, tying up my first round of work with Genevieve. At least, I expected so—much of what would be left we could accomplish by phone, by email, by Facetime. That thought, though, did not make me happy—in fact, quite the opposite: I would miss the elderly woman, with her sharp wit, the voice that could drop so low it was nearly a growl, the dark eyes sharp as knife blades. She had contacted me to be her biographer, her amanuensis, because she had decided, long before we met, that we were, to use her word, *simpatico*. After our initial series of interviews, I knew she was correct. I had never felt such a complete connection to any person other than Micheline.

But then, when had I found Genevieve to be incorrect? She, like me, prided herself on her accuracy. The only misinformation she provided was intentional.

As, I supposed, looking across the banquette at Paul's closed-down face, it was with me.

The first order of business, of course, was to find our guest house, located about a third of a mile away from the central train station. It was in a strange little side street called the Polygon, which was not, to my way of thinking, the least bit polygonal. The guest house was perhaps halfway along, a tall narrow Victorian building with wedding-cake trim, harkening back to the days when Southampton was the port of call for the giant trans-Atlantic luxury liners, and passengers needed a place to stay before embarking with the tides. Paul and I were given rooms next to each other on the third floor, deluxe en suite singles. I was getting quite used to sleeping single in a single bed. I couldn't speak for my nephew.

It was early afternoon. While Paul settled himself, I called the number I had for the Hambleside Yard, the place where Shep had stored the *Màquina de los Vientos* the winter before he'd sailed. Paul had not argued when I suggested I do it rather than he, as I claimed that my journalist's credential might open more doors for us. I was able to make an appointment for the morning with the yard manager—perhaps he was also the owner? I was a bit unclear. Then I put the dying phone on the charger and went to wash the travel from my face.

When I knocked on the door to Paul's room, there was no answer. I let myself back into my own room to call him, in case he'd fallen asleep.

"I'm in a pub," he said, when he at last answered, after several rings. "I'll meet you for dinner. At six, in front of the guest house." There was a surge of noise on his end, and then we were cut off. I stared at the phone in disbelief.

He had hung up on me.

• •

Discouraged and upset, I thought of Genevieve's coping mechanisms and decided to walk. The SeaCity Museum, with its *Titanic* display, was only a few short blocks away, and somehow I didn't think that was the sort of place Paul would want to visit in his present state of mind. Hell, I didn't want to visit it in my present state of mind. The ghost of Shep was too close, too real; I could almost hear his footsteps, in tandem with mine. Instead, I browsed the rack of brochures in the entryway of the guest house on the way out, finally lighting upon one for Tudor House and Gardens on Bugle Street, down near the quay. The map indicated that it was not even a mile away. I'd dug out the portable charger and plugged it into my phone, shoving both into the depths of my cross-body bag. Now I wished for one of Genevieve's blackthorn sticks, so I could whack it against the pavement on the way, out of sheer bad temper.

The afternoon was sparkling with sunlight, the white Victorian villas along the Polygon shining like cruise ships or whitecaps. I was not appeased, however, and pushed my hands into my pockets. My nephew had hung up the phone on me. My nephew had left me at the hotel, to wander out to a pub without me. My nephew, for whatever reason, was angry with me, and would not tell me why. I thought of Genevieve's words: *You need to watch him carefully.* Difficult to do if he slipped away while you were making a phone call for him, while you were washing your face. Difficult to do anyway, as he was no longer a boy, but an adult. An adult teetering close to the edge, but that hardly seemed to matter.

I felt like crying. I looked at the time on my Fitbit, then counted back five hours. I could call Micheline—I *should* call Micheline. But to say what? That I'd lost her son, that he'd hung up on me, that he was angry with me for some reason I couldn't figure out?

In the Tudor House, I paid my entry fee and wandered about desultorily, staring at things without registering them, half-listening to voices as they remarked upon this feature or that. The place felt cold to me, as though haunted by half a millennium of ghostly voices, the stomps of boots, the swishing of long skirts. Eventually I wandered out into the gardens. Even here I felt disconnected, the sun too bright, the air too warm, the scents too cloying. I found a bench and sat, defeated. Walking down here had been a waste of time. I usually enjoyed such places—the Tudor period, all uproar and brashness and turmoil, had always been a favorite historical exploration—but I simply couldn't find any empathy to spare this afternoon.

It was pointless. After a time, I struggled to my feet and headed back to the guest house. I could work on drafting the magazine version of Genevieve's story, or at least at outlining. I was good at that. Interpersonal relationships, not so much. I'd never been good at those. Which might have explained why I'd shied away from any romantic entanglements for twenty-odd years, save for that crash-and-burn summer with Gio. It was better to avoid relationships if all they did was cause pain, confusion, and—let's face it—near-professional ruin.

I had noticed an Italian bistro on my slog down to the quay and back again, and suggested it when I met up with Paul at six. He didn't seem to care one way or another. His face was pale, his eyes bloodshot, and his shoulders slumped. I'd hoped, after his interest in cooking with Genevieve, that the prospect of well-cooked and presented food might arouse some feeling in him: appetite, curiosity, something. Anything.

The restaurant was small and crowded, with red-checked cloths on the tables and candles jammed into the necks of wine bottles. The napkins were crisp and white, and I placed mine over my lap before I took up the menu. "Focaccia for a starter?"

He grunted, and I decided to take that as assent. I inhaled deeply and steeled myself, determined to talk on as though he were responding, as though we were having an intelligent and equal conversation. The waiter came by, a dark-haired, dark-eyed young man who might have passed for Italian if one squinted in the dim light; I ordered our starter, and a glass of the house white, while my nephew ordered a pint. "You should really try a glass of wine—I'm sure this place has a nice Italian you might like."

"I don't know anything about wine."

"Now's a good time to start learning."

No answer. He turned his head away. I refocused my attention on the menu again.

"Oh, this looks good." I pointed to the page. "Did you see this wild mushroom ravioli?"

Again the grunt. This was all uphill work.

"I don't know if I want that, or the seafood special. Mussels and prawns: and when anybody mentions garlic, you know how I get."

This did not even elicit a smile.

The drinks came, along with the focaccia and oil. I took a sip of my wine, for fortification more than for anything else. Then I took up the warm bread, dipped it, and took a bite. Across the table, Paul took up a piece of focaccia and began, methodically, to crumble it over his bread plate.

"Aren't you hungry?"

A shrug.

The waiter returned, and I chose the seafood. Paul did, too. When the waiter smiled at him and winked, my nephew returned the grin. The grimness returned, however, once the young man had sailed off toward the kitchen with our order.

"He's very handsome," I offered. Another tack. I wondered at the tiny exchange between the two. Paul had had a girlfriend in high school—Valerie? Mallory?—but I hadn't heard of anyone steady in college. Perhaps he was on a proverbial voyage of discovery. This gave me pause: if Paul came out as bi, or gay, Micheline wouldn't have any trouble with it at all; but what about Shep? He had been a decent sort, and I had always been very fond of him. But I didn't remember that this subject had ever come up for discussion between us. I had no idea how accepting Paul's father would have been, though I hoped he would have embraced his son's identity, whatever that turned out to be.

I looked after the waiter, now bowing solicitously over an elderly couple at another table, pointing to something on the menu, then something else. *One of our tribe,* my gay friend, John, would have pegged him, but I had known John to make mistakes before. Besides: I was getting ahead of myself. The waiter and Paul had smiled at one another, which meant, basically, that they had smiled at one another. I was reading things into the exchange that probably weren't there.

I finished my wine, and thought I could probably withstand another glass, though I very rarely had more than one—but I wasn't driving, I reminded myself, merely walking around the corner to the guest house and my bed. Paul ordered another pint as well, though he had probably had a couple in the afternoon at whatever pub he had been hanging around in. I watched for signs between him and the waiter, but saw very little more than a professional interaction. Well, I sighed, that didn't make the waiter any less good-looking. If flirting with a good-looking server made my nephew feel—and behave—better, I was all for it. Hell, if flirting with a good-looking server made *me* feel better, I was all for that, too.

The seafood plate, when it arrived, was all I'd wished for. Shrimp and mussels in a creamy garlic sauce over pappardelle, piled high in a shallow bowl and garnished with rocket. I leaned forward into the steam rising from the bowl and breathed in deeply, closing my eyes. The scent was rich with garlic.

"Paul, learn how to make this," I urged.

This time when he didn't answer, I glanced across and saw him savoring a bite from his own dish. His eyes were not closed, but they might as well have been, for he was not looking at anything in particular—or at least not seeing anything. He was chewing slowly, and concentrating. I thought of Genevieve's words the other evening, about tasting the food she ate, really tasting it, and knew that Paul was trying to emulate that.

I breathed a long sigh of relief, and addressed myself to my plate once again. If Paul had the will to think about his food in the way Genevieve had spoken of, he could not be all lost. He still had the wherewithal to save himself. There was something affirming in that. I threw out a silent prayer of thanks to Genevieve, back in Scarcroft Road, sitting down to her own evening meal. And not surprisingly, I missed her.

Nineteen

The appointment at the boatyard was for ten a.m. Paul, still monosyllabic and pale, picked his way partially through his full English breakfast before giving up and addressing himself to his coffee. I wasn't really looking forward to this side visit, but I'd promised him we would do this, the one thing he'd specifically asked for on the trip—and, if the truth be told, I was a bit curious myself. So when the taxi arrived at twenty minutes past nine, I checked my bag for my notebook, phone, and recorder, less from habit than just in case Paul needed the professional coverage.

I was glad for the early start, as traffic slowed considerably for the tolls on Central Bridge. Soon enough, however, we came into the village of Hamble-le-Rice; a couple of turns later, and we pulled up at Hambleside Yard, a forest of white masts, blue-tarped boats in cradles, and a large red building with a door prominently signed, OFFICE.

"Shall I wait?" the cabbie asked, but I shook my head as I paid him, not knowing how long we would be. He gave me a card. "Call if you need me again." Then he was off.

The man who opened the office door to us was grizzled, wearing a red polo shirt with the Yard's logo on the left breast. "Phil Newlan," he said, sticking out a hand. I shook it, and when he turned to Paul, his sunburned face broke into a smile. "And you're the Genthner boy. I'd know you anywhere. You've the look of your father about you. Come on in, have some coffee."

The front office, where a secretary glanced up from her computer and smiled, was spare and neat, but Phil led us through to a cubby of a private office in the back. The walls here were covered in charts, schedules, photographs of boats large and small. Phil went directly to a spot between two windows looking out over docks crowded with dingys and ketches; he brushed aside some papers to reveal a small photograph tacked to the woodwork. I saw the expression on Paul's face even before I drew close enough to realize I was looking at the *Màquina de los Vientos,* with Shep in sunglasses standing feet apart and arms akimbo on the deck; beside him, Phil Newlan's smiling face was partially shadowed by the peaked cap he wore.

"The day they sailed, Shep and the *Màquina.* Beautiful morning, wind just freshening, tide just on the cusp. I'd brought him a bottle of champagne, luck for the trip." Phil's expression faltered, and he let the pages flutter back into place, then stepped quickly away to fumble with the coffee maker atop a file cabinet. "Damn near broke us all here to hear what happened, son. I'm sorry. Shep was a good man. One of the best."

Paul had stepped closer, moved the papers aside again; he prised the tack out of the woodwork and took the photograph into his own hands, which shook a bit. He stared down into his father's face.

"He looks happy." There was an immeasurable well of sadness in Paul's voice, and wonder, as though at the idea that such a happiness had existed.

Phil handed me a cup of coffee, and pointed to the sugar and creamer packets. Then he brought a cup to Paul, and joined him in looking down at the photo. "I think you know how much Shep loved sailing. He and I—we had such talks when he was here. Such talks. I was pleased and proud that he chose us to care for the *Màquina,* to ready her for the sail. He told me stories of all the times he'd made the trip across the Atlantic with others: he was so very ready to solo. So ready." His repetitions had a singsong quality to them, as though he were setting a cadence.

Paul nodded. His eyes were wet. I felt myself tearing up; I wasn't sure whether I'd be able to handle it if he cried. I sipped my coffee—it was bitter, and abysmal, but I didn't care—and stepped to one of the windows overlooking the Hamble. A small motor craft was cruising down the river toward the Southampton waterway. I wondered where it was headed. The Isle of Wight wasn't all that far; if I were on that boat, I'd be headed there. Cowes? Yarmouth? My island geography was hazy. Probably Shep would have known.

"What about his route?" Paul allowed himself to be led to a chair before a wide desk covered with charts. "Did he tell you about sailing that way before?"

Phil settled into a wooden chair that creaked comfortably under his weight. He moved a compass aside and dug around for a chart, setting aside a couple before he came upon the one he wanted. He spread this atop the pile between himself and Paul and leaned forward, running a tanned finger along a line through the ocean. I came closer, leaned over to look.

"It's a common one," Phil said. "Your father and his friends had sailed back and forth several times. You know that. He knew all the tricks. He was familiar with the weather patterns, and timed the sail accordingly. The excitement for him, this time, was the idea of conquering the route by himself. Pitting himself against the wind and the water and coming out victorious. He was a strong sailor, your father, and a cautious one. He and I went over that boat so many times, so carefully. Checked everything. Provisioned everything. Stowed everything. With his experience, and the seaworthiness of the *Màquina*—" Phil's voice trailed off, and he wiped a hand across his face, staring down at the chart. "That's why I just don't understand—"

"Why it—he—failed."

Phil lifted his lined face to look up at Paul. "There are always factors you can't account for—that's what makes the challenge, right? Sailing the Atlantic is not a walk in the park. But everything that could be planned for, everything that could be practiced for, *was*. Shep was as ready for this as any sailor could be. He wasn't one of those amateurs you hear about who think it would be a lark to sail across the ocean—the ones who leave it late and get caught in hurricane season, for example, or who don't plan for any contingency beyond a day sail; the idiots who don't file their plans with the authorities, who don't apply for the proper permits for layovers in the Azores—things like that. Your father knew to take care of all those things, and I'd swear on anything you like that he *did* take care of those things. So I keep asking myself: what went wrong? What did we miss? What the hell happened?"

His voice was raw with frustration.

Paul could only shake his head, his grip tightening on the photograph in his hands. I looked back out at the Hamble. Everything Phil said about Shep was true; I knew that from experience. He had never been one to leave *anything* to chance. So what the hell *had* happened?

An idea slithered into the back of my mind, a serpent, a danger. I forced it back. I would not allow myself to think like that. I would not. But if we took away the possibility of accident, what was left?

We talked a while longer, and then Phil took us on a tour around the boatyard. At the far end, three levels of storage, with an enormous crane to lift boats into their berths. I had seen this before, when I was researching in Alaska, but I was still fascinated by the way the crane could maneuver craft into their slots, tucking them away like Genevieve had tucked away her F. A. N. Y. cap: babies into bed. On the opposite end of the yard were the cavernous barns in which work was done on these boats: there were two sailboats inside now, and I heard shouting and metallic clanking. The rest of the yard was taken up by cradles, most empty at this high season, though some sailboats were still stored there. I wondered at people who owned such craft and didn't have them in the water in summer; but several of them, as we circled, sported signs advertising them for sale.

"Do you sail?" Phil asked me, a hand shading his eyes from the bright sun.

I shook my head. "I've only sailed as a passenger. Shep tried to teach me, quite a long time ago, but that was a fiasco." I laughed ruefully. "But Paul sails."

"Used to," he corrected quickly.

Phil drew in a sharp breath. "You haven't quit."

"I hate the ocean," Paul said.

"They all come back," Phil said quietly to me as we waited for our return taxi. "Eventually. The sea is a cruel lover, but she's irresistible." He was looking at Paul, who again held the picture of Shep on the deck of the *Màquina de los Vientos,* with some pity. Shep, who apparently couldn't resist the sea, his lover, and paid the absolute price for that.

"I don't know about that happening," I demurred.

"I do." Phil's tone brooked no argument. He smiled to himself, as though privy to a secret held between him and the sea, something someone such as I could never quite understand. I was willing to let it go.

Up the hill, I could see the dust thrown up in the lane by the approaching taxi.

"Can I come back?" Paul asked without looking up.

Phil threw me a knowing look. "Of course you can, lad. You'll always be welcome here, anytime."

Paul nodded, his Adam's apple working. I turned my attention back to the cab, swinging about before the doorway as it slowed.

"Wait," Phil said as I stepped forward. "Wait." He sounded as though he had come to a decision, or remembered something important. "I have something."

Paul was in the process of replacing the photograph on the wall between the windows.

"Take that," Phil said gruffly. "Take it, if you want it."

Paul stuffed the picture quickly into his jacket pocket, as though worried Phil would change his mind.

There was a grate and squeal as Phil dragged open the bottom drawer of the furthest battered file cabinet. From it he drew a small metal box, a bit smaller than a cash box, discolored and with a padlock affixed to the latch on the front. He kicked the drawer closed again with a foot, and brought the box to me.

"You need to take this. I don't have the key. I don't know who would have it, either—Shep's wife? Your sister, isn't she?" He coughed, wiped his hands down the front of his blue jeans, as though wiping his hands of responsibility. "Shep left it here with me."

"Why?" Paul demanded sharply.

Now Phil held up his hands. "No idea. He said something about my saving it for him, or—" and he coughed again, uncomfortably— "giving it to his family when they came calling."

My palms were sweating. I licked my lips. Paul's hand had gone convulsively to the photo in his pocket.

"So take it with you. Do what you need to do."

We thanked him and climbed into the cab. When we drove away, I looked back, and Phil was still standing before the office door, staring up at us. His face was shadowed.

Twenty

"We could probably break the lock easily enough with a pry bar," Paul said, examining it with narrowed eyes. His need was rolling off him in waves. "Even a long-handled screwdriver would probably work."

It was the longest string of words he'd put together for me in several days. I was grateful for that, but at the same time I was fearful of the box, of its contents, of the things Shep had decided to leave for his family, should they come calling. He was obviously aware of the possibility that he would not be returning himself to collect it.

"We don't have the tools," I protested.

"We can go to a hardware store and get them."

"Or we could just go to a locksmith's shop and have him pick the lock for us."

Paul frowned. "That's not suspicious or anything."

I shook my head. "We just tell them we've lost the key. Because it's the truth. I don't have it, you don't have it, Phil Newlan doesn't have it."

"Maybe Mum has it."

I shot him a look. "Do you want to wait until we get home to open this box, then?"

That was how we ended up on the doorstep of a locksmith half a mile from the guest house. There, the proprietor took down a ring of dingy keys from a pegboard behind the counter, and, squinting at them, began trying one after another.

"It's a Yale," she said cheerfully, "and there's no point in breaking the lock off if we can just open it." She wore a pair of rimless half-glasses, tinted blue, over which she glanced at us. "If we find a good key, I'll just cut you one, shall I? You might need to use the lock again."

Paul shoved his hands into his pockets. I knew he was touching the photograph of his father, a sort of talisman. I watched the locksmith's deft fingers, tipped with incongruously pink nails, trying one key, trying another. After a few moments, she replaced that ring on the pegboard and took down a different one. This time it only took a couple of tries, and then the lock snapped open.

She smiled. "There it is, and there you are."

"How much do I owe you?" I asked, reaching into my bag.

She shrugged. "Buy the key, and we're even."

"Fair enough." She took the key back to the machine, and slotted it into the cutter. It was a noisy process, but quick. She traded the key for my cash, and we were out on the street again.

We sat at a melamine table out on the back terrace, squeezed between our guest house and the fence belonging to the next. My hands were shaking. I pushed the tin box toward Paul. "You open it."

He bit his lower lip and did as he was told.

I leaned forward.

Inside the box were two envelopes. The top one bore Paul's name, written in blue ink in Shep's squared-off handwriting. Paul reached in hesitantly, picked it up as though he were picking up a poisonous snake. For a long moment he held it, stared at it, his mouth working. He said nothing. Neither did I.

I looked in at the other letter. It was addressed to Micheline.

"I don't know if I want to read this," Paul whispered.

"You don't have to, not right away." I picked up the second envelope, then put it back down and closed the cover of the box on it. "You really don't have to read it at all, if you don't want to. And you don't need to decide right now, either."

Paul nodded, blinking a few times. He reached into his pocket and pulled out the photograph, then held them side by side, looking from one to the other. "I don't know if I can deal with what he had to say, not now. Not right now. I don't know if I want to read about his secrets."

Secrets? I wondered, biting my lower lip. Would Shep tell, after all these years? After death?

I only nodded. We sat in silence. I slipped the padlock into the hasp and snapped it shut.

"You're not going to read the other letter?" Paul asked.

"It's not mine," I said. "It's your mother's."

His eyes hardened. "That never stopped you before."

With that cryptic remark, he shoved back his chair and banged back into the guest house. I could only stare after him.

Twenty-one

I had convinced myself that I could give Paul to them, hand him over to my sister and brother-in-law and simply walk away.

After all, I was only an egg donor. I had allowed the harvest, which had been surprisingly uncomfortable, had waited until the *in vitro* fertilization with sperm from Shep had transformed itself into a viable embryo, and had allowed that to be implanted inside my body. I was a carrier; from the get-go, this was Micheline's child. I was helping, only because she was desperate after that complete hysterectomy, and I would do anything for my twin sister. *Anything.* That included bearing her child if she asked. She did, and so I did.

Both Shep and Micheline had been present for the birth. The nurse had laid the lanugo-covered, squalling, squirming body on my stomach, and I wasn't prepared for the sudden rush of—*maternal?*—instinct which washed over me. *My son.* I was horrified, though, and shoved the thought away with all my might. He wasn't my son. *He wasn't my son.* He was my sister's son. And because in terms of DNA, her long-lost eggs were identical to my otherwise unused ones, this child might have just as easily been hers genetically as mine.

Besides. I had made a promise. I just hadn't realized how progressively harder it would become to fulfill that promise. When I had forced myself to hand the baby over to Micheline, it was the

125

first and only time I'd felt anything *negative* about my twin sister. Jealousy. Resentment. That horrified me as well. It took a long time for me to bring myself to take the baby in my arms again.

It grew easier to recognize my role as aunt the more I absented myself from that nuclear family. The two years I was researching and writing the book in Alaska were the years when Paul was learning to walk and talk, and I saw him infrequently. Thus I was able to convince myself, once the manuscript had been submitted to my publisher and I'd screwed my courage to the sticking point and descended upon them for Christmas, that Paul was an entirely different child, not one I had carried in my body for nine months.

Paul was not my son. Paul was my sister's son. Paul was my nephew.

Right now, he was a man who seemed to have developed some strange misconception about my relationship with Micheline, and I had no idea what it was, how he had come by it, nor how to counteract it—without telling him the secret we three had kept from him since that day, twenty-three years previous.

I remember a day—Thanksgiving—when I'd come to stay with Micheline and Shep. Paul, who might have been five or six at the time, was playing in the yard in his brilliant safety orange—it *was* hunting season, after all—thrashing about in the leaves. He'd build up the pile, and then hurl himself into it, rolling around until the orange, yellow, and brown were once again strewn across the dying grass of the big lawn. I was struck, as I stepped out onto the veranda with my cup of coffee, by his self-sufficiency: his mother was in the kitchen, slaving over the proverbial hot stove; his father in his study, holiday or no, typing up some business emails. Paul pushed the leaves together with a rake he could barely handle, tossed that rake aside, and then dove into his pile with a single-minded recklessness that I had to admire.

"Avi!" he shouted in his high child's voice, throwing an armful of maple leaves into the air so that they fluttered about him. His round face under his orange cap was reddened and full of laughter. "Come jump with me!"

I set the mug on the railing and joined him. The leaves crunched underfoot, in our hands, against their counterparts on the ground.

"Make a big pile," he ordered, handing me the rake. I did as I was told, gathering the leaves from the parts of the lawn he indicated apparently held the best ones. He used his hands, collecting as many between his palms as he could, and tossing them into the pile. When he was finally satisfied, he took the rake from me and threw it aside. "Jump!" he ordered. Then he did. His round face looked up from the pile, the only part of him visible. Carefully, I leapt in beside him. The leaves smelled of that overripeness bordering on rot, a precarious balance I adored. I buried my face in their scratchiness.

"What are you doing?" he demanded.

"Smelling the leaves." I pressed more to my face. "Smell them, Paul."

He did as he was told, his expression a study in curiosity.

"What do they make you think of?"

He cocked his head, then threw himself backwards so he was staring at the sky. He held a particularly large specimen of maple leaf before him, and put his hand against it, his fingers spread out toward the five lobes. "I don't know."

I lay back, too. The leaves rustled companionably beneath me. Paul handed me his leaf.

"Your hand is bigger."

Indeed, the leaf and my hand were nearly the same size. It was a bit more veiny than my hand was, and I pointed that out.

"Mom doesn't play in the leaves with me," Paul said after a moment. He sniffed at another handful of leaves. Then he squirmed closer until his head was on my arm. When he spoke

127

again, it was a whisper. "I wish you were my mom, Avi."

For a long moment I could not breathe.

A movement caught my eye from the house, and when I turned my head, I saw Micheline. My sister was behind the glass of the veranda door, a face rippling and blurry, but there was something incredibly haunted about her expression, and my chest hurt. I stared hard at her, willing her to step outside, and slowly, ever so slowly, she did.

I kissed Paul on the head then, and extricated myself. As I passed Micheline, I handed her my jacket.

"I'll finish the dinner," I murmured. "Go play with your kid."

I answered her call, just before dinner.

"There was a box," I told my sister on the phone now. I'd called earlier, left a message, and she was just now getting back to me. "At the boatyard in Southampton."

"Shep's?" Micheline's voice caught when she spoke her husband's name.

"He left it with Phil Newlan, the yard owner."

"He knew we'd come for it eventually."

I couldn't help but think that he'd known *I'd* come for it, since I was the investigative reporter. I didn't say that, though. If Micheline wanted to include herself, that was fine—Shep was *her* husband.

"Paul and I took it to a locksmith and got it opened." The box was on the bed next to me, locked again; the new key was on my keychain, in my bag. I stared now at the padlock. "There's a letter inside addressed to you."

I heard her suck in her breath.

"I didn't open it. I don't know what you want me to do with it."

For a long moment Micheline didn't answer.

"Don't," she breathed at last. Her voice was raw. The sharp pain scraped over the three thousand miles between us. "Don't open it."

"Okay." I nudged the lock with a finger, lifted it and let it fall back. It made a hollow metallic thunk. "Do you want me to mail it to you? Send it back with Paul when he goes home?"

There was a sound that might have been a sob.

"Don't mail it. What if it gets lost?" Now there was a real, recognizable sob. "That there's a note—from Shep—that he left before he—died—"

Micheline didn't finish, but I knew exactly what she meant. What if, knowing now that he had left her the letter, she asked it to be forwarded, and then it was lost in its journey across the ocean, lost just as Shep had been lost? It would be too much for her to bear.

"All right, then. Paul can take it when he goes next week."

Slowly her gulps lessened and finally subsided. "Paul," she gasped. "What did he think of the letter?"

"There was a second one in the box, addressed to him."

"What did it say? What did Paul say about it?" Her voice now was strident. Urgent. Fearful.

I told her about his unwillingness to open it just yet. "He's thinking about whether he can bear to read what his father had to say to him before he sailed. He's working up his courage."

"Oh, God, that poor kid." Then suddenly, "Aventurine. Do you think—do you think Shep wrote about you?"

Oh, God. Her thoughts always traveled the same routes as mine. That Shep might have written to his son about his conception, his birth.

"No. No, I don't think so." My words came fast, tumbling over one another. "He didn't know he wouldn't be back." *And you promised each other. And I promised you both.* Another thing I didn't say.

"But Shep was hedging his bets," Micheline protested. "If he had completed the sail, he simply would have gone back to claim the box, wouldn't he? From this Phil person? The only reason you and Paul have it—and have those letters—is because Shep never went back for it." Her voice was climbing. "Avi, Paul can't read that letter before we know what's in it. You've got to get it away from him."

I caught my own breath. "Mick. I don't know how I can do that. I don't know that I *can* do that. He has it now. He's trying to decide what to do. He won't listen to me at this point anyway. He's getting worse with me, angrier and angrier."

"I thought you said he was all right the night he cooked dinner with your spy."

I licked my lips. "I think it might have been the company. He's so angry with me, and I don't know what's triggering it. Maybe—if *you* asked him to hold off?"

I could imagine my sister pacing the floor in her dining room, the one room in her house long enough to accommodate her anxious movements back and forth. I could almost hear her steps on the hardwood flooring, unmuted by any rug.

"I could try. I could." She sounded as though she were desperate to convince herself.

"Call him," I urged. "Try."

I knocked on Paul's door an hour later, to ask about dinner. I was thinking maybe just a pizza—I wasn't all that hungry, and my head and stomach both were reeling. Stress, I thought. Tension. I had left my room and then had turned back, trying to find a hiding place for the small box and the letter inside. I couldn't begin to explain to myself why, suddenly, it seemed so imperative that I hide them somewhere safely away. I did know, however, that leaving the box perched on the bed near the pillows was not something I was comfortable with.

I knocked on Paul's door again. I hadn't heard him come back along the corridor after he'd stormed away from me on the terrace earlier, nor had I received a call or text from him. He didn't answer the door. I knocked a third time, my heart sinking. He wasn't back. Somehow I knew he wasn't.

I sent him a message. *Dinner? Pizza? Meet me somewhere?*

After a moment the little checkmark appeared: the message had been read.

I waited. There was no reply. The little dot remained at the edge of the screen, however. Paul was online, but he was ignoring me.

With some misgivings, I tried the handle to his door. It was locked. I knocked one more time, hopelessly. There was no answer; there was no reply to my message.

I turned toward the stairs. I felt the tightness all up my spine, across my shoulders, into my neck. I felt the impending headache.

Please, Micheline. Talk to him soon.

Twenty-two

The music festival, featuring both Mobius and Gio on the program, had been my idea; as Paul had always been eclectic in his musical tastes, I had suggested it in the hopes that he would find it a diversion. We picked up the rental car after breakfast, and headed out on the A33. Paul, coffee from the Costa's in Above Bar Street in hand, was as morose as ever, but, concentrating on driving on the left as I was, I had no time to pay much attention. The soothing British voice of Nigel the SatNav directed me toward the motorway, and I gritted my teeth and drove.

I had driven in the U.K. before, but not often enough. I was grateful to find that the roads leading toward the festival were not the narrow lanes that so unnerved me, the kinds with the pull-offs on the shoulders to allow passage of traffic from the other direction. Still, the countryside was green and unfamiliar, and I had to fight against my normal reaction of peering to the sides, at houses, at shops and pubs, at people walking their dogs, at public footpaths winding off the road into fields and copses. *Drive,* I told myself, following the voice across the roundabout, taking the second exit.

At the gate I showed the attendant the tickets on my phone, and she gave us a couple of wristbands before directing us along a rutted track to the field where cars were already serried. I grabbed my pack from the rear seat, with water bottle, a blanket I'd borrowed from the proprietor of the guest house, and sunscreen. Paul didn't wait, but, his hands jammed in his pockets as usual, wandered off toward the arrow under the trees at the edge of the parking field; he'd obviously had enough of my company, silent or not. I sighed, mentally planning to call my sister again once we'd returned to Southampton this evening, to let her know he seemed to be getting worse and not better.

Don't let him read that letter, she'd said. Somehow I knew that if I asked him about the envelope from the lockbox, my question would be unwelcome. Ignored at best, triggering an unpleasant reaction at worst. I watched his retreating back, biting my lip, and locked the car. I wished desperately that I knew what Shep had needed to tell him.

Already sweating, either from the heat or from stress, I followed the sound of ukulele music, big, as though thousands of instruments were being strummed by thousands of hands. I made note of the workshop tent nestled among the trees just over a tiny bridge, then turned to the right, following the straw-covered path beneath the trees. My wristband was checked again at a gate on the end of the path, and when I emerged from the shade, I found a much smaller field than the one used for parking, with a stage at one end, encircled by stalls. This was obviously a really cuddly music festival, and I liked it already. Even this early, people had staked out their ground on blankets, with chairs, with umbrellas to shade them from the sun. I found a place at the end of a curved row and unfolded the blanket. I had lost Paul, but in an arena this size, he would be able to find me easily, should he choose to look. Of course, there was always the possibility that he would not choose.

The sun was blazing. I slathered myself with lotion: legs, feet, arms, shoulders, face. Even the tips of my ears, which I usually forgot, much to my later discomfiture. I'd only have to do it again in an hour, I knew; I looked longingly at the umbrella under which my nearest neighbors sat, tapping their armrests along with the ukulele tune. Off to my right was a stall with a sign that read: TOOLS FOR SELF-RELIANCE. I sighed and stood up to investigate. I desperately needed some of those tools.

There were indeed tools: hammers, saws, scythes. I wandered slowly around the perimeter of the arena, until I found a stall selling hats. Almost as useful as an umbrella, I decided, at least as far as the health and welfare of the skin on my nose was concerned. I tried on several under the watchful eye of a woman wearing a pink fedora, before plumping for a straw hat with a flower on the wide brim and a pale blue ribbon trailing down the back. It seemed somewhat frivolous, and maybe that was why I liked it— when was the last time I'd been frivolous? At six pounds, it was a bargain, as far as frivolity was concerned. I pulled it over my hair and continued my wandering.

A soap tent, where I asked the woman about her recipe: all vegetable oil, with goats' milk. I bought a couple of bars of lavender, my favorite, and shoved them into my pack before moving on to the used book and record stall next door. This one was double-sized, with tables and tables of hardcovers and paperbacks, on edge with spine up; there were bins of vinyl with worn covers toward the rear. I found a tattered copy of Gaiman and Pratchett's *Good Omens*, then kept on browsing until I came to non-fiction, where I scanned the offerings for familiar covers. None of mine that I could see, and in a tiny vain sort of way, I was disappointed; my sales in the U.K. had always been pretty strong. I comforted myself by thinking that perhaps no one who bought my books was getting rid of them to second-hand sellers—I hoped it was true.

The proprietor here was a woman, too, and she approached me from her lawn chair out front when she saw that I'd pretty much looked over all she had to offer.

"Price inside the front cover, dear," she said. I flipped it open to show the penciled-in amount, and fished the coins out of my pocket. "Ta." But she did not move away, and when I looked over, she was examining my face. "Sorry, but I think I'm supposed to know you?" Her brows were drawn together.

I felt my skin flush, as it did when anyone actually recognized me from jacket covers, or readings, or the rare television appearance.

"Sorry," the woman said again, leaning a bit closer and frowning more fiercely. "But aren't you the writer lady?"

There were a lot of us writer ladies wandering about in the world. I thought it would be rude to point that out, though.

She was waving to a man seated in a chair next to her own. "Jack," she shouted. "*Jack!*" When he turned, she waved her arms again. "Jack, bring that book over. The one next to my chair. No, not that one, the other one."

Jack lumbered to his feet, adjusted his suspenders over his capacious belly, and carried the book across to her. This cover I recognized: a backlit photo of a band, the players only silhouettes against the blaze of lights. The book I'd done a couple of years ago about a year in the life of a British folk band, the year I had hit so many music festivals in the U.K. that my head pounded and my ears rang for a long time after. A book that had sold particularly well in this country—maybe not surprising it should find a new life in a used book tent at a festival. And this was the hardcover edition. Taking the book into her hands, the woman turned it over to look at the photo on the back jacket. Not one of my best—in my critical estimation, it was more of a grimace I wore than a smile— but for better or worse, that was definitely me. The woman looked from it to my face and back again.

"This," she said, jabbing a finger at it. "It *is* you."

I nodded, making a wry face. "It *is* me."

Now she turned to the man, who was scratching his beard thoughtfully, frowning. "See? That man. He wasn't kidding. He said she was here somewhere." She looked back at my face. She wore a straw hat, the brim even wider than my own, which cast her own eyes and cheeks into shadow. "That man who just was here—did you see him? He brought me the book and told me you were here, at the festival, and I should get you to sign the book. He said it would make it worth more."

I didn't know if that were true.

"What man?"

She rummaged in her pocket for a pen. "Would you?"

I flipped the cover open and turned to the flyleaf. Under my name, I scribbled my signature, and added the date for good measure.

"What man?" I asked again. I could feel the sweat beading on my forehead, under the band of my hat. Maybe it had been Paul. I looked around for him, but he was nowhere to be seen. "What did he look like? Was he young?"

The woman waved vaguely in the direction of the stage. "No. Middle aged. Maybe?"

The man shook his head, tucking his thumbs under the red suspenders. "Fortyish. Not much older than that, I wouldn't think." He looked me up and down. "Older than you, I'm guessing."

Which I supposed I could take as a compliment. I took my leave of them and headed now toward the beer tent, *Good Omens* tucked into my bag. Uneasily, I patted it for luck.

At the bar in the cool of the tent, I ordered a pint of something brown, paying extra for the reusable pint cup. As I turned away, I scanned the crowds, again looking for my nephew. If he was still here—and where else would he be?—he had successfully gone to ground. Not at the food tents as far as I could see. I was beginning to get anxious.

Then it hit me: the band. The book. *A Year in the Life of Mobius.* I had purchased tickets to this particular festival because I had wanted to see them again, and they would be playing at some point in the evening. One of them—some of them—must have arrived early; one of the members must have been the man the bookseller had spoken to. Of course. Possibly Peter Breedlove? Of the four members, he was the one most likely to scope out a book tent; he was the one who had read voraciously all during the tours I'd followed them on. *All the better to write lyrics,* he would say, wetting a finger and turning a page.

I immediately sipped my beer and felt better. Besides—it couldn't be Neil. What would he be doing down here, ten miles from Southampton? We'd left him in York. Somewhere. There was no reason to believe that he'd be anywhere down here in the south.

But. *But.* There was no reason to believe he'd have been in York, either. No reason to believe he'd have been in London. No reason to believe he'd have known that we were going north, no reason to believe that he would follow. But that simply could not have been coincidence.

No, I told myself. It wasn't Neil at the book tent. It was Peter Breedlove. It was Mobius. They were here somewhere, and I would find them, just to reassure myself.

Just over to my left was the merch tent. I ducked in and paid six pounds for the weekend's program, then headed past the food tent—fish and chips sold out already—to find a place at the picnic tables beyond. I didn't see Peter, nor did I see Paul. I settled with my pint and began thumbing through the program for the page with the schedule times. Saturday: Mobius was on at 7:10. I checked my watch; it was still only early afternoon.

I flipped to the center page, where there was a map of the festival site, including possible walks. I was tempted, sorely tempted, channeling Genevieve in my anxious restlessness. I took another drink from my pint. It was either a long walk at this point, or another pint—or ten. I closed my eyes, feeling the sun on my shoulders, feeling the sweat trickle down my spine. Yeah, that would probably be brilliant, to drink myself into oblivion even before Mobius did their set. I finished the pint, rinsed the glass out under a spigot nearby, then tucked it into the front pocket of my pack, and examined the map before setting off.

I chose the longest route on the map.

It led me through a churchyard, the kind that is mown perhaps once or twice a season, to allow growth for birds and butterflies; the path was clearly visible through the tall grasses, which waved gently around me as I passed. Butterflies fluttered up, performed intricate ballets, and settled back into a yard punctuated by worn and leaning stones; I knew nothing of butterflies, yet another topic of ignorance, and wished fervently that I had learned at some point. The church itself was weathered stone, with pointed windows, a porch to one side, and a belfry that leaned slightly away from vertical. For a moment I toyed with the idea of going inside for a look, but I'd been sitting uncomfortably with myself back at the arena, and was too restless to make that mistake again. I pressed on along the path. I had all weekend to explore.

After walking a bit further, I entered a glade, and the sun strained itself through the fluttering leaves above to fall in diamonds on the track at my feet. The air, too, was cooler in here, and I felt my breathing grow easier. The sounds of the festival had long since disappeared into the distant background, to be replaced by birdsong and the whisper of a slight breeze through the trees. I had forgotten how a ramble along a public footpath could have such a soothing effect. Every once in a while I heard the sound of a car on an invisible road somewhere to my left, so I obviously wasn't far from the village. Still, it was easy, under these trees, to forget.

The path meandered its way up a small rise, and I became conscious of the sound of laughter ahead. My heart sank. Of course there were other people out here—the map was laid out for anyone who paid the six pounds for the program. I pushed on, crested the rise, and below me lay a pond of sorts—more like a place where the stream I'd heard burbling earlier widened out before rolling on. Three people floated there, a woman and two men. Wild swimming.

"Avi!" the woman shouted. I lifted my sunglasses. Linny Breedlove, Peter's wife. Her brother Alan, and Peter. Alan raised a hand, and then promptly sank under the green water. He surfaced quickly, shaking the water from his hair, sputtering.

I hadn't seen any of them in a couple of years. Linny's screech, though, was unforgettable. She'd always been loud and joyous, I'd found in the year I'd followed them, even in the lean days, when the band was having a hard time getting their songs out there to the listening public, when they were opening for second-tier acts, when they were just scraping by. As I stood there, she shouted my name again. "Get in here! Plenty deep!"

I knew what that meant, and I didn't need a second invitation. Laughing, I threw my bag and map to the ground, tossed my hat aside, then pulled my loose shirt over my head. In shorts and camisole, I hurtled down the hill toward them and leapt in with the biggest splash I could muster.

The water was bracing, and I, too, sputtered as I surfaced. I wiped my eyes just in time for Linny to splash with both hands into my face. Alan put a hand on her shoulder and dunked her. It was like being with a group of kids, and I found myself laughing for the first time in days.

"God, I've missed you guys," I choked out. I ducked under the water, then burst out again toward the sun, throwing my hair back.

"How'd you find us?" Peter asked. He was floating on his back in the water, cycling his feet desultorily.

"Serendipity," I laughed. It was the name of my favorite Mobius song.

"Oh, God," Alan groaned.

"You'll just have to work that one into the set," Linny said airily.

She looked around, pushing the tangled blonde hair from her eyes. "Wish we'd thought to bring along some drinks." She paddled a bit. "You haven't brought any, have you, Avi?"

I had to shake my head. "If I'd known you were going to be down here, I should have done my best." I dunked again. I was growing used to the temperature, and the water now felt delightful against my skin. I felt washed. Baptized. "I thought you all were going to call my cellphone when you arrived."

Peter shrugged. "Meant to, but it was so hot after the van. Thought we'd come through here and cool off, then give you a ring. But you found us anyway."

"It was meant to be," Alan intoned. He swam to the bank, then drew himself up into the grass.

"But—where's Brian?" Only three, when there should be a fourth. Mobius's drummer was missing.

"Left him sleeping in the shade," Alan said, shrugging. A shirt lay nearby on the grass; now he gathered it up and began toweling his hair with it, and I hoped, as an aside, that it was his own and not someone else's. Like mine. Everything tended to be communal property with these people, a matter which had frustrated me endlessly during my year in the van with them. "He stayed out late last night after the gig. Think he might have found a new true love."

Brian, as I documented in *A Year in the Life*, was a kind of hopeless romantic, always finding a new true love, sometimes marrying her—he'd been married and divorced twice—and always rediscovering that true love took work to stay true. I had always thought of him as a cork: no matter what took him down, he always popped right back up to the surface, with that cheeky smile breaking across his good-natured face. He'd tried it on with me once or twice, but never seemed too upset when I brushed him off. There were, after all, other, more accommodating sorts in the next town, or the next.

A cloud had made its way across the sun, and in its shade, the water seemed suddenly colder. I saw Linny, across from me, shiver; then she too swam to the edge of the pond and clambered up onto the grass beside her brother. She had a tank top on over her shorts, but now she pulled a too-large shirt, which was probably Peter's, on over it, and lay back in the grass.

"What time is it?" Alan called over.

Peter's watch apparently was waterproof, for he lifted his arm from the water to have a look. "Half three," he said. "Probably should get back in time for sound check." However, he made no immediate move to get out of the pond. "I'd kind of hoped to get over to that book stall beforehand, but I guess that's out."

Alarm bells.

"You haven't been over there yet?" I demanded.

My tone must have alerted him. He turned to me, his eyes narrowing. "What is it?"

I took a deep breath. "It must have been Alan or Brian, then."

"What?" he asked again.

"Someone told the woman at the stall to hold out my book about the band, because I'd be along to autograph it today." I gulped in another lungful of air. "I thought it might have been you. You're the reader."

Peter shrugged, kicking back toward the bank. "Not I. Like I said. We got here, lit out for this pond—it'd been a long drive in this heat. Brian, though—it might have been him, if he woke up and felt like wandering off for some hair of the dog."

I followed the rest of them out of the water, and, like Alan, took up my shirt to towel off as best I could. Then I pulled it on over my camisole—wet as I was, it really didn't matter. I was starting to feel anxious again. I hoped Peter was right. I hoped it was Brian. But the drummer had never been much of a reader, I'd noticed over the course of our year's adventures together: he was far too busy trying to find the new love of his life. In fact, I had written about one time when Brian and Peter had got into it, at one of the low points of the winter tour, because Brian had moved his book to make room for a woman he'd invited back to the green room at a tiny venue in Shropshire, and had somehow lost it. No, it didn't seem at all likely that the book stall was among the first places Brian would go exploring when he woke up with a pounding head.

We started back toward the festival, leaving the leafy oasis behind. The sound of fiddles, mandolin, and guitar grew louder as we passed through the grassy churchyard and continued toward the back gate. The three flashed their artist wristbands and hustled me through before anyone noticed I was an imposter. The van—a much newer and far less beat-up one than they had had seven years ago—was parked at the edge of the lot under some trees with its awning pulled out, and a few plastic chairs scattered around it. Brian Orwell lay sleeping on one lounge chair, a hat over his eyes.

"Gi-yup," Alan said, nudging the chair sharply with a foot. "Sound check, you lunk."

"Look who we found in the woods," Linny crowed.

Brian sat up slowly, blinking, as though unsure of where he was. His pale eyes settled on me. "Hello, Avi," he said, squinting. "That you?"

"I'm changing. I don't want to get electrocuted," Linny said. "Stay out a minute." She slammed the van door behind her with a thunk.

Brian rubbed his eyes and yawned.

"You been to the book stall, you yob?" Alan demanded.

Again the yawn from Brian. "What the hell are you on about? I don't read books."

Twenty-three

The members of Mobius set up their instruments and amps onstage, Brian's drum kit taking up the far right, beside the set-up for the band headlining after them. I listened to the sound check from my blanket over by the far gate, watching the four mark their spots and test their feedback on guitar, fiddle, electric guitar, mandolin, drums, voice. It was a familiar dance, one I had watched many, many times, and it always fascinated me. Their eyes directed to the board off to the side, each pointed up or down as they checked mics and amps. Linny, on her fiddle, tested by following along to the music playing over the system, piped in during the break; the song was "Mr. Blue Sky" by ELO, and as always, she nailed it, laughing, her blonde hair swinging around her shoulders.

I leaned back on the blanket. From somewhere wafted the sickly sweet smell of pot, mixing with the scent of grilling meat from the food tent. The sky above the arena was indeed deep blue; Mr. Night would not be making an appearance this English summer day for several more hours. I took a deep breath, staring upward.

Neil *couldn't* be here, but there was no other explanation. Not for the first time did I wish that the proprietor of the book tent had been just a bit more observant. Over forty? What about hair color? Eye color? Clothing? What did his voice sound like?

If in fact he was here, he was playing a long game, and the

thought of that made me—who knew exactly what kind of long game Neil was capable of—incredibly nervous. I cast my mind back to the guest house in Southampton, where my computer, my digital recorder, and all my notes were locked in my room. Locked. Right? I closed my eyes and tried to remember whether I had double checked the door to make sure it was indeed secure when I left; that had become such habit with me over the years, and was so commonplace an act, that I could not quite remember my hand on the door, my turning the knob and pushing with my knee. I *had* done it, right?

But if it were Neil, he was here, not there.

Right?

Right?

I sat up again, quickly, and scanned the crowd around me. Of course I didn't see him. If he was here, I would only see him when he wanted that to happen. What he wanted to do in the meantime was just this, what he had always known how to do, and what—I admitted it to myself now—he had, somewhat sadistically, always enjoyed: to send me into an anxious spiral. He was succeeding. If he was here.

The sound check was done, and my friends were leaving the stage; they would not return to it for several hours. We'd agreed to meet over at the beer tent, and then get dinner and catch up. I scrambled to my feet again and made my way around the back of the crowd toward the rear of the arena.

They had beaten me to it; of course they had. Where I was a lightweight and knew it, the four members of the band were pint-drinkers of the professional variety. Linny was waiting outside the tent, leaning back against one of the picnic tables, her profile outlined in the afternoon sun. She jerked a thumb toward the lines inside.

"I sent 'em in to do battle," she said cheerfully, tossing her hair back. She'd changed into a flowered sundress that left her shoulders bare. "I told 'em I'd wait for you."

I sat on the picnic table bench and looked toward the band on the stage, another quartet: a banjo, guitar, fiddle—now, two fiddles—and the cajón. I was not familiar with this bunch. I hoped they were lively. I could use lively at this point.

"You look like you could use a pint," Linny continued, peering into my face. Perhaps reading my mind. Her own freckled face was wide and good-natured, the gap in her teeth making her look exceedingly young. She was, I knew quite well, only four or five years younger than I; our birthdays were two weeks apart. "I hope it's still the brown you like, because I told them to get you the brownest they could find."

"The festival special is pretty good."

"Let's see what they figure out. Sometimes they mean well, but it doesn't come off."

I knew what she meant. Part of the theme of my book about them was the accidental nature of their success—they always meant well, but a series of strokes of luck, rather than of genius, or even of planning, had always seemed to find them in the proverbial right place at the right time. When Peter had finished reading the draft of the book, he had handed the manuscript back to me with a shaking head. *Bunch of fuck-ups,* he'd said. But there had been wonder in his voice: a kind of *how the hell did we pull that off?* It was probably their communal good nature: I'd told them the story might not cast them entirely in a good light, but they didn't seem to care. *It's publicity, isn't it?* Linny had demanded, and she had been right.

The men returned from the bar fully laden. I took a pint from Brian, while Linny kissed Peter in payment for her own.

"No kiss for me?" Brian asked sulkily, looking up at me from under his obscenely long eyelashes. Women always swooned for those eyelashes.

"I've got cooties."

We moved on to the food tent. Now on the board outside not only was fish and chips crossed out, but so too was shepherd's pie. Everything seemed to be served with a side of chips. Just inside the tent flap, a table was laden with bottles of ketchup, jars of mustard, vinegar, and bottles of HP sauce. I ordered the bangers and chips, then paid and stepped aside while the others made their decisions. Once we had all we needed, I found myself back at the picnic tables I'd huddled over only a few hours earlier.

Brian sat across from me. He had liberally salted his chips, which surrounded a bubbling square of lasagne on his paper plate. "You working on something new, Avi?" he asked, examining his fork critically, which appeared to be made of balsa wood. Eco-friendly, but he seemed to doubt its ability to be efficacious with his dinner of choice. "We haven't seen you in ages."

"She should come out with us more often," Linny said stoutly. "I mean, just look at her. Tired out, she is. Look at her eyes."

I did not mention that they'd wear me out further, with their nocturnal hours and their cheerful drinking.

Brian made a noise. "She's all right, isn't she? Still turning down every offer of my irresistible self." He sighed, and jammed the fork into the lasagne. It did not break. Neither did the lasagne. "You'd think I'd have worn her down by now."

"Brian, shut it," Alan said. He'd got the sausages as well, but had had the foresight to pick up one of the balsa wood knives from the table in the tent. He cut a sausage up, ran a chunk through the puddle of HP sauce on his plate, and ate it. "Not every woman finds you attractive. You got that one from last night, you hardly need to juggle anymore." He ate a bit more sausage, then followed it with a few chips, also dipped in the sauce. Then he turned his hooded eyes on my face. "Thought you were supposed to be here with your nephew."

Before I could answer, a woman in full tie-dye, including turban,

interrupted, asking for an autograph. She held out a CD and a pen.

"Shut it, Brian," Alan said out of the corner of his mouth, seeing Brian perk up at the woman's expectant smile. I looked at Linny and smirked. She winked.

They took turns signing the cover of the CD—*Bailiff's Lament*, I read on the cover, their first released album. They all looked so young in the photo on the back, like kids trying to appear sophisticated and worldly for the photographer, trying to strike the "serious artist" pose. I had seen pictures of Paul trying to do that at age twelve, posing moodily in what he hoped looked like a windswept landscape.

"So, the nephew?" Alan prodded again. He followed his mouthful of chips with a long drink from his pint. "Like to meet him, if he's around."

I shrugged noncommittally, made a face. "He's going through a tough time right now—his father died last year."

"Moody, is he?"

You could say that again. "Up and down. Mostly down. I think he's kind of mad at the world today. Doesn't seem interested in talking to me. Probably not to anybody else, either."

Linny leaned into me sympathetically. "I'm sorry, love. I know how those kids can be." Linny and Peter had two, a son and a daughter, who were both at university now. Back when I'd first known them all, the kids had accompanied the band on the festival tour, and were rather self-sufficient. I didn't, however, remember either of them being moody. A tad rebellious, maybe. But then, they had been all of twelve and thirteen then, and who wasn't rebellious at that age? The boy, Artie, as I recall, had been infectiously cheerful, taking after his mother.

Speak of the devil and he shall appear. Linny and I were facing the arena, though the picnic table we had all chosen was toward the back of the little yard the food people had marked off with advertising. A familiar squaring of the shoulders caught my eye, and I looked up to see Paul, several yards away, talking to a young man his age. As I watched, he smiled and ducked his eyes, then flicked his hair back from his forehead. The other young man laughed, and touched Paul lightly on the shoulder before dropping his hand quickly, as though somehow trespassing. I squinted, looked more closely. It was the waiter from the Italian restaurant. An interesting plot twist.

"There he is now," I said, and raised both a hand and my voice. "Paul!"

Either he was intent upon his conversation with this dark-haired young man, or he was pretending not to have heard me, for they both turned away and started across the arena, weaving between the rows of people seated on the grass. I watched until they passed the control booth and out of sight.

"That went well," Brian said.

"Shut it, Brian."

The party broke up at the impatient summons of the band's manager and sound engineer, Ruth, who looked a bit cranky—but she had always, as long as I'd known her, looked a bit cranky, since herding this pack of cats around the countryside was never easy. I had a bit of my pint left, though the sausages and chips were long gone, so I stayed, moving down the bench to allow a couple to take the far end of the table. It was nearly five-thirty, nearly time for the evening sets to begin. I tried to remember who was opening the night's festivities, but couldn't quite picture the line-up from the program. With a sigh, I drained the last of the festival ale, and stood to rinse the reusable cup at the spigot next to the performer's gate.

Instead of trying to get back to the blanket by following Paul's example and threading my way through the crowds, I circled around the back, past the book tent, past the soap tent, past the tent with tools for self-reliance. The crowd was bigger than it had been earlier; the evening acts were, after all, more well-known. I spotted my blanket after a moment, my books and other assorted detritus on it. No sign of Paul. I made my way to it, and dug out my sunscreen again, applying it liberally. It was probably too late, though; whatever I'd put on earlier was probably washed off from the wild swimming. At least I had the hat.

The first act was taking the stage, the announcer introducing them. The Little Crumps, from Bognor Regis. I was surprised, and looked up curiously; I had lost track of them ages ago, after the melee at the concert in Upper Snodsbury, and the tragic death of their drummer. From where I sat, I could see that people were already assembling down near the rail; I knew enough to realize that, once Mobius appeared in an hour and a half, it would be virtually impossible to get to the front. And I was enough of a festival aficionado that, to be anywhere other than the rail for my favorite acts, was simply not done. I capped the sunscreen, shoved it back in the front pocket of my backpack, and clambered to my feet once again.

As I was making my way past the gate, I caught sight of Paul and the other young man again. I lifted a hand in greeting, but did not stop. That made me feel rather petty; but I was tired of being treated like the enemy by my own nephew. At the same time, I felt guilty about feeling that resentment, because I knew what an emotional mess the kid was. All the same, I was determined to have one evening—one show—with my friends, who appreciated me, before I had to go back to being the concerned aunt once more.

I was rather surprised, then, when, as I drew up to the rail, I turned at a touch at my shoulder to find Paul and his companion.

"Hey," I said.

"Lance, this is my aunt, Aventurine," Paul said. He sounded nervous. "Aventurine, this is Lance."

The young man had even darker eyes than I remembered

beneath curly dark hair, and a rather endearing crooked smile. He shook my hand. "Delighted," he said.

"As am I." I looked between the two of them, and had a quick flash, back to the other night at the Italian restaurant, and to Lance, who might or might not have been flirting with Paul. With whom Paul might or might not have been flirting.

"I've just been telling Lance that you wrote a book about the band that's coming up in a bit. Mobius." Paul seemed to be holding himself carefully away from Lance, but—I don't think I was being fanciful here—the air between them seemed to hum.

"I did. They've become great friends of mine."

"I don't know them," Lance said, glancing up at the stage, where a duo was singing in close harmony now. "But Paul says they're good. He says they owe a lot of their following to your book, too."

I almost laughed. "I think they're pretty good. But I might be a bit biased." This surprised me, too, that Paul was telling his new— friend?—about me. Still, when you are just meeting a person you desperately want to chat up, any topic of conversation is a good one.

"A bit." Paul laughed nervously. He looked at Lance, blushing— unless his reddened cheeks were from sunburn, or the early evening heat. "That's why she wants to be at the rail. Because they're her friends." He shifted back and forth, his eyes flitting between Lance and me. Was he looking for something? Approval? Reaction? How changeable he was, too: in the morning not wishing to have anything to do with me, and now bringing Lance to meet me. I preferred this Paul to that. He cleared his throat. "We're just going to get a pint before they come on. You want one, Avi?"

Under the bad influence of my friends, I'd had more today than I usually did, and probably I didn't need any more. However, it seemed churlish to turn him down. "Can you refill my water bottle? I still need to drive home."

"Lightweight." Paul laughed as he took the bottle; the teasing was more a show for Lance than anything else. "Be back. Save our spot."

I looked after them. I admit it: with some concern, though a far different concern than the one I'd been dealing with. If this was attraction, I hoped it wasn't a kind of rebound, out of hurt and anger at Shep. At me. I wondered if this was a coming out moment, or if there had been one before at some time, and I'd just missed it. I hadn't really kept up since Mallory or Valerie, or whatever that high school girlfriend's name had been.

Should I ask my sister? What if she had no idea?

I probably should have gone for another pint of festival ale.

Twenty-four

It was, as always, an energetic show—this time including some new material, which, Alan promised us, the adoring audience, would be available on a new CD come November. The old standards were included as well; Linny laughed and waved down at me when Alan introduced "Serendipity," and I sang along lustily. It felt good to just belt out the lyrics: suddenly I felt just how much I'd been holding back, not just on this trip, but for some time now. Every once in a while I noticed Paul glancing my way, at times looking surprised and a bit puzzled. Mostly, though, when I looked to my right, I saw him swaying with Lance; sometimes their hands would touch.

There were two bands on after Mobius, to finish off the evening. I was thinking about giving up my position on the rail and retreating to the blanket when Ruth appeared, slipping out from behind the stage to come across to us. She still looked annoyed, the familiar frown visible in the lighting from the stage, etched between her brows under the bandanna.

"They've gone to the merch tent to sign. Come back over to the band gate and meet us there."

Then she was gone, back the way she had come.

"Wanna?" I asked Paul. He looked to Lance, who shrugged.

"There'll be free drinks."

At this, Lance tipped back his head and laughed, his teeth gleaming in the semi-darkness. His parents, I thought inconsequentially, must've not had a lot to spend on orthodonture. "I'm not going to say no to free drinks," he said.

We left the rail and headed toward the entrance on the far side of the arena, beyond the food stalls. Paul and Lance walked beside me, and a little bit behind, but even so, I was able to see them out of the corner of my eye, close, their arms occasionally brushing. Something definitely was happening there. I only hoped it was something that could bring Paul out of his funk.

Sorry, Lance, I thought guiltily. *I'll use you if I have to.* But of course, it wasn't really up to me.

The after-party, though, didn't really last all that long. Under Ruth's watchful eye, the band members toasted their successful show, their successful CD signing, their successful sales of band T-shirts. The crowd had been large and appreciative, and even the taciturn Peter seemed happy with their showing. Or perhaps he had already had enough to drink to make everything all right.

"We've got to get back on the road in a bit," Ruth warned them. She was wearing a baseball cap now, the bill to the back. The only thing missing from her big-mama persona was a cigarette dangling from the corner of her mouth, but Ruth didn't smoke. To the best of my knowledge, Ruth didn't drink, either, and sometimes—like right now—that was probably a good thing. Now she looked at her watch, the dial glowing on her wrist. "I want to get to Oxford by midnight." Ruth had done all the driving for Mobius since the night Alan had fallen asleep at the wheel and put the old van in a hedge. Well before my time with them, thank God. She turned to me. "We've got another festival over to the west tomorrow evening. Why'n't you come along?"

I shook my head. "We'll stay, thanks. Gio is on tomorrow night."

Linny's head spun and she looked over at me with delighted expectation. "Gio? *Gio?*" She set her pint glass down on the picnic table. "Aventurine Morrow, are you holding back on us, then?"

I shook my head. "No, Linny. Just, no. Gio and I were over a long time ago."

"You haven't started back up?" She frowned, her disgust with me obvious. "Avi, the man is to die for. Still."

I only smiled, took a sip of my own drink, which I was nursing slowly—I really didn't need it. Off to the side of the van, Alan had handed Lance, who was seated on an overturned bucket, a mandolin, and was now walking him through some fingerings. Paul hovered nearby, his eyes never leaving Lance. None of them seemed to be paying any attention to us.

"Avi, you're pretty thick sometimes," Linny said despairingly, her head in her hands.

"Gio and I are friends," I protested lightly. "It's better that way. We had fun, and then we realized we could never work. So we went back to friends."

"With benefits?" Linny lifted her eyes hopefully.

"You have a one track mind."

"But it's a hell of a track," Brian said on the way by, carrying a drum case. He leaned into the open door at the rear of the van, made an adjustment, and slipped the case inside. Then he tapped the assorted cases, naming them under his breath.

"Shut it, Brian," Peter muttered.

"You're a pig, Brian," Linny called after him. She didn't seem at all perturbed. After all these years touring from gig to gig in the confined space of the van, they were all used to each other's vagaries. She turned back to me. Perhaps it was the free-flowing alcohol that had loosened her tongue; but it was more likely that Linny had never had many inhibitions to begin with. After my being part of the cramped confines of the van for an entire year, she didn't bother to hold back. "Gio Constantine is the real deal, Aventurine.

Talented. Good-looking. Makes enough money to support you in the manner to which you should become accustomed. I don't know what your problem is, unless it's that stupid man you lost your heart to all those years ago. The thief. The bastard."

She was probing, in that shameless way she had.

"I didn't lose my heart."

"She doesn't have a heart," Brian said on the way by, bringing yet another bag to the back of the van. "I know. I've been trying to find it forever."

Over my shoulder, a voice rose, tenor, light, but true. I turned. It was Lance, singing. Paul's face was in shadow.

"No," Alan said abruptly. "Like this." He reached toward Lance's hand on the frets.

"Get yourselves organized," Ruth called from the driver's seat, where she was adjusting the sat-nav. "We've got to take off."

They hadn't much out on the picnic tables save a few empty wine bottles and some glasses. Peter set aside the book he hadn't been reading, and began gathering up the mess.

"Aventurine." Linny was standing before me now. I slowly stood to face her. "Don't do it, Aventurine. Don't waste your life pining away for that asshole. If you won't jump Gio's bones, find someone else's. Life's too short to die alone."

I felt my eyes widen. "I'm hardly planning to die soon, Linny. Calm yourself." I laughed, but somehow the laughter was forced.

"That bastard isn't worth your time."

I shrugged, looked around. "I think he's here at the festival, actually." Stupid. Of course he wasn't in the performers' enclosure. He didn't have my connections.

Still, the words surprised me with their taste in my mouth. I hadn't voiced that fear, not yet, not to anyone. That didn't mean it wasn't there. It was, and was growing.

"Here?" Linny made a face. "What an idiot. He must know you don't want to see him." She leaned forward, tucking her hair behind her ear, and looked into my face, her own expression wide and curious. "You don't, do you?"

I shook my head.

"Good. Keep it that way." She turned away, and then just as quickly came back again. She threw her thin arms around me in a quick hug. "Take my word for it. It's never good to go back to assholes. They don't change. Things don't get better. They only get worse." Another quick squeeze, and then she was headed for the sliding door of the van. "Stay away from the slime ball, Aventurine. Listen to your old Auntie Linny, who knows what's best for you. And get back with that Gio. Seriously."

"I'm walking Lance back to his friends' car," Paul announced as we watched the taillights of the van disappear through the gate toward the road and Oxford and Mobius's next festival in the west. He did not look at me. "I'll meet you at our car over in the field." I hadn't seen Lance with these friends, but perhaps he'd thrown them over for Paul, who might just be a better one?

Lance wished me goodnight, adding that he might see me tomorrow, and I watched the pair of them head back toward the gate. Shoving my fists into the pockets of my shorts, I too headed toward the arena, where the music was suddenly climactic, and the crowd noises peaking. Must be the end of an encore. I looked at the time on my Fitbit and saw that it was past eleven. Probably Ruth wouldn't be getting that wild bunch to Oxford by midnight; but with my experience of her and her wily ways, I knew she really meant to be there by one, and had just insisted on twelve because her charges couldn't ever seem to get out of their own way anyway. I snorted to myself.

When I passed through the gate, I found that, indeed, the final act of the evening was waving, preparing to leaving the stage. The announcer came out to the mic and wished us all a forceful good evening, with thanks, prodding anyone who seemed disinclined to move. In the scattered lighting from the stage and from the edge of the arena, the people standing, stretching, gathering their belongings: they all looked ghostly, moving in slow motion, having no feet. Again I snorted at my own fancy, picking my way across to the place where my blanket lay bereft, my backpack opened, the bottle of suntan lotion off to the side. I hadn't been back to it since the Mobius show, but Paul must have been looking for something. Car keys? I had those in my back pocket. There wasn't much else in the pack, so it hardly mattered.

Take that, Neil, I thought contemptuously. *If you're here, you didn't find anything in my stuff this time.*

And then. Suddenly. There he was.

He approached, smiling, a pint in each hand. Before I could say anything—punch him, kick him, turn my back on him—he held out one to me.

"Cheers, Aventurine," he said. His smile was wide, deceptive, wolfish. Or maybe that was just me.

I stood, turned to stone, holding the folded blanket in both hands. I said nothing.

"You look shocked," Neil said, freeing one of my hands and pressing the pint into it. In the half-light from the bulbs strung about the periphery of the festival grounds, his face was shadowed, but his eyes gleamed like a wild animal's, and the odd light glinted on his teeth.

I grasped the beer, a reflex. I looked down into it, at a loss. I *was* shocked. *Stay away from him,* Linny had warned. From the stage came a shout: a roadie, then another roadie called out a garbled reply. From somewhere—the beer tent?—wafted the sound of guitars; a voice was singing, vaguely out of tune.

Neil's eyes continued to glitter, too, as he sipped from his plastic glass, measuring my reactions over its rim. He said nothing. Waited. I really had no words. All I had was anxiety. I hadn't laid eyes on him in years. Nearly twenty-four years, to be exact. The summer before Paul was born. At the going-away party at our friends the Rowells's apartment in Brooklyn, before they left us for their new life in San Francisco.

I opened my mouth, closed it. I couldn't speak, couldn't even drink the pint.

"Avi?"

In the noise and crowds, I had not heard Paul's approach. He was alone, no Lance.

Neil took a slight step away.

There was an uncomfortable pause. They looked at each other and away again, as though trying to avoid meeting each others' eyes. I barely registered the strangeness of that interaction, but then it was over, and I was left thinking I had imagined it.

"Paul Genthner," my nephew said, holding out a hand. His glance slewed between the pair of us. "Are you—Gio?"

"No. Neil." They shook hands. I wondered fleetingly why he did not give his surname, as Paul had done. "Not quite in Gio's class." There might have been a sneer in his voice.

"My nephew," I said. My lips felt numb.

Neil rocked back on his heels. "Of course," he said. He took another drink from his pint. "Shep and Micheline's boy."

I felt Paul tense beside me. "You know my parents?" His voice sounded odd. Then, more quietly, "You knew my dad?"

The past tense fell heavily on my ears. Yet the words seemed hollow, almost rehearsed. As though Paul had practiced saying them, perhaps before a mirror. I shook myself; I had no idea why I should think that.

I was losing my grip.

Neil did that. Neil had always done that.

"Yes. Yes, from quite a long time ago. College." The eyes still glittered in the dark, but slid up and down Paul's lanky frame, a measurement. "How are your parents? Haven't seen them in a while."

I sucked in my trepidation.

"My father—" Paul took a ragged breath. "My father is dead."

"No. I'm sorry." The words were quick, but even though I hadn't seen Neil in years, I felt the edge of insincerity behind them. "I didn't know." But how could he not? Surely Neil knew about Shep's disappearance, the debris from the *Màquina de los Vientos;* for a while the story had been big news: *Investment Banker Disappears in Bermuda Triangle.* Before the rapid news cycle washed that story away like so much flotsam. It was almost as though—and I flinched away from the thought—Neil knew exactly what he was doing asking that question, and was probing for some sort of reaction. The random cruelty: I recognized that, even after all these years.

I handed Paul the pint; I hadn't taken a single sip. He downed it. The atmosphere was still strange, charged. The anxiety raged, and I was sweating with it.

"Listen," Neil said. "That was a pretty good showing, wasn't it? Mobius. You wrote a book about them, didn't you, Avi?" He knew I had; of course he knew. I felt the ground underfoot shifting like sand. "And more tomorrow. Can I give you a ride somewhere? Into Southampton?"

Before Paul could answer, I shook my head, laid a hand on my nephew's arm, which he shrugged off. "No, thanks," I said hurriedly. "We're all set."

Neil knew we were staying in Southampton.

I shook myself. Everyone who wasn't camping here at the festival was staying in Southampton.

I don't know if Neil believed me, and I didn't care. I turned away, hearing, 'nice to meet you,' directed at Paul, who fell in beside me. When we made it to the south gate, where one of the strings of lights was buzzing and turning itself off and on, with no further sign of Neil, I paused. "Sorry about that. Just had to get away from him."

Paul set the cup atop an overflowing rubbish container. "Not all that good a friend of Mom and Dad, if he didn't know."

I shrugged, unwilling to say anything further. "We were all friends a long time ago," I managed at last. "I haven't seen him since before you were born."

"Asshole," was all Paul said. His voice still sounded strange. The encounter had unnerved him. Probably had erased any good the evening spent in the company of Lance had done. I hated Neil for that.

We followed the path past the workshop tent, where a few voices still lifted in a shaky rendition of "Lillibulero." Then we were across the little bridge, and into the field where most of the cars had already gone.

Well after the exposé on Malvern appeared, and after the story won that National Press Club award, I only saw Neil once more, at a going away party for our friends, the Rowells: Jacob had taken a position as a visiting professor at a small college outside of San Francisco; Liz was still looking. Just a small party, we were promised; otherwise—I was feeling especially run down that day, I remember—I probably would have begged off and let Micheline and Shep go along without me. *Down* is actually a far too tame word for what I was feeling, of course; there was still hurt, there was still fury, there was a mix of far too many emotions to name them all, but all of them were bad. How, after all, does one overcome that kind of treachery, on the personal, the emotional, and the professional level? How long did it take? The hormones hadn't helped; I was a total emotional wreck. I hated being alone with my thoughts, I hated socializing. I hated thinking that there was always a possibility that I would go out and see Neil, whom I had banished from my bed, from my heart, from our apartment.

Heavily pregnant by then, I was wearing the green that day and Micheline the blue. Of course people confused the two of us, but that was what we meant to do: after all, it was Micheline who was the pregnant twin, not I. When Neil appeared, with a debonaire bow for Liz and a bottle of scotch for Jake, I felt the nausea rise up in my gullet—an all-to-familiar feeling lately—and hid in the pantry. Micheline just gave him the cold shoulder, walking away as he approached, ignoring him when he spoke. With apologies to me for making me face him, my sister and brother-in-law made our excuses to our hosts (*my wife is not feeling well*) and left early.

I had not seen him again.

Until now.

I still felt nauseated. The sweat beaded my hairline.

I leaned my head against the steering wheel for a moment, breathing as heavily as though I had run a marathon, before twisting the key sharply in the ignition. I didn't have the excuse tonight of suffering from morning sickness, but the roiling in my stomach, and the creep of acid up my throat, was nearly more than I could bear.

"You okay to drive?" Paul asked. He almost sounded concerned, rather than furious and resentful.

I nodded. "Yeah."

I could have said more. I could have agreed with Paul's estimation of Neil's character, that he was, in fact, an asshole. I could have told Paul the story of my sad and stupid and disastrous relationship with Neil Barrett. But I did none of those things. I just threw the Renault into gear and bumped it along the track after the others toward the exit and the road to Southampton.

Twenty-five

I did the math. It wasn't quite nine there, at my sister's. My hands shaking, I dialed Micheline anyway.

No preamble; no greeting. "Are you all right?"

"You're going all twin sister on me."

It was a play for time, and we both knew it. I had never smoked, but now I thought of the way I'd seen my sister's hands shake as she put a cigarette between her lips, struggled to light it. There was something beyond habit with that: it was ritual, and ritual was what we needed to get through the hard stuff. Shake the cigarette from the pack, put it in your mouth, strike the match, draw that first lungful of smoke, closing your eyes while you do. I almost wished I could do that, as I knew, when I heard the scrape of the match across the miles, that Micheline was doing it.

"What happened? Is it you? Is it—is it Paul?"

"Has he called you?"

A long pause. I envisioned Micheline tipping her head back and blowing the long stream of smoke upward, toward the kitchen ceiling.

"He called early this morning."

"Did he sound all right?"

Her laugh was tight. "What does 'all right' sound like?"

I frowned. I was lying on my back on the bed, staring up through the darkness at the high ceiling, which I couldn't see. The window to the right was open, a breeze moving the white net curtains gently, restless ghosts in the darkness.

"He's just been so angry with me, and I still don't know why."

"Have you asked him?"

"It seems as though I haven't seen much of him. He's off at every opportunity."

"And has he read the letter?"

"I haven't asked. I told you. If he wanted to tell me, he would. But—" and I sighed. "He doesn't seem to want to tell me anything. Mick, I'm just so worried and discouraged. He's never been like this with me. It's like he *blames* me for something, but won't tell me what it is." I rubbed at my eyes with the ball of my free hand. They felt hot and gritty. "I can't fix it if he won't tell me what it is. I can't defend myself."

"What about today? You went over to the festival to see that band. Did he go with you?" Micheline sounded desperate, as helpless as I felt; and it had to be so much worse for her. She was so far away from us, reaching out blindly in the darkness.

Now I closed my eyes, imagined the white smile in the dark face: Lance. *Lance what?* I didn't even know his last name, and I wish I'd asked. One hell of an investigative reporter I was. "He came. I didn't see him for most of the day, though—he took off. Met up with him around dinnertime, to see Mobius. He had found—someone—to hang around with."

My words hung out there like they were hung on a line, blowing gently back and forth like the curtains at the window.

From the other end of the telephone connection, I heard another scratch, another match. Micheline was lighting up yet another cigarette.

"*Someone.*"

I took a deep breath. "His name is Lance. They seemed—quite taken with each other."

Again my sister's laugh, and there was an odd quality to it. Relief? "You can say the words, Avi. You can ask the question."

I felt my cheeks flush. "That's not it," I protested. "I just didn't know how *you'd* take it."

"Oh, for God's sake, Avi." The tight laugh again. Micheline sounded borderline hysterical—like I felt. "This is my kid we're talking about. And you're my sister—my twin sister, in case you've forgotten—and you should know my thoughts by now. It doesn't matter, Avi. *It doesn't matter.* What matters is that boy's happiness. He's had precious little of late."

I shrugged, though there was no way she could see me. But we were *twin sisters*, so probably she could sense it, right? "Of course, it's a bit premature. I mean, they met at a restaurant the other night. Lance was our waiter. They hung out this afternoon. And here we are, thrusting them into a long-term relationship."

"Long-term relationships aren't necessarily what they're cracked up to be." Micheline's voice was beyond sad, skirting around bitter. "Maybe a couple of kisses and getting laid are what it's all about."

"Yeah, well, I wouldn't know about that." Abruptly I sat up and stumbled toward the bathroom and a glass of water.

"No? I thought you were seeing that Gio Constantine tomorrow. Wasn't that the extent of your relationship with him? How many years ago?"

The water was cold, but the inside of my mouth felt furry, as though I'd just awakened with the hangover of the century— despite the fact that I hadn't even fallen asleep yet. I ran the faucet again and downed another glassful.

"Gio—he's a good guy. He knew what we were about, he and I."

"Which was a couple of kisses and getting laid."

For some reason, this teasing, if it was teasing, made me uncomfortable, and I didn't know why. I had told Micheline all about Gio when we'd had the fling, but that was all it was. They hadn't met; the closest they'd come had been a night at a pub in

London, when Gio had steadfastly refused to come inside, playing his scene for all he was worth. Not much emotional entanglement for either Gio nor me, and we'd both appreciated that. Still, it wasn't as though I'd kept any of it a secret from Mick. Hell, I'd never kept anything a secret from her—I wouldn't have been able to had I tried.

"I think Paul and Lance have plans to get together again tomorrow," I said, trying to steer the conversation away from my non-relationship with Gio. George, his real name was, but he'd prefer everyone forget that. Didn't sound star-quality. But, if the truth be told, I would much rather see Gio, or George, star-quality or not, than Neil. Who might just show up again tomorrow as well. I might be forced to use poor Gio as a kind of shield. I hoped he was up to it.

I didn't realize I'd caught my breath until the sound echoed from my sister. "What is it?"

"Neil." The name fell between us like a bomb. Long after it had left my lips, I felt the shockwaves.

A long pause. I took the opportunity to drink yet another glass of water; this time it wasn't to combat the furry taste in my mouth, but rather the acid taste in my throat at speaking the name. At this rate I was going to keep myself up all night, using the bathroom, downing antacids like candy. Still, that would be something to keep my hands occupied, since I didn't smoke.

"You sound certain now."

"I am certain now."

"You'd better tell me."

So I did. About the request from the bookseller that I autograph *A Year in the Life*. About the open backpack, the bottle of suntan lotion lying out on the blanket. Then about Neil himself, appearing with a pint, as though he hadn't been forcibly banished from my life for twenty-four years. As I described the scene to Micheline—the beer Neil thrust into my hand, the strange almost-taunts he threw at Paul about his parents—my confusion grew. Something was so wrong there; something about that encounter rang false. Of course, with Neil, everything was false—there was nothing about that man that a person could trust. But I couldn't help but think that there was more. Layers. Depths I sensed, but didn't understand. And—I shook my head, unwilling to consider the idea—it had something to do with Paul. Something in the shift of his eyes.

"One good thing," Micheline mused once I had finished. "He's slithered out from under his rock now. You know what you're dealing with."

"Out from under his rock. Apt. He's a snake."

"Or a vampire. He only became visible after dark. But listen, Avi." Now her voice grew serious. "Listen to me. Stay away from him." Echoing Linny.

It was my turn to laugh. Knowingly. Bitterly. "Oh, I will, Mick. Don't you worry about that one."

"No, Aventurine." She took a deep breath that echoed down the phone. "I mean it. *Stay away from him.*"

"Mick—"

"*Don't take him back.*"

I lay awake long after we had broken the connection. The room was hot, despite the oscillating fan whirring away on the bedside table. The curtains had long ago ceased their gentle movement: the night had become heavy and humid, lowering on us all in Southampton like a wet blanket. From outside, I heard the honk of car horns, and the bark of a faraway dog. Then, a long roll of distant thunder.

Don't take him back.

Now I really wished I smoked, so I could take a few angry puffs and then jam the cigarette butt violently into an ashtray.

My own sister. My own sister who knew better than anyone the betrayal I had suffered at that man's hands. How she could even

166

think I would consider something like that—*damn it*. I ran my own hands up into my sweaty hair and massaged my aching head. How she could think I would ever let that poor excuse for a man back into my life, and—I knew what she was saying without her saying it—back into my bed? The greatest sex in the world wasn't worth being emotionally and professionally eviscerated. I knew that well.

The thunder was rolling closer. I stared up into the darkness and waited for the rain.

Twenty-six

In the early hours, to clear my head, I stepped out into the Polygon, the uneven pavement still damp from the rain overnight. I turned right, and headed to the traffic circle, and then the park beyond. In the brightness of the morning, everything sparkled with lingering wetness: the trees, the grass, the gardens. If I stared long enough, the raindrops on the green resolved themselves into individual emeralds. Hands clenched at my sides, I kept my head down as I chose the paths along the north side of the park, skirting statues without looking at them, avoiding meeting the eyes of people walking their dogs or jogging in the other direction.

I had not slept well.

Damn them all. Micheline, Paul. And Neil, mostly, and that smug smile as he thrust his way into my life one more time.

He would no doubt show up again at the festival today. He had a plan, a poker hand he was holding close to the vest. While he might have made himself visible at last, his plan was still shrouded in darkness. Again, I had the sense of standing on shifting sand, as though he had already laid some of his gaslighting groundwork, and things that I thought I knew could morph into something totally unrecognizable at any moment. I didn't like that. I didn't like not knowing where I was, or what was going on. I didn't like not feeling in control, and I sure as hell didn't feel in control. Not after last night, with its meeting, its phone call, its thunderstorm that finally broke and kept me awake until it rolled out of town in the wee hours. I thought now of Genevieve, and the fierce control she held over every aspect of her life; I thought of her mother, with no control save for her cooking. I knew which life I preferred to live.

I passed the Cenotaph, then crossed Above Bar Street into East Park. Something here made me turn again to my left, and this time, at the memorial, I stopped to stare upward, hands still in pockets. It was curved, with benches below a striding angel, who in turn was flanked in relief by engineers manning their doomed posts. I did not approach any further, squinting only to read the carving below the angel:

> *To the memory of the engineer officers*
> *of the R. M. S. Titanic who showed*
> *their high conception of duty and their*
> *heroism by remaining at their posts*
> *15th April 1912*

Despite myself, I felt the tears well up. I squeezed my eyes shut and lifted my face to the sky, hoping to stave them off. An entire crew of men, working frantically to pump out the hull as bulkhead after bulkhead failed, knowing that their work was in vain, hoping to stave off the inevitable in order for as many people as possible to escape before the ship slipped below the waves. Pretending to control, even as all control was lost, along with their lives.

Yet, they weren't for the engineers, the tears, and despite trying to convince myself, I knew they were for Shep, who perhaps had time to try to save himself, and perhaps had not—and no one would ever know. The investigation had been closed, Shep's death deemed by misadventure, and there was nothing left to do but wonder. *What happened, Shep?* Phil Newlan couldn't imagine that it was an accident that befell Shep, but if not, that left intention. But whose? Who would want to sabotage Shep and the *Màquina de los Vientos*? Because that would, of course, lead to the disabling—or as it turned out, the sinking—of the boat. And that would mean that Shep had enemies. Enemies who had access to the boat, while it was here, in Southampton. Yet Phil Newlan was adamant: Shep had gone over the *Màquina* thoroughly before setting sail; Shep had left nothing up to chance. If someone had tampered in some way with the boat, Shep would have known, and would have corrected the problem before he'd set off. Phil would have told us that, too: *The funny thing was, Shep found—* whatever it was Shep would have found. Unless Phil's entire story was a fabrication; but to what end? Phil, too, had seemed genuinely grieved by the loss of someone he apparently counted as a friend.

The only other possibility—and it made me break out in a cold sweat just to think of it—was that the sabotage had been done by Shep himself.

Micheline spoke of Shep frequently, long before I met him, and I have to say that I took her ravings about his intelligence, his good looks, his kindness, with the proverbial grain of salt. No one could have possibly been that close to perfect. If I hadn't known her better—better than anyone in the world—I would have suspected her of making this guy up. Who the hell was named *Shep* anyway?

I called him all sorts of things, just to drive her wild. Sheep. Chip. Shrek. Sherpa.

"Shepherdson," she'd say calmly, not looking up from her book; she, like I, always had a book. "His name is Shepherdson."

"What the hell kind of person is named Shepherdson?"

Then I met him.

My sister, like me, did not have any tendencies toward dissembling. She had not lied about Shepherdson. Shep. He was dark where we were fair; he was tanned where we were freckled, but like us, he had the green eyes—though his were sparkling, where ours tended to be opaque, hiding our thoughts. He greeted me warmly, bending to kiss my cheek and expressing his happiness that we'd finally met; then his gaze had swept on until it found Micheline, and his entire demeanor softened. When he looked at my sister, it was plain that she had become the center of his universe. Never mind that we were identical twins, had been mistaken one for the other since the day we were born. Shep knew which one of us was which, even without our habits of green and blue clothing, and he knew which one of us he loved.

With that realization, I felt the flicker of jealousy spark up, the tiniest of foul flames.

Now, where there had been two, there were three. Or rather, where Micheline and I had been two, now she and Shep were two, and I was, for the first time in my life, only one.

And I had developed an almost immediate crush on the man who, after a few years, became my brother-in-law.

It was still early. Breakfast wouldn't be on yet in the dining room until 7:30. I forced myself to turn away and continue along the park walkway. In the center of East Park was the Queen's Peace Fountain, surrounded by flowers. I felt like soaking my head, as though that might possibly clear it, but kept on. Eventually I came to a pergola from which emanated a scent so strong I thought it might knock me down. The flowers that covered it were white, the small petals pointed. I knew it wasn't wisteria—it was too late in the summer for wisteria, and the flowers weren't right—but I had no idea what it was. For the second time on my walk, I closed my eyes, but this time I breathed deeply, trying to let the smell steady me. No success: the scent was too overpowering. Holding a hand out like a person unable to see, I brushed through the pergola and out the other side, as though pushing my way through curtains.

What if Shep had scuttled the *Màquina* intentionally?

That would mean Shep had killed himself.

I stepped off the curb at Above Bar Street without looking, and a car horn sounded frantically. An angry voice shouted at my back.

Shep had killed himself.

He had left letters for his wife and his son.

Suicide notes.

Had Paul opened his yet? *Don't let him read it,* my sister had pleaded.

I quickened my steps.

"Not yet," he said, cutting a bit of his good British back bacon. I watched his hands, tanned and long-fingered. He had picked up the British way of handling his utensils, too: fork steady in the one hand, rather than the American way of shifting knife and fork back and forth between both hands. He didn't look up, but instead stared down intently into his plate. "Why?"

I scrambled for some answer to this. I hadn't thought the conversation through, and cursed inwardly. "Your mother—"

"Your sister," he cut over me, but with only a hint of the rancor of our previous conversation about this.

"Yes. Mick." I took a breath, followed it with a sip of black tea. No milk, so any good Brit would recognize me for the foreigner I was, even if he was able to pass. "Has she said anything about the letter to you?"

He slewed a look up to me, then returned his attention to his beans and grilled tomato. He was going to be no help.

"She wants you to wait. To open it. Until you're together next week, and you can open your letters together."

"You could always open it for me."

I closed my eyes for a moment. *What the hell is going on?* I wanted to demand, but didn't. Instead I reached for the tea cup again. My grip was unsteady, and it clinked against the saucer, the tea spilling over.

"I haven't opened your mother's letter. I've told you. That's between your father and your mother; it's nothing to do with me."

I could almost hear his eye-roll, it was that pronounced. If I drank the tea, I wouldn't be able to retort. I poured more into my cup from the pot, and picked up the cup once again.

Abruptly Paul pushed away from the table, his breakfast abandoned. "Are you ready? I told Lance I'd meet him at the workshop tent at eleven."

Suddenly I wasn't hungry, either. I drank the last of the tea and stood up.

Twenty-seven

It was early for a pint, and fortunately I didn't mind warm beer, because mine was slowly growing warmer. I found a bit of protection from the late morning's already brilliant sun under the awning beyond the food tent—not hungry yet, maybe never hungry again—and sat to troll through my program. There were a couple of workshops I was half-heartedly interested in, but as far as I knew Paul and Lance had that place staked out, so it was safer to avoid it. Hedgepig was playing in the mid-afternoon, just before the break; I remembered the kindness of the mando player with particular fondness. In the heat, I thought with longing of the wild swimming of yesterday, and wondered whether I was up to it alone. I lifted my straw hat and brushed the sweaty hair away from my forehead. I didn't know whether I was up to anything alone today, now that Neil had come out into the open. He was here somewhere—if he wasn't here now, he'd be here eventually. I needed to be with others, even strangers, when he appeared, for my own safety, for my own sanity.

Just the thought of his presence made my skin crawl. I was sitting at a table to the back of the picnic area, facing the arena, and now I scanned it, looking for the figure, the walk. I didn't see him. Still, I really didn't have to see him for him to have the desired effect. He could be here; he could be back at his hotel room, wherever that was. Just the fact that I was looking for him, that he had destroyed any peace of mind I might have built up—that would be enough for him. I could almost hear him laugh.

I downed my beer, rinsed the cup at the tap near the gate, and shoved it into my bag again before heading out on the path I'd taken the previous day.

There was a man sitting on the bank, back to, as I came up. I tensed, my panicky mind trying to fit the familiar figure into various molds until it found the correct one. The flight instinct had kicked in, despite the shape being all wrong—Neil's appearance had made me that paranoid. Then the figure turned at the sound of my footsteps, and of course it wasn't Neil. It was Gio Constantine, who smiled delightedly, and I felt myself go absolutely limp with relief as I slumped to the grass beside him.

"Knew you'd come after me at some point," he chuckled. I didn't have to see the lines crinkling around his eyes to know his expression, I knew his face so well. However brief our fling had been, he still had a physicality that was burned deeply into my memory. "Knew you wouldn't be able to resist my magnificent self for long."

"Go to hell." The sun reddened my closed eyelids, so I pulled my hat over my face.

He laughed, a rich baritone, which he, professional that he was, knew how to use to best effect. "You're going soft in your old age, Avi. *Go to hell?* Whatever happened to 'Gio, you flaming bastard'?"

"*My* old age? You're older than I am."

"I'm perennially young, ridiculous woman. Just ask the pretty young stylist who dyes my hair."

He plucked the hat from my face to kiss my cheek, then dropped it back. After a moment, though, he lifted it again, and I felt his eyes on me.

175

"Hell, Avi, you look wiped out. Are you sick?" Gio's voice was rich with concern, and even after all these years, I could tell he wasn't feigning.

I wiped my palms down my cheeks. When I opened my eyes, he was only a silhouette against the brilliant sky, so I closed them again. "Not sick. Tired." I was; that was no lie. The lack of sleep last night. The anxiety, mixed with a vague resentment, where Paul was concerned. The worry for my sister. The grief over Shep. And the fear that the biggest bogeyman of my entire life was back. Back with a vengeance.

"Tell me." Gio lay down in the grass beside me, tucking my head into his shoulder. Not quite like old times—when we had been lovers, the contact had been fevered; but now it was just a warm touch between friends. It made me want to cry, it was so gentle. Well, everything right now made me want to cry.

So I told him about Paul. I couldn't quite bring myself to say anything about Neil.

"Ah, Avi," he said into my hair when I'd finished. "I've got nothing for you about your nephew, except that he's got to figure out how to get past this, which he'll do in his own time. It's a terrible way to lose your father, and, if you add that on top of his coming out, if that's what he's doing, he's probably not feeling too steady right now, is he?" Slowly Gio sat up and drew me to sit beside him. "So give him all the space he needs, and walk away when he wants to fight with you."

"Which is apparently all the time, all of a sudden."

Gio shrugged. "Because you're safe. He doesn't have to pretend with you, and so you have the pleasure of witnessing his acting out."

"You make him sound like he's four years old," I said dryly.

This time Gio laughed gently. "We're all four years old. Deep down inside. We just want to cry and lash out when things are bad, but we've learned the world is not good to us when we do that. But that doesn't make us want to do it any less." He brushed a bit of hair from my forehead, then reached for my hat to replace it on my head. "You want to do it now."

I snorted. A self-defensive sound.

"Am I wrong?"

I didn't answer right away, and he waited, his head tipped to the side. His good side, where the dimple showed.

"Okay," I admitted grudgingly at last. "You are not wrong. I want to punch somebody right now, and I want to cry."

The smile was back, the one he used so expertly, which I had fallen for that summer, and just as quickly, realized was his intent all the time: that people—I—should fall for him. "I'd rather you didn't punch me, of course, but you're more than welcome to cry on my shoulder."

I smiled in return, but it felt small, forlorn. "I don't think so. I do that, and I'll find myself appearing in your songs."

The laugh was now uproarious. "Oh, Aventurine. What a monumental ego you have."

"Am I wrong?" I taunted.

He shook his head. "You are not wrong."

We had met, Gio and I, the August I was at the Wickham Music Festival with Mobius. Ironically, he had mistaken me for a member of the tech crew, as I had graduated, early on, to wearing black and dragging equipment around under Ruth's growling direction. *Might as well make yourself useful if you're going to take up space,* she'd said more than once.

"Could you take this?" he'd asked gruffly, handing off a gig bag and a guitar case. His eyes, as I'd learned they did, had hardened and narrowed as he considered the stage and imagined his set-up. He barely registered me, I was certain, as a human. I'd heard around that Gio was an insufferable *artiste* sort, but after the previous couple of months with the band, I'd learned to recognize that single-minded look: it was all about the music.

So I took the gig bag and guitar and lugged them up to the stage, handing them off with a shrug to the real techies. Linny and I took in the show from the VIP side of the red marquee, I with some curiosity: I'd heard some of Gio's music; in fact, had listened to Peter play some of his songs while we rode through the night in the van. From our vantage point, Linny and I saw Gio from the side, his strong nose and shimmering halo of hair; the bank of speakers down here brought us the music clearly. He sang the songs I knew from the van, but one I'd never heard before caught my ear.

My love lives behind a blue door:
My love—for that she is—
Walks the lanes at twilight.

It was haunting, and hopeful, and heartbreaking all at the same time. I felt the lyrics in my veins: I hadn't had a love in a long time, and every word rang true. When the song finished and Linny began clapping vigorously, I simply clasped my elbows and felt incredibly lonely.

At the end of the show, Linny and I left the tent to find everyone else commandeering a pair of round plastic tables at the side of the VIP enclosure. Brian kicked out a chair for me, which caught in the hay strewn across the ground—it had rained the previous day—and tumbled over.

"Have a seat," he said. "Can I get the ladies anything, or are they too starry-eyed over the incredibly handsome soulful singer-songwriter?"

"Jealous, Brian?" Linny scoffed.

He shrugged in the half-light from the party bulbs strung around the enclosure. "I just never made the mistake of assuming Avi was a techie, that's all. And she jumped to do his bidding." Brian's voice held the peevishness of a teenager with his feelings hurt.

I felt the closeness behind me. A touch on my shoulder.

"You're not a tech, then." That melodious baritone. I saw Linny feign melting, her eyebrows climbing up her forehead, before I turned.

"She's a writer," Peter Breedlove corrected. He stood slowly, unfolding his lanky frame from the plastic chair, and the two men exchanged handshakes and introductions. Then, "Aventurine Morrow. She's doing a book on us."

It was difficult to see Gio's eyes in the semi-darkness, but his teeth shone when he smiled. "My apologies, then, Miss Morrow. Miss?"

"Miss," Linny breathed, at the same time I corrected him: "Aventurine."

"The least I can do after that grievous error is to buy you a pint."

I felt Linny's speculative gaze on my back as Gio and I wandered, pints in hand, through the artists' entrance and out into the brightly lit lot beyond the marquee. The stewards at the gate giggled at his gallantries, and so did I, recognizing it for the show it was. We passed out onto the lane, still talking, then cut through the muddy campground and meandered toward the scattered lights that were the village. He told me of his summer tour; I told him of my research project with Mobius. He told me of his family; I told him of mine. When my phone pealed in my pocket as we turned the corner into the village square, all buttoned up for the night save for the pubs, and I plucked it out to read Linny's number on the screen, Gio simply took it from my hand and answered.

"Hi, Linny. Gio. What? No, all's fine. Tell Ruth you can go on ahead. I'll make sure she gets back to you. What hotel? All right, then. Cheers. See you soon."

He handed the phone back, grinning wickedly. I slipped it back into my pocket, feeling the warmth creep over me.

"What if I hadn't wanted you to bring me back? What if I wanted to get back to the van with the others now?"

Gio was still grinning. In the shadowy lot, he ran his free hand

179

along my jawline and into my hair, then pulled me into a kiss. Not a long one. Just a hint. A promise.

It had been awhile for me. I liked it.

"You don't want to get back to the others in the van now, do you?"

He was incredibly handsome. Incredibly charming. His hand was still in my hair, his thumb gently caressing my earlobe.

"Not really," I said.

When he delivered me to the hotel in Fareham at 6:00 the next morning, he kissed me once, breathlessly hard, then lifted a hand and turned away, the early sun a corona around his head. I thought I'd be the one late to the van for a change, and was prepared to bear the brunt of Ruth's wrath, but I felt revitalized, despite the lack of sleep, and I didn't care. It hardly mattered, of course: Ruth had wanted us there at 6:00, knowing that the band would be unable to load themselves up and get away until at least 7:00. I leaned against the tailgate, waiting for the rest of them, touching my tender lips gently in the early morning light.

That had been the beginning. Romantic, and delightful, and fevered, and decidedly very welcome. Even as I knew that, I recognized that that wild beginning contained the seeds of the end. A couple of kisses and getting laid? All right, but when Gio and I did that, we did it well. And with no real further expectations, which, quite frankly, made it all the more pleasurable.

We took a quick swim. Gio had brought a towel, and we took turns drying off with it. The sun was still blazing, and without a judicious re-application of sunscreen—I'd left the bottle back at the blanket in the arena—I knew I was going to be fiery red within a matter of minutes.

"Here." Gio carried the towel to the shade of a tree at the point where the stream widened into the pond; he spread it out on the grass, and waved me to it with the sweep of a hand. Before I sat, though, I stopped and looked up into his handsome face, bearing a few more lines around the eyes. If his hair was going gray, his stylist did indeed cover it well for him.

"Here," I said. I opened my arms, and, with a surprised laugh, Gio moved into them and lowered his mouth to mine.

Eventually Gio's watch alarm urged us back to the arena. There was something comforting about walking side-by-side with him, who had once been my frantic lover, and who now was at that level of friendship where everything is known and nothing really matters enough to get in the way. All the things which had made me crazy about him during that one wild summer now had faded into quirks which made me think of him with a fair helping of loving amusement. As I glanced over at him from under my straw hat, at the strong profile and that definitive nose, and at the towel draped around his neck in a way that somehow looked debonaire, I thought I probably loved him more now than I had then. It was an easier love, too. I rather liked it. After a moment, as I knew he would, he slipped a glance toward me, to make sure I was admiring him.

"Linny Breedlove told me she thought you were still hot stuff," I told him, and winked.

He lifted his dark eyebrows. "And where is our delightful Linny Breedlove of whom you speak?"

"Off to another festival with her husband and her band."

"Damn it."

"I'm sure you'll find someone equally adoring here," I consoled him, leaning into his arm, wondering fleetingly how I'd feel if he *did* find someone at the festival. We had reached the gate, where Gio did not deign to lift his arm to exhibit his artist band; I don't know why he deigned to put the damned thing on, quite frankly.

He expected everyone to recognize him, and for the most part, they did. "Other than me, of course. Besides. You should be too tired out now."

"Sometimes you're such a bitch, Avi," he growled. As if to prove my judgment of his stamina wrong, he smiled disarmingly at the two women manning the checkpoint; one of the two actively preened. Perhaps she would be the equally adoring one? I resisted the urge to ask her what she was doing after her shift at the gate. Gio might be recovered by then. "I'm half-inclined to tell these charming people that you're some pesky groupie who's stalking me, rather than my friend," he added.

Still, he winked at the women, and led me through.

"I think they liked me," he whispered, and I couldn't help but laugh.

Gio would be playing his set solo this evening, and had only come down with a car. He opened the trunk now and revealed two guitar cases and a gig bag.

"That's all?"

He made a face. "It's all I need. And I can move fast."

"You make it sound like you're on the lam."

He shrugged, frowning, as he opened the bag and sorted through assorted cords and kits I didn't recognize. "It'll make it easy for me to get home to Oxford tonight. Not too late. I've got a radio gig lined up for tomorrow afternoon."

"So you're not staying tonight?"

Again with the dark eyebrows. "Is that an offer?" He leaned in close, mock-suggestively.

"Don't be an ass, George," I countered, emphasizing his real name. I shoved him back, then waved a hand in the direction of the gate. "Seriously. You're making that lady fiercely jealous over there. She thought you and she had a thing going."

"Do we?"

"Probably not, if you're going back to Oxford tonight."

"Damn." He zipped the gig back up again, and wrestled it out of the trunk of the car. Then he took one of the guitar cases in his free hand. "Can you get that one?"

Reminiscent of our first meeting: me as techie. I lifted the case out, and slammed the trunk shut.

"And you're sure you don't want to bring me home to your charming guest house tonight?"

There was a tented area to the end of the lot, which I hadn't noticed. He led the way toward it.

"A very wise person of my acquaintance—*several* wise persons of my acquaintance—have advised me in recent days to stay away from my old loves. They have pointed out that going back is not healthy." Never mind the exception Linny made for Gio; never mind the slight one I'd just made for him myself.

"Are they wrong?"

From the stage I could hear the breaking down of the afternoon's acts; I had missed Hedgepig. The announcer was inviting everyone to partake of the victuals offered by the food tent during sound check for the evening. Fish and chips and shepherd's pie were still sold out.

"They are not wrong," I said. I thought of Neil, out there in the arena somewhere, and shivered. I'm not sure why I still said nothing about him to Gio.

Twenty-eight

I saw Gio off after his set, helping him tuck his guitars and equipment into his car boot as gently as someone could who was only impersonating a techie. It was nearly nightfall, the lot shadowy, though streaks of dying summer evening light, red, orange and pink, painted the sky above us, an impressionist's dream. In the east, however, where the moon should have hung, there was nothing but clouds.

"Sure you don't want to come up to Oxford?" Gio checked that nothing would shift during the journey, then slammed the trunk shut. He turned to me, his face in shadow. The hawkish nose, though, was unmistakeable, even in the dramatic lighting. "Just for old time's sake?"

I leaned into his chest, chuckling. He was persistent, but more out of habit than any burning desire. He wrapped his arms around me, and I did the same to him.

"I've no intention of following old tracks," I said into his shirt. I felt rather than heard him laugh.

"At least any further. Give us a kiss, then, Aventurine."

It was a satisfying kiss, easy and friendly, and again, with the knowledge of each other which made me wistful, but not quite enough to consider a quick trip to Oxford. Then we released each other, slipping apart until only our hands touched—and then that contact was broken as well. He climbed into the driver's seat, waved ironically, and was off. I held my hand up until his taillights disappeared.

I had caught a few fleeting glimpses of Lance and Paul wandering about the arena, pints in hand, and at one point, thought they were heading outward in the direction of the pond. As was the case yesterday, they seemed quite engrossed in their conversation, leaning toward one another, listening intently as the other spoke. Now, in the inconsistent lighting of the evening, I knew I'd never find them—but Paul knew where the blanket was, very close to the spot of yesterday. I made my way to it, circling the crowds, and settled. This time my pack was closed, all ship-shape. Still, I felt my neck prickle, as though I were being watched. I glanced around, but, with the only real lighting coming from the stage, I could make out nothing but shadows.

I had picked up dinner at the food tent on the way by, and another half-pint. Now I sat cross-legged on the blanket, listening to the group performing on the stage, a trio of young men whose name I didn't recognize. The front man, in a striped T-shirt, alternated between guitar, banjo, and bouzouki; to his left, a man wearing a baseball cap backwards played a double bass, and a drummer, partially obscured by his kit, went about his business energetically. I used the bamboo fork to eat my rapidly cooling lasagne—served, in that British festival fashion, with chips—and hoped I didn't drop pasta and sauce down my front. Still, it was dark enough that, if I did, no one would see.

The prickling on my neck did not abate, and, even though the temperature had dropped quite a bit with the lowering of the sun, I felt uncomfortably sweaty. Still, I could see no one: wherever Neil was, and I just knew he was here somewhere, he was out of sight.

So too were Paul and Lance. As the set progressed, and they did not make their appearance, I wondered whether they were among the crowds down at the rail. I squinted against the stage lights, trying to find a profile I recognized; but there were so many people, and all in motion, dancing, bouncing up and down, hands in the air. Not that I would blame them; the trio were lively, cranking quite a bit of sound from those few instruments. Frustrated, I set the plate aside and reached for the half, which, in the darkness, I knocked over. No more beer for me. I swore under my breath. It had been my only beer since the one I'd bought on my arrival, and I was hardly going to thread my way all the way back to the other side of the arena this late, and in this crowd. I searched my pack for my water bottle and pulled it out: empty. Damn it.

The band finished with gusto, and waved their way offstage. The lights did not dim, however, and the crowd's shouting reached a crescendo, holding it for a minute or two. Then the three reappeared, manned their instruments, and leapt into what was probably their most requested number—even I thought I recognized it. I realized I was rolling my paper plate over and over in my hands, crushing it ever smaller. There was no sign of either Paul or Lance. I looked around again, but everything was shadow to the edges of the arena, where the stalls and tents glowed, still doing business while they had the chance. *Tools for Self-Reliance.* I needed those more than ever. Frustrated, I scanned the figures at the rail once more, for a movement, something, I could recognize. No luck.

Two songs worth of encore, then the band said its final goodnight. The lights came up, and the stage announcer approached the mic to wish us all a very pleasant good evening, with a reminder of what was on the bill for the next day. I stood, plucked the blanket from the ground, and shook it vigorously, to rid it of grass and ants and crumbs and whatever else. I folded it slowly, letting the crowds pass around me as though I were parting the Red Sea. The arena emptied fairly quickly, leaving only the tech crew moving about purposefully, shutting the place down for the night.

Still no Paul.

Maybe he'd gone ahead to the car. Maybe he was saying a quick goodnight to Lance, away from my prying eyes? At Lance's car. Did Lance have a car?

I tucked the folded blanket beneath my arm and unzipped my bag, searching inside for the keys to the car. Futile: I couldn't find them by touch. I pulled out my phone and used the flashlight function to look inside. There were no keys there. Slightly panicky, I dropped to my knees again and unzipped my pack, using the flashlight again to examine each of the pockets. No keys.

Paul must have them.

He'd driven us over in the morning, even though he wasn't on the rental contract. I hadn't wanted to argue about it. What did he do with the car keys once we'd arrived? I closed my eyes, trying to envision him getting out of the driver's side. Slamming the door, hitting the lock button so I heard the click of the tumblers behind me. Striding off toward the copse and the workshop tent. He hadn't handed the keys to me, hadn't tossed them over. He must have just dropped them into his own pocket without thinking.

Quickly I zipped the pack up again, but left the flashlight on. The arena was nearly empty now; a small electric lantern glowed over at the gate, where the two volunteers were wishing people goodnight, their voices hushed. I answered in kind as I passed, then turned to the right, following the rough path behind the backs of the stalls. I had to slow my steps, not so much because of the uneven ground, but because of the tipsy couple ahead of me, pushing a cart mounded with their festival-going paraphernalia, some of which kept falling off and causing hysterical laughter.

There was singing coming from the workshop tent, the open flap of which was draped with colored fairy lights. I paused long enough to stick my head through and look at the stragglers, most of whom appeared slightly drunk, and sounded that way too as they swayed and sang. I could see neither Paul nor Lance there, and my anxiety mounted.

Paul's at the car, I told myself. *He's waiting at the car.*

But when I crossed the little bridge into the field, I found that almost everyone was gone there, too. When I turned in the direction of the place we had parked, I saw no rental car.

My steps slowed. I looked around desperately.

Maybe I had simply forgotten where we'd parked. It was a big field.

By now there were only six cars left in the parking area. I took a few more steps into the field. Our rental car was a Peugeot. A silver Peugeot. Only one of the six was silver, but it didn't look right. I walked toward it, confused. I'd been driving about in that rental car for a couple of days now; surely I could recognize it? As I moved forward, though, the car started, spun around in the near-empty field, and headed away toward the gate.

The car was missing. Paul was missing.

I was standing in the middle of a field, at midnight, in the English countryside, alone. I looked up at the sky, in which dark clouds now obscured the stars.

Had he left without me? Why would he do such a thing?

Was he *that* angry with me?

I still had my phone in my hand. I dropped everything else and keyed in Paul's number. It went straight to voicemail. I tried again: same result. Either his phone was dead, or he was ignoring me.

"All right?" A couple wearing yellow vests and carrying flashlights approached. "Need any help?"

I felt myself flush. "My car—I can't find—" My voice trailed off. I know what I sounded like, standing out there. I sounded like someone who'd been cheerfully drinking away since the beer tent opened twelve hours ago, who now couldn't find her way home. "Is there a taxi company around anywhere?"

A laugh. "In this village?"

"It's just that my nephew seems to have taken the car." That sounded stupid as well. If I wasn't drunk, he must be, having driven off and left his old auntie in a field. I saw the pair look at each other, though it was too dark to read their expressions. It didn't matter. I knew what they were thinking as well as if they had been flashing neon lights.

"Have you got any friends down in the camping field?" the woman suggested. "Someone you could doss down with tonight?"

I should have taken Gio's offer. I should have.

"No."

They looked at each other again. How could they see each other in this darkness? I felt their impatience like a hum on the humid air.

"How far do you have to go?"

"Back to Southampton." I tried to keep the desperation from my voice, but the words still formed themselves into a question.

The man shook his head. "Maybe you could call for a taxi to come get you. From Southampton."

I nodded, fumbled in my pocket for my phone, dropped it on the ground.

"Avi."

Just as he had appeared last night, Neil was at my shoulder. It was so sudden that I jumped.

"I can give you a lift back to your guest house."

I reared back.

He smiled, first at the stewards, then at me, and the light cast from the flashlights lit his face from below his chin. I felt his gaze like hands on my skin, and I rubbed my arms.

"That's settled, then," the woman said, relieved of this burden of responsibility, and the two of them moved off toward the bridge, leaving me alone in the field with Neil. I fought down the urge to call after them, to beg them to help me.

"I told Paul I'd see you got home all right."

Now I could feel a dull fury welling up from my gut. "You did *what?*"

Neil shrugged. "I saw him earlier, and that young man he seems to fancy, and I told him if they wanted to take off, I'd take care of you."

He'd take care of me. The words themselves made me nauseated. Beyond that, it was so like him, ordering other people's worlds for his own ends. But what were his ends? I thought I knew. Yet with someone like Neil, did you ever really know?

"You didn't," I sputtered angrily. "You had no *right.*"

Now he put a hand to his hip and leaned back. "Come on, Avi. Surely you're not still hating me for something that happened twenty-five years ago."

"Happened? *Happened?* It didn't just *happen,* Neil. You *did it.* You damn near ruined my life. You stole my story. You attempted to build your own success on my work."

"That's all, then? Your story?" I could hear the sneer in his voice. "I didn't, oh, I don't know—break your heart?"

"Go to hell."

"It's just a ride, Aventurine. Just a favor." Neil threw up his hands then, and turned to walk off toward a dark car at the edge of the field. "Take it or leave it. But I've got to get back to Southampton. I need my beauty sleep."

And then, as if the entire world were conspiring against me, I felt the first raindrop. Then the next.

Just a ride.

I cursed at the first flash of lightning and hurried after him.

Twenty-nine

We were at the first roundabout when Neil started coughing, a rough, wheezing smoker's cough. He waved a hand toward the back seat.

"Water bottles," he gasped out. "Can you reach me one?"

There was a paper bag on the floor behind his seat with several in it. I held one out, and he waved a hand again, still coughing. "Can you open it?"

I unscrewed the cap, which resisted, but then gave way with a satisfying crack. Neil took the bottle and took a quick slug, his eyes on the thin traffic ahead. He coughed again, but with less intensity. After a moment he took another drink.

"Warm," he said. "Bought them this morning. They've been in the car all day." He downed the rest, then tossed the empty bottle over his shoulder into the back seat. "Can you get me another?"

I was just grateful he wasn't going to crash, having been unsteadied by the coughing spasm. I groped in the bag for another bottle, cracked it open, handed it to him. He drank some more.

The inside of the car was uncomfortably warm—or maybe it was just me—so I pushed the button to open the window just a bit.

"I could turn up the air conditioning," Neil said. Even that sounded, to my anxious ears, like an echo of a long-ago criticism.

We were coming up on another roundabout. The roadway was dark, and glistened with the sporadic rain; the windshield wipers scraped the glass intermittently. Around each taillight ahead of us flared a corona, making vision difficult. We came up to the roundabout behind a produce truck—Sainsbury's or someone's— whose lift door was decorated with fruit: bananas, apples, a peach. I wondered fleetingly about my chances of making it safely to Southampton, should I leap out of the car and throw myself on the mercy of the truck driver.

"Need air." I had accepted the ride, but with all the bad grace possible, and I certainly wasn't going to make small talk with this man. He made me that uncomfortable. I had never thought what having my skin crawl would feel like, but now I knew.

Neil gestured with his bottle. "Help yourself."

I reared back. "I'm not accepting a drink from you. I fell for that once. What kind of an idiot do you take me for?"

My retort was so swift and sharp that I half expected Neil to pull to the shoulder and tell me to walk the rest of the way. Even in the rain, even uncertain of the way back, I didn't reject the idea out of hand. Instead Neil just laughed, took another drink from his bottle of water. "You're probably wise there. Though I did give you a pint last night, with no ill effects."

"I didn't drink it."

"You took it."

"And I gave it to Paul. He drank it. You saw him." *You goaded him about his parents.* "I'm not *stupid*, Neil. I know what you're capable of."

"You think I'm going to get you drunk and take advantage of you? I'm not a rapist, Aventurine."

"Not a physical one, no."

"And you've got a pretty high opinion of yourself at your advanced age." It was as though he hadn't heard me. Or was ignoring me. We were on the motorway now, and he flicked the directional and changed lanes. "Of course, Gio Constantine is rather an ego-boost, isn't he?"

If we hadn't been hurtling down the road in the darkness, I would have slapped him. "Leave Gio out of this," I hissed.

Neil laughed. "Of course, you did seem to be enjoying each other's—*company*—around by that pond on the footpath."

I sucked in a breath. I felt Gio's arms around me, felt his five-o'clock shadow on my skin. And I felt somehow shamed, wondering what Neil had seen, had heard. The worst thing about it was that I knew he meant to dirty the afternoon. He meant to dirty everything. I gripped my hands together fiercely in my lap, wishing for this interminable journey to end.

"Tell me," Neil continued, his voice lowering. "Does Gio like that birthmark of yours? That sweet little one on the inside of your thigh? It always drove you crazy when I kissed you there. Does Gio do that to you, too?"

I recoiled, even knowing he meant me to. My entire body burnt hot with mortification. "Stop it," I cried out, pressing my hands to my ears. "Stop it. You have no right." I absolutely shook in my fury.

At my anger, he backtracked, chuckling a little. "Sorry. Sorry. Old habits. I always did like baiting you. You always came back so hard. You're a little off your old game tonight, Avi. What's happened?"

"Just shut up. Shut up." Even the sound of his voice was too much to bear. Still, he was right about one thing: in hindsight, I had come to recognize that all his teasing, when we were together, always had a cruel edge, one that I had been willfully blind to at the time. Closing my eyes now, I brushed a hand across my sweaty forehead and tried to regain control. I opened the window a bit further.

"Just get yourself a bottle of water, Avi," Neil said after a moment. He seemed to have deflated, the fun having gone out of infuriating me. "I haven't opened any of them. You could tell with these two— you broke the seal when you opened them. They're safe. They're all safe."

I was terribly thirsty, and very, very hot, though mostly from the violence of my anger. There was a sudden flash of lightning to the south, and then a resounding crack of thunder following almost immediately. The rain was spattering now, coming through the open window. I wished I could stick my head out into it.

I reached into the bag, pulled out yet another bottle, and held it up to examine it by the green dashboard lighting. It looked fine. I checked the cover. It appeared unopened. When I twisted it, the plastic cap resisted until it finally let go with a crack, just as the others had. The bottle had not been opened, had not been tampered with. Even so, I sipped the lukewarm water cautiously.

"There," Neil said encouragingly. "See?" He took another sip from his own water, then set it in the cupholder. "There's even room for yours."

I think I might have dozed. I don't remember much of the entrance into the city.

It was raining harder. I couldn't get my eyes to focus. My brain was fuzzy, my thoughts vague and overwhelmingly anxious. I became conscious of the water bottle slipping from my hand as though in slow motion, and I tried to stop it, but my fingers were unresponsive. *Bend,* I thought, trying to concentrate, but it was no use. I felt the water splash out over my feet, run into my sandals; I heard it gurgle its way out of the bottle.

"Now, look what you've done, Avi," Neil chided. But he didn't sound too angry. There was satisfaction in his voice.

Up ahead on the side of the street, a police car. What did they call them here? Some animal. Koala. Panda? Something. The green glow of the dashboard lights was too intense, and it was making me nauseated. I gulped for air. Should I wave from the window, attract the constable's attention, plead for help? But then we were past, before I could formulate a solid plan, and I'd missed my chance.

We pulled up in front of the guest house, though I wondered vaguely how Neil knew which one was mine. This was mine, wasn't it? In the dark and rain I thought I should remember the ornate Victorian trim, but it was hard to tell, and harder to worry about. What was the name of the place?

I shook my head to get rid of the sleep, but even when I stopped, the world outside the windshield kept moving. Spinning. Dizzyingly.

Oh, no.

I threw a look over at Neil. He was pushing open his own door. "My place is just along there," he said, and his voice sounded thick to my ears, as though he were speaking through cotton wool. "I don't think I'm going to be able to get a parking spot any closer, do you?"

Suddenly panicky, I shoved open my own door, but the pavement was rolling, and I stumbled out of the car, onto my hands and knees.

"Avi?"

He was around the front of the car. I looked up at him, and he loomed, too tall, too dark, a shadow from my past rather than a man in the street. I tried to get up, and fell again.

Neil laughed. He reached down for me, dragged me to my feet, and put my arm over his shoulder, his arm around my waist.

"You really shouldn't have had so much to drink at the festival, Avi," he said. "You never could hold your beer."

Part IV

Aftermath

Trust no one. Least of all yourself.

—Honoré

Thirty

My head was pounding, my eyes were crusty, and my tongue was furred and too big for my mouth. I kept my eyes closed, but the light glowed red through my eyelids. The bed was spinning. It was a hangover for the ages.

Except. I'd kicked over my last half-pint during the last show. All I'd had to drink from Gio's set onward was that blasted bottle of water, which had been unopened. I'd pulled it out of the bag myself, after I'd pulled two others and opened them for Neil, who had downed them.

Neil.

Oh, God.

The room was otherwise vacant, the curtains billowing, the sun shining brightly. I felt my stomach turn, and hurled myself out of bed and across to the tiny bath, falling to my knees before the toilet just in time. Then, heave after heave, mostly empty, just bile. Only bile. I lowered my head to the cold porcelain of the toilet bowl, weeping silently. The bowl was cold against my breasts, and I shivered. Then I jerked away in horror as the realization washed over me.

I was naked.

I'm not a rapist, Aventurine.

I don't know how long I sat, back to the wall, in the bathroom, a towel clutched around my nakedness, as though that would help.

I didn't remember anything after falling in the street. Someone speaking words that made no sense, something about my being drunk, Neil laughing.

From somewhere down the street beyond the park, I heard the ringing of church bells. A vilely cheerful prelude, then twelve evenly spaced notes. Twelve. It was noontime. I had no recollection of the last twelve hours, until now, waking up in my room in the guest house alone and naked. I could see, through the doorway, my clothes scattered on the floor: shorts, shirt, cami and pants on top the pile. Had I taken them off last night before I fell into bed?

I remembered, hazily, Neil picking me up from the cobbles, draping my arm over his shoulders. Nothing after that. I didn't remember getting my key from my bag. I didn't remember letting myself into the guest house, climbing the four flights of stairs. But I didn't remember Neil bringing me up to my room, either.

I buried my face in the towel, the material rough against my skin, like an unshaven jaw. I sucked in a breath, almost remembering something—but there was nothing. My hands hurt—my knees, too. From the fall? I looked: one knee was scraped raw, some gravel still adhering there. Both my palms as well. There was dried blood on my hands, and one of my nails was broken, blood beneath it.

The weeping started again. Frustration—and fear.

What had happened?

Oh, God.

I dragged myself to my feet slowly, using the toilet, the edge of the bathtub. Then I ran the shower just as hot as I could bear it, and climbed in. I soaped my washcloth and scoured every inch of my skin, no matter how much it hurt.

• •

It was while I was toweling off, gingerly, that I realized how it must have happened.

Nearly parallel to twenty-five years ago. *Parallel.*

I stumbled out into the bedroom. There I tore through my backpack, my suitcase. Then, my insides curling up, I forced myself to backtrack, to go through my things more slowly, more methodically.

My recorder was gone. My notes. My portable hard drive. The thumb drives. The iPad. The laptop.

De ja vu.

He'd taken everything.

I couldn't bear the thought of breakfast. It was way too late, anyway. After the second bout of dry heaves, I felt turned inside out.

When I grabbed my bag to get the phone to call Paul, it felt light. I knew what I was going to find—what I *wasn't* going to find—and sure enough, the cell phone was gone. My wallet, filled with pound notes and bank cards, was there, as was my passport. Just the phone, gone.

I dragged on my jean jacket, slung my bag over my shoulder, and took one last horrified look around the plundered room.

Then I saw it. On the bedside table. A photo print, the edges curled, and the note written on paper torn from a small notebook. My notebook. I left the door open and approached the table warily, knowing that this was a bomb, one planted by Neil on his way out after pillaging my story.

I had never seen this photograph before, but I recognized the occasion immediately. The going-away party at the Rowells's, the last time I had seen Neil before this trip. We were outside on the fire escape, and there we all were: the couple in their *bon voyage* sashes and pointy hats, as well as Shep, Micheline, and me.

A heavily pregnant me.

Everyone had glasses in hand, save me; pregnant, I hadn't been drinking. At the back, Micheline, her face in profile, smoking a cigarette, blowing smoke into the early evening. One of the few times we'd gone out together once my pregnancy had become obvious; but we had been careful to change colors. I wore green, the color Mick had favored since childhood, and she wore a blue tunic she had dug out of my closet. We all looked so young. So young.

I picked up the note. Two lines.

You never smoked, Avi.

And *I showed Paul.*

Thirty-one

I pounded on his door. No one answered.

It was long past time for the breakfast room to be opened and closed again, but I peered around anyway. No one there; only the brilliant red eye of the coffee maker. The idea of coffee nauseated me. I felt my stomach clench again.

I didn't even know where the rental car was. Where the keys were.

I didn't want to go back to the festival anyway.

As I had done the previous day, I went to the end of the road, crossed at the intersection, and made my way blindly into the park.

I showed Paul.

I needed to call my sister. I needed to call Genevieve.

I desperately needed to find my nephew. But where would he have gone? I wiped at my face with my scraped palms, wanting to claw at my skin with my nails. I wasn't weeping now; I was fairly certain there were no more tears left in me, just as there was nothing left in my stomach. Just as there was nothing left anywhere.

Neil had taken it all.

Again.

I saw them at last, appropriately, near the *Titanic* memorial. Paul and Lance. They were seated on one of the granite benches, engrossed in conversation, leaning toward each other, their faces animated. There was fire in my nephew that I had not witnessed in ages.

Paul looked up, and his glance fell on me. The change was immediate. He stiffened, straightened his back, his face becoming as stoney as the monument before which they sat. Lance followed his gaze, then put a hand on his arm.

So many ways to open the conversation, and all I could come up with was, "Thanks for taking off without me last night."

Wrong, wrong, wrong. That put him on the defensive immediately. Paul's eyes narrowed.

"Your friend Neil said he'd bring you home."

"He's not my friend."

Paul shrugged.

"Don't," I heard Lance murmur. He still had a hand on Paul's arm.

The look Paul cast him might have been meant as reassuring. "It's all right," he said. "I'm all right." Then he turned back to me. "He said he really wanted a chance to talk to you. That things hadn't been good since your relationship ended."

My laugh was short, sharp. "He got that right, anyway." The midday sun was blazing down, and I felt the sweat beading at my hairline. The light stabbed into my eyes, no matter how I squinted against it.

"He said he had a hard time forgiving you for what you did to him."

I fell back, as though shoved by an unseen hand. "What I did to him?" It was hard to breathe. The park was swinging around me like a carnival ride; I felt like I was looking at Paul and Lance through the wrong end of a telescope. "What *I* did to *him?*"

The nausea, never far away, rushed back in full force. I clapped my hand to my mouth, suddenly fearful of vomiting here, in this park, on this afternoon. What I had done to Neil? Neil, who last night—I hadn't a clue how—had managed to slip me something;

Neil, who had done who-knows-what while I was unconscious; Neil, who had stolen all the available work I had on my story about Genevieve. Neil, who had done, again last night, exactly what he had done twenty-five years ago. And I'd fallen for it this time, exactly as I had the last time.

Paul's expression twisted; he looked as though he found the sight of me repulsive. "Yeah. When you went behind his back. To sleep with my father. Your brother-in-law. Your twin sister's husband."

I staggered back from the depths of his fury. Staring. My eyes hurt in the brilliant light, still gritty from this morning, and it was hard to focus.

"I never did—"

"Don't." Paul held up a hand to stop my protests. "Just don't, okay?"

"Paul—" Lance protested.

This time Paul shrugged off Lance's hand, unwilling to be calmed. He got to his feet abruptly, as though he could not longer stand to be still. "No. Okay? No. I saw the picture. Do you get it now, Aventurine? *I saw the picture.*"

"It's not what you think."

"Bullshit. Okay? That's bullshit."

His voice was climbing the register. A pair of women passed by, and I felt their scrutiny on the back of my neck.

Everything was upside down. I felt dizzy and sick and unable to defend myself. "I would never do that. Especially not to my sister. I love her, Paul. More than you could ever know. I would do *anything* for your mother."

"My mother?" Now Paul turned his head and spat. "You're my mother, aren't you, Aventurine? You're the one who gave birth to me. You."

"Paul—"

It would fairly rip my heart out to deny it, so close had I held the idea of this child, the one made from my egg and borne of my womb. And yet—I knew this much to be true: I had given birth to Paul, but he was no more my son than Lance, standing by helplessly, his hands outstretched, his mouth agape.

"Your mother raised you. Your mother loves you."

"Deny it, then." He glared at me, his face mottled in anger, his fists clenched as though he wanted to hit something. "You can't, can you?"

I took a moment too long.

Paul spun away, his arms flailing the air. "See?" He spat again. "He told me. When we first met. And I didn't believe him. I wouldn't believe him, because I thought I knew you. But then I saw the picture last night."

When they *first* met.

I knew it all, then.

"In Haworth," I breathed. "He was in Haworth. Neil."

Paul lifted his chin, but did not answer.

"You were coming out of it. Your mother and I thought the trip was working, and you were getting past the darkness. Then you went to Haworth, and everything changed. You met Neil there, didn't you?" I gulped for air, in an agonized awe about the range of Neil's manipulation. He had been playing a long game. I had figured that much. Still, I had not realized that he was willing to use Paul as a pawn in that game. "How did he do it, then? He surely just didn't walk up to you and say, 'hey, let me tell you something about your father.'"

Paul said nothing.

"He followed you, you know."

No answer.

"Think about that, why don't you?" I insisted desperately. I had to get through to him somehow. I had to get Paul to listen to me. "Somebody from *my* past, following *you*. Why do you suppose he would do that?"

"Maybe he thought it was about time I knew the truth."

"Truth." The word was bitter in my mouth, and I spat it out. "Neil doesn't know the meaning of that word. He's a liar, a thief, and possibly—" I sucked in a breath— "a rapist."

The word was a bomb.

Paul stilled, staring off toward the street, where cars passed by on their way to somewhere else, as though this dreadfully important scene wasn't playing itself out here in the park: they only saw us in their rearview mirrors, if they saw us at all.

Still seated on the bench, Lance turned slowly to face me, his face a painting of shock. "A *rapist?*"

I didn't have time to wonder why the word should inject such horror into Lance's voice. He lifted a hand, then quickly clasped it with the other, as though to still its shaking, and pulled it back.

"Don't listen to her, Lance," Paul said over his shoulder. But there was a crack in his voice, a note of uncertainty. "She's got all the reason in the world to lie."

"And Neil doesn't?" I tried to drive the wedge into that tiny gap of uncertainty. My head was absolutely pounding. "He stole from me, Paul, twenty-five years ago. A story I was working on for the newspaper I was writing for. He took it all, and won a prize for it, a prize which should have come to me."

"You're just jealous of his success."

"Paul. *Who* is the successful one here? I've got books. I've got prizes. I'm making damn good money with my writing. For God's sake, it was Genevieve who came to *me*." I took a deep breath. I wanted to reach across the divide between us and shake Paul, shake some sense into him. "Had you ever even heard of Neil before he insinuated himself into your life?"

"He just hasn't had your breaks, is all." But Paul's voice now was that of someone drowning, someone throwing out a lifeline to save himself.

"I *made* my breaks, Paul, and don't you ever forget it. I've hustled all my life. Your new friend Neil tried to destroy that twenty-five years ago, and he wasn't successful. I didn't let him do it. And I won't let him do it again this time, either."

"I don't—"

"Paul."

The single word was from Lance, low, but authoritative.

After a moment, Paul turned to look back at Lance. His face was mottled, twisted, as though he were trying not to cry.

Despite my anger, I felt a pang of pity, the pity borne of love, for Paul. In so many ways, he was still a boy. A boy still grieving for his father. That Neil would take advantage of that grief—I felt the bile rising again. Horror at the kind of person Neil had become—had always been—and disgust that I had ever let him into my life.

"Listen to her, Paul," Lance said. He still gripped one hand with the other, as though he were the only safety he knew. It was an odd gesture, one that made me wonder. "Just listen to what she has to say."

We were connected, the three of us, at the base of the monument, by the tightest of filaments. Any more stress, and I knew we'd snap, and break apart, perhaps never to be connected again. I curled my hands into tight fists at my sides, gripping at the cuffs of my shorts, pressed my lips together until they hurt.

"I don't—I can't—"

"Just listen."

After another second in which we all became stone like the monument, Lance raised his dark eyes to mine. Then he nodded.

Everything about this day was just too bright, too much. The birds calling to one another in the trees overhead were too loud. My head was pounding, my stomach churning. I had to get this right. This could be my only chance to undo the damage Neil had so carefully wrought. I closed my eyes briefly, and took a deep breath.

"Neil stole my work again last night, Paul."

He steadfastly refused to look at me. Still, at least he was no longer interrupting.

"He slipped me something on the ride home from the festival. I don't know what. I don't even know how." I looked now at my palms, scraped and raw, where I had fallen on them in the street the previous night. I had opened the water bottles. I had held on to mine, had only set it in the cup holder between the seats.

I had set it in the cup holder between the seats.

I had been so stupid.

How easy it would have been for him—how easy it *had* been— for him to slip something into his own bottle, to mix the two up in the cup holders. Quick switch. Of course. I only had to pick up the wrong one. I don't know what he used; I hadn't tasted it, I didn't think.

I bit my lip. But what *if*? What would he have done if that plan had not worked out? How desperate was he? What was he capable of at this point? The sweat on my skin was suddenly incredibly cold.

"How do you know? Maybe you were just drunk." He spat the word, contemptuous.

"Paul." It was Lance again.

I pressed on. "I had one half pint yesterday. I bought another one, but didn't get to drink it." He looked like he was going to protest again, and I pretended not to notice. "Besides. When was the last time you saw me drunk? Never, right?"

Paul turned his head.

"We got back to the guest house, and I fell down. In the street. That's the last thing I remember until noontime."

When I awoke, naked, sick, and confused.

I felt the sweat again tracking down my forehead, under my arms. The sob surprised me, and I choked it back. Out of the corner of my eye, I saw Paul glance at me and away again just as quickly.

"Go on," Lance said quietly.

"Everything is gone, Paul," I said wretchedly. "Everything. All my notes, my hard drive, my thumb drives with all the pictures Genevieve had me copy, even my telephone. Neil ransacked my room and took everything." *Again.* But I didn't have to say that. I couldn't bring myself to, anyway.

Slowly Paul seemed to deflate, his fight leaving him, the anger dissipating, to be replaced by confusion. He stumbled to Lance's side, and sank onto the bench beside him. Lance took his hand.

"I don't understand," I heard him whisper.

"Is that all he took? Is it all he did?" Lance asked me. His voice was soft, but somehow urgent, and—sympathetic? His dark gaze had depths I wasn't sure I recognized, wasn't sure I wanted to.

I dropped my own gaze to the stones beneath my feet. "I don't know. *I don't remember.*" The sobs were back, despite my attempts to stifle them. I put a hand to my mouth, felt my abraded palm rough against my lips.

Thirty-two

The two held hands on the way back to the guest house, Paul gripping Lance's fingers as though staving off chaos. He held himself carefully away from me, and that was fine. I didn't want to be touched by anyone, *anyone*, even someone I loved as much as I loved Paul. My skin still prickled, felt dirty and raw. The shower hadn't helped. I wondered if any shower would ever help.

At the top of the stairs we found my room being cleaned by the chambermaid. She straightened, holding the vacuum wand aloft like a weapon. "You want me to come back later?" she asked, brushing her dark hair away from her sweaty forehead.

"No," I said quickly. I wasn't sure I wanted to go back in there. "Thanks. Do what you have to do."

Without a word Paul led the way along the corridor to his own room. He fished the key from the pocket of his jeans and let us in. His room had already been taken care of by housekeeping, the bed made, the curtains tied back to let in the brilliant afternoon sun.

"We've got to call your mother," I rasped.

"You do it."

"He took my phone." *He.* I couldn't say his name. I couldn't. At least he'd left me my passport, my bank card. I could get another phone, here, somewhere. A sim card. Something. I tried to convince myself that I still had some control over the situation.

211

Paul threw himself down on the narrow bed, then tossed his phone onto the bedspread beside him. Lance closed the door behind us, then handed me the phone before sitting on the edge of the bed like someone who was familiar with the room, the occupant. Of course, I thought stupidly, he must have spent the night here.

"It's locked," I said.

Mine was too.

For a moment my mood lifted, but crashed just as quickly. My phone was locked, too, and so was the hard drive. The thumb drives had not had a locking feature. But Neil would still have a difficult time getting into the phone and hard drive, at the very least. Not the digital recorder, though, with the hours of records of Genevieve's deep ironic voice. My thoughts ricocheted between the possibilities.

The phone made its way back through Lance to Paul, then returned to me. I quickly opened the contacts and selected *Mom*.

Mom. My sister. Paul had his arms crossed over his chest, and he stared at me with his hard eyes. There was irony in his look, too, and a challenge. So much damage between us, still. He couldn't quite trust Neil, but Neil had made it so that Paul felt he couldn't trust me anymore. The questions, all his questions, lay between us like open wounds.

Across the Atlantic, Micheline's phone rang and rang, and then went to voice mail. I could have screamed in frustration. "It's me," I said hoarsely. "Call me on Paul's phone. Mick, it's an *emergency*."

I pressed the red phone icon to end the call and stared at the screen, the unhelpful screen. My vision blurred, and I blinked.

Then the cell phone lit up with Micheline's number, the ringtone a song I didn't recognize. I slammed a finger onto the keypad to answer.

"Avi, what is it? *What is it?*"

Once again I took a second too long to answer.

"Avi, where's Paul? Is he okay? Where is he?"

"He's here. He's okay. Sort of."

Micheline sucked in a quick breath. "What the hell does that mean?" The anger borne of fear swelled her voice.

"He's fine. No, he's fine. We're in his room at the guest house in Southampton."

Paul was staring at me, still with that challenge in his shadowed eyes.

Another deep breath. "Southampton. Avi, he's opened the envelope, hasn't he? The one from Shep? Oh, God."

"No," I said quickly, and then wondered if it were true. "I don't think so." I had forgotten the envelope, and without thinking, I searched the room with a distracted gaze, then turned to Paul. "Have you opened your father's letter?"

He sat up slowly, his eyes never leaving my face, and reached a hand to the drawer in the bedside table. He pulled out the envelope, the flap now unstuck, and handed it to Lance, who in turn handed it to me.

"He's just given it to me, Mick." I tucked the phone between my ear and shoulder, and gingerly pulled the single sheet of paper from the envelope. It felt weighty, and it was difficult for me to unfold, my hands were suddenly shaking so hard. I cast one more look to my nephew before scanning the page quickly. Shep's familiar spiky handwriting. I caught my breath. I was holding the words of the dead: if this is how it affected me, how had Paul felt? The pity gripped my chest again.

"What does it say?" Micheline's voice was climbing in panic. "Aventurine, tell me."

"Hold on." There was a single chair, and I stumbled to it, sat.

Paul,
I have always loved you. More than life itself. In that moment when they first placed you in my arms in the

hospital, I knew that it would never be possible for me to love anyone as I loved you and your mother. You have made us the proudest parents possible. I've always tried to do my best for you, to be the person you could look up to. Please always remember this. And no matter what you may hear about me, I need you always to understand how much I love you, how much you mean to me, and how grateful I have been to have you in my life since that day in the hospital.

It was signed simply *Dad.*

Paul was lying back on the bed again, his arms crossed as though for protection; his eyes, though, were clenched shut, as was his mouth. He looked as though he might cry, and was fighting the tears. I understood, feeling the burn of tears behind my own eyelids. Lance put a light, long-fingered hand on Paul's knee, and left it there when Paul made no move to shrug it off. I was shocked at the pang of jealousy: that there was no one to comfort me; that I was not the one to comfort Paul.

"'No matter what you may hear about me,'" Micheline repeated in my ear. Her voice, from three thousand miles away, sounded as though she were being strangled. "Oh, God. Oh, Shep."

"What does that mean, Mick?"

But she was full-on sobbing now. In my mind's eye I could see her, her eyes clenched shut just as her son's were, and with her free hand pressed to her lips. She would be rocking back and forth, in an attempt to comfort herself. I wanted to take Paul in my arms, but more than that, far more than that, I needed to hold my twin.

"Oh, Shep," she gasped again.

"Micheline," I whispered. "Oh, honey. Tell me."

The sobbing, after a moment, lessened slightly. "Put him on," Micheline said. "Paul. Put him on the phone."

I held out the cell phone as directed. "Paul. Your mother wants to talk to you."

"*Mother.*" And to my horror, Paul turned over on his side to face the wall.

"What is it?" Micheline demanded. "Aventurine, what's going on?"

I licked my lips. "He doesn't want to talk to you. He barely wants to talk to me, Mick." I took a deep breath: I had to tell her. "There's something—"

"I'm coming over," she said, cutting me off. "Aventurine, don't let him out of your sight. I'm on my way right now."

"Mick—"

But she'd cut the connection.

Thirty-three

"I hope her letter's still here," Paul spat. "I hope you didn't lose that, too."

I flung the phone on to the bed next to him and jerked the door open. Down the hall, the chambermaid was just backing her way out of my room, and I barely acknowledged her before dodging around and inside. I dropped to my knees beside the bed and groped beneath. My fingers found the box, but when I slid it out, I discovered the padlock missing, and the latch bent.

Empty.

The hollowness of the metal box Shep had left us, the missing letter he had left for Micheline, the *absence* of everything, kicked me in the gut. I fell back on my heels, my scraped hands between my knees. Neil had found the letter and had taken it, along with everything else of value.

"Something wrong?" the housekeeper asked from the door, her tone concerned, and perhaps a little defensive, fearing that she'd be blamed for something.

I shook my head. "No," I croaked. "No. Nothing."

Everything. Though nothing the chambermaid could help with.

Lance was behind me, at the door, a long-fingered hand on the woodwork.

I opened the box once more, as though I could make the letter

216

reappear. That didn't work. I put a shaking hand inside, touched the cold metal of the bottom. Then I squeezed my eyes shut.

"It's gone," I whispered.

I heard a small gasp from Lance.

"He took it. The bastard took it. It's gone."

I left the box on the floor, then stood and stumbled to the bed. There I sat, stupidly staring at the emptiness, which might have been in the box, which might have been in me.

The last letter Shep had written to his wife.

It was probably a love letter. The idea of Neil opening it and reading it with his rapacious eyes, touching it with his thieving fingers, appalled me. The fact that the universe had entrusted it to me, to deliver to my sister, and I had failed in that duty, made me sick. She hadn't wanted me to read it; she had wanted to be the one to open it, to read the words Shep had thought to leave for her, if he did not return. *And he had not returned.*

Neil touching it. Neil reading it. Neil making it dirty.

I thought again, nonsensically, of that monument Micheline and I had played upon as kids, up the road at the old cemetery. A monument to a man lost at sea, a grave that was marked and yet empty. *Shep.* I stared down into the box, which might as well have been Shep's empty tomb.

The bed creaked as Lance lowered himself down beside me, not quite near enough to touch shoulders.

"He's going to be so angry," he said.

I laughed bitterly. "He already is. He understands none of it, and hates me for all of it."

"Thanks to this guy Neil."

"Thanks to Neil."

I should have felt a blazing anger, but all I felt was cold. Failure. Worthlessness.

• •

Had I not been in such a bad place after Neil had stolen all my work twenty-five years ago, would I have agreed to donate the egg? Would I have agreed to be the surrogate?

I had felt so useless. So stupid. So worthless. I had trusted, and it had turned out that I had not trusted well. A judgment blow, that. How could I have been so blind, to have chosen a person who, without a thought, would betray me to such depths as he had?

Then Micheline and Shep had come to me, holding hands, desperate, asking the unthinkable, and I had agreed. Because I wanted to be worth something. I wanted their love and approval, and because of Neil, I knew then that I was not worthy of love and approval unless I served some purpose. After years of therapy, I knew, intellectually, that my sister would not have loved me any less had I told her I was unable to agree to their request. We were twins, for God's sake, and there were no two people in the world with a closer bond. Oh, she might have been disappointed, but she would have gotten over that. Still, that was what I knew *intellectually*. What I felt, deep down in my gut, was that I had to perform this great service for her to keep her love. Neil had done that to me.

I have no idea how long I sat, dumbly, beside Lance. I did not cry, not now, not anymore. Everything I thought I had worked through in years of talking to the counselor, everything I thought I had examined and rid myself of: it was all back, as though I'd only been lying to myself, hiding things in some dark basement of my mind. Wave after wave of loathing. Absolute *loathing*.

I was so stupid.

Micheline was on her way. She could catch a flight at 10:00 tonight and be here in the morning. We'd have to meet. We'd have to talk. She would learn the depths of my failure to her. I didn't know how I would be able to bear it.

Someone would have to go to Heathrow to pick her up. Or she'd have to find her own way to us. She'd have to call—

But I had no phone.

She'd have to call Paul. Who might or might not answer.

"I've got to get another phone," I said at last.

It was something I could control. I grasped at the idea as though it were my last proverbial straw.

"Another phone?" Lance frowned.

"Where's the closest place to get a cell phone? Do you know?"

He thought for a moment. "There's a Carphone Warehouse down at West Quay. I think that's the closest?" Though he didn't seem too sure. "EE's down there, too."

"How do I get there?" Under normal circumstances, I would simply follow my phone's directions. I looked down at my empty hands: these were definitely not normal circumstances. I wished for simpler days, when I could just follow a computer printout, or before that, when I could pick up a paper map at a corner shop.

It didn't take Lance long to pull up a map on his own phone; the two places he'd mentioned in West Quay were about a mile or so away, on the way to the car rental place. I could find that.

"I'll need the keys to the car."

Wordlessly, Lance left the room. In a moment he was back. "He's got them in his pocket. He's sleeping. I don't know if I should wake him." He glanced from me, down the hall toward Paul's room, and back. He pushed his dark hair back off his forehead, suddenly looking particularly young.

I didn't know, either. I closed my eyes. I could walk down there in fifteen minutes, do my business, walk back. I could be back in an hour. An hour's sleep might make all the difference in the world in my ability to communicate with Paul.

"I'll walk down. I'll be back in an hour." In my head, I heard Micheline's frantic voice: *don't let him out of your sight.* But I couldn't do everything. "Watch him," I said to Lance. "Stay with him. His mother and I are trusting you. And give me your phone number."

• •

To the corner, across the park, down Above Bar Street. Past the Costa's and the casino, and there was EE. There was only a moment's wait before a salesman was available; I told him what I needed, got a sim card, a number, gave him my credit card, and was out within twenty minutes. Perhaps he sensed my frenzy, for, rather than wishing me a nice day, he shouted, "Good luck!" as I fled the store.

On the pavement, I dug out the slip of paper with Lance's phone number, and plugged it in quickly. On his end, it rang and rang, and then went to voicemail.

"It's me, Lance. Aventurine. Call me. I'm on my way back."

I desperately wanted a coffee, but even more, I desperately needed to get back to the boys. I couldn't get past the growing fear that something was happening, something awful, back up there, with Paul, while I was away. Micheline had told me not to let him out of my sight, and as unstable as he seemed, he could even now be doing something terrible. But what? *Stay asleep,* I begged him, the words echoing over and over in my head. *Stay asleep. Please.* I hoped Lance could hold it, whatever it was, at bay, though perhaps I was putting far too much faith in a young man I—and Paul—had only known for a few days. But I needed his help, or my sister's, or anyone's at this point. I was at a loss. As I hurried back towards the Polygon, I punched in Micheline's number. That too went to voicemail. I repeated the urgent *Call me,* and hung up.

Then I broke into a run.

I had to dodge the rubbish men with their big truck and yellow safety vests. I stumbled up the steps and unlocked the door to let myself in, and came face to face with Lance, pacing in the foyer.

"I'm sorry," he gasped. "He's gone." His face was mottled.

"*Gone?* Where?"

Lance threw up his hands. "I don't know. We had a fight—"

Oh, God, he was fighting with everyone.

"—and he took off. Ran down the stairs. I heard the door slam."

I still stood in the doorway, and now I spun to look into the street. "How long ago, Lance? *How long ago?*"

"Five minutes? Ten? Not long. But Aventurine—he took the car."

And sure enough, as the garbage truck eased its way past, I looked to the spot where the Renault had been parked, and it was no longer there.

Thirty-four

I called his number, and there was no answer. Voicemail.
"Where are you?" I demanded. "You're scaring me."
Lance called as well. Voicemail.

We sat in the empty breakfast room, phones in hand, waiting for ideas. The coffees Lance had brought over from the sideboard—always the waiter, I guessed—slowly cooled, untouched.

"Your story," Lance said at last.

I had been so wrapped up in the personal that I hadn't really fully considered the professional. I had been trying to do damage control for me, for Paul, for Micheline. I hadn't really thought of the story, except as peripheral.

"That's wrong," Lance said now. There was a sharpness in his deep brown eyes, and an intelligence I hadn't really appreciated until now. "We're looking at it all wrong."

I waited.

He licked his full lips, as though working at his words. "Hurting Paul wasn't his main goal. It was just a cruel sort of sideline. Neil's main goal has always been you, and the story."

"I've shut him out of my life since he stole my work twenty-five years ago."

"But he's not had any real successes since, and he's hungry."

That was true. I had not seen any bylines from him in the nationals for ages. "Starving might be the right word." I knew very well that once a writer has that recognition, they crave it again, more and more. At least, that's the way it is for me. I'm forever thinking ahead. I love the process—the research, the interviews, the writing. But I love, too, knowing that my work is well-received. And maybe this one—*this one*—could win the National Book Award. But if not, there is always another project lining up somewhere.

"And now he's taken your work about that lady spy."

"Genevieve. Genevieve Smithson."

Lance frowned, biting his lower lip. He really was a good-looking boy. And intelligent. I didn't wonder that Paul was rather taken with him. "Talk me through this," he said, setting his phone face down on the table between us. "He took your notes—what else?"

"Flash drives, hard drive, phone, recorder, laptop, iPad." I ticked my missing tools off on my fingers. "Written notes."

"Where did you back up your work? You *did* back up your work, didn't you? Please tell me you did." Lance had the worried look of a young person talking to an elderly person about the electronic world.

"Yes. Everything. I even scanned my notes with my phone and uploaded them to the cloud. I've got copies of everything."

Lance nodded. "Good. Excellent." Again that characteristic swiping of hair from his forehead. "And your phone, that's got a passcode."

"And the hard drive does, too. As well as the iPad and the laptop."

"Does the recorder?"

I shook my head. "No. He can get in there. He can listen to my interviews with Genevieve. He's taken the flash drives with her pictures and documents, so he can access those."

"So. You've got most of your research so far, and he has access to some of it, but not all."

I nodded. I dropped my face into my hands, discouraged.

"So, at best, he can write a half-assed article."

"But even a half-assed article would ruin my chances with this story." And what about Paul? What did any of this have to do with his disappearance? My insides were screaming, but my only tenuous link right now to my nephew was through this boy.

For a moment, Lance drummed his long fingers on the table, then he wiped a hand across his face. "He'd have to write an unauthorized version, though. I mean, Genevieve's *your* girl. She's hardly going to give him access when she chose you to write her story."

I looked up at him sharply.

He shrugged, smiled a bit self-consciously. "Paul told me that. He was rather proud of that bit. And he was quite taken with your Genevieve."

I thought of them cooking together in her well-appointed kitchen, him moving at her direction. A careful choreography, with delicious results. Yes, he had been quite taken with Genevieve. Who wasn't mine, wasn't anyone's but her own.

Now Lance returned to business, frowning deeply again. "There are ways to crack passcodes, people you can hire to do it. I think you've got to face the fact that it's going to take Neil a while to get into your phone and hard drive and stuff, but he'll probably get it eventually, if he's that determined."

"Oh, I think he is."

"So the only thing that could throw a spanner into his works would be if you and Genevieve were to put up a fuss."

I shuddered. What fuss could I put up?

The touch of his fingers on the back of my hand was surprising. I lifted my eyes.

"*Think.* What if Genevieve wasn't able to put up a fuss?"

His words fell like stones in deep water. I stared stupidly at him for a moment before I began to feel the panic: my eyes grew wide and hot, my breathing became shallow.

"What are you saying?"

Lance only met my eyes silently.

"*What are you saying?*"

Lance took a deep breath. "Aventurine, you said Neil might be capable of—" his dark glance slewed away quickly, and then he forced himself to look back at me. "Rape. You said he might be capable of rape. Well, then, why not murder?"

"He wouldn't hurt Genevieve," I protested, holding my hands up to fend off the terror of that thought. "She's an old woman. He wouldn't kill an old woman."

"If everything else you said is true, then he might be willing to try. And to his way of thinking, why not? Precisely because she *is* an old woman, and she might stand in the way of his success in publishing this story as his own."

"But—"

Lance was relentless. "Who's to say, if the subject is dead, that it's an *unauthorized* biography? No one. Your word against his."

"I've got her agreement. In my files."

"So he claims she changed her mind. Liked his offer better. What then?"

The panic was taking hold.

"Lance—"

He indicated my new phone. "Call her."

"You're saying—"

"*Call her.*"

Part V

I'm an old woman, Aventurine.

—Genevieve Smithson

Thirty-five

"I'm fine," she said.

My relief at hearing her words when she answered the phone was immeasurable. The irony in her voice brought me back to her parlor, her cake, the way she had of tipping her head and fixing me with that gaze that felt like surgery.

"The Germans didn't get me, remember."

I could see her expression: the patience, the eye roll that wasn't an eye roll. That firm set of her determined jaw.

"You were sixteen. You're not sixteen anymore."

"True. But training is training, isn't it?"

I clawed at the fake wood of the tabletop in frustration. Lance, his expression mirroring my helplessness, was pacing the breakfast room, peering out the side windows into the alley that led to the minuscule car park behind the guest house, the one that never had enough space to park in. He had his phone in hand, and looked at it each time he turned.

"You need to promise me to be careful."

"I need to do nothing of the kind. Aventurine, I haven't had a mother in more than seventy-five years. I certainly don't need one now."

"Just promise me."

A gargantuan sigh from York.

• •

"I've found him," Lance said, when I ended my call.

I caught my breath. "Paul? Where is he? How did you find him? Did he answer?"

Lance shook his head. "He still won't answer. But he forgot: back at the festival we were fooling around with the Find Friends feature. He's logged into my phone indefinitely. So I pinged him."

I pushed back from the table so hard my chair hit the wall with a crash. "Where is he?" I peered at the screen of Lance's phone, but it reflected the windows, and I couldn't make anything out. I probably would have been unable to understand what I was looking at anyway.

"You're not going to like this." Lance's dark eyes, when he met mine, were anxious.

"Tell me." I had visions, horrible visions, that flashed through my mind, one on top of another.

"He's heading north. Toward Oxford."

I frowned, trying to think. "Oxford? What the hell's in Oxford?" Gio? Paul didn't know Gio. They hadn't met.

Lance made a noise, tapping away at the screen of his iPhone. He frowned, then held the screen out to me, so I could see it clearly this time.

Something I recognized. A map. The blue line was nearly straight, northward up the M40 to the M1 and onward. Straight, the old Roman road. To York.

"He can't be," I whispered. "He's not even supposed to be driving that car—he's not on the contract." The statement, at this point, was totally nonsensical, but I felt, inside my head, any intelligent thought fracturing, shards flying outward as though from an explosion. "Why?"

Lance shrugged. "Genevieve. You agreed he was quite taken with her."

"Yes, but—"

"Look, Aventurine," Lance cut in. His voice was rising. "He's not a kid anymore, he's a wildly intelligent man. If we can figure out that Genevieve might be in danger, he obviously could, too."

"Lance—"

"Listen. He's lost so much. Right now he thinks he's lost everything. He trusts Genevieve in some strange way. She's probably the only one left in his world he *does* trust. And if he thinks she's in danger, it makes sense that he's going to go to her."

For someone who had known Paul such a very short time, Lance seemed to have his pulse. Again I looked at him with respect. Lance was obviously worried about him, too, something of which I approved.

"But there's something else we might not have thought of," Lance added slowly.

"Something else?" There was too much already.

"Your phone's an iPhone, isn't it?"

I held the phone from EE up to show him.

"No. The other one. The old one."

The one Neil had stolen.

"Yes."

"And Paul has you on the Find Friends app, right? Connected indefinitely?"

I nodded, beginning to see where this was heading, and not liking it one bit.

"What if he's following *your* cell phone?"

It didn't take long at all to clear out our rooms. I threw all my things—what was left of them, anyway—into my bag, while Lance did the same with Paul's belongings, of which there hadn't been many to begin with. We met at the foot of the stairs, bumped our way out into the street, now tinny with the light before a rain.

"He's taken the car. I don't know if they'll let me rent another one."

Lance threw me a look. "I can rent it."

"Are you old enough?" He didn't look it. With his narrow face creased in worry, he looked all of twelve years old.

"I'm twenty-seven."

A cab inched its way between the cars bumped up on the pavement. It had its light on, and I threw up a hand.

"Let's do it," I said. "You rent it, I'll pay."

I let him drive, too. The compact car he chose had an onboard navigation system in the dash, and I kept his phone in my hand, watching the blue dot that was Paul make its way toward Oxford. In no time we were on the A34.

The traffic was slow. I could only pray that the tailback was as bad where Paul was, several miles ahead, and where my own phone, even further ahead in Neil's pocket, led the way.

Thirty-six

"What did you argue about?"

We had been driving for more than an hour in deathly slow traffic, both of us mostly silent, anxious, uncomfortable. I had spent the time staring at the blue dot on the screen in my sweaty palm, which, at times, had slowed to a crawl. Sometimes we seemed to be gaining ground on that blue dot; sometimes not.

For a long moment, Lance didn't answer. His eyes flickered from the slowed traffic ahead, to the side mirror, the rearview, and back again. "You," he managed at last.

"Oh." I wasn't sure how to answer that.

"I told him—I probably shouldn't have said anything, probably shouldn't have got involved. I mean, it's not my business—"

"You told him what?"

A big sigh. "That he was being unfair to you."

Defense from a surprising quarter. I felt myself warming to Lance. "Thank you."

"Who is this guy, Neil, anyway? Some stranger who insinuates himself into Paul's life and starts telling him things, feeding on his insecurities and his grief and his anger, trying to come between him and his family: you, his mother, his father. His *dead* father." Lance pounded the steering wheel once with the ball of his hand. "It's a dick move, that is."

It was a dick move. But the kind that Neil was expert at. Perhaps the only kind he was capable of.

"I take it that didn't go over well." I blinked several times against the glare from another car in the lane to our right. "Your defending me."

Lance slowed behind a black Land Rover. "No. I told him it wasn't fair that he'd listen to the stories of an absolute stranger, but not the side of someone he's known all his life. Someone he met on a *bus*. Over you. He didn't like that at all."

Paul's instinctive stubbornness. I knew it well. I wasn't at all surprised at his reaction, because, after all, I *had* known him all his life. Lance, in the scheme of things, was still a newcomer in Paul's world, and, I supposed, couldn't be expected to read him so well, so soon. And yet—he did. Very well, considering.

"He's really angry," Lance said now, his voice full of wonder at the depth of that anger.

"Yes," I agreed. I had felt that same wonder at first, but now I was beginning to feel—just tired. Tired of being in the wrong with that boy, tried and convicted without being heard. I knew—*I knew*—that it was a scattershot anger: the root was his father's death, and all the unanswered questions surrounding it; but Paul was unable to focus that anger, and it sprayed everywhere. I was just an innocent bystander, as it were. That didn't make it hurt any less, however.

I blinked again several times, but this time not against a glare. I tried to refocus on the screen in my hand. The blue dot seemed to have stopped its movement entirely. I used two fingers to enlarge the map, and saw that Paul's identifier was now off the motorway, in what looked to be some sort of roadside services.

"He's pulled over," I said.

"Where?" Lance leaned forward, as though he might be able to catch sight of Paul if he strained hard enough.

I squinted at the cell phone. My eyes were so tired. My head was pounding. "In a motorway services." I checked the location.

"He can't need gas yet." Quickly Lance checked the gauge in our car, which I could see registered nearly three-quarters of a tank. "Maybe he needs coffee. He didn't sleep well last night." He bit his lip, his face flushing.

I bet.

"Or the toilet," I agreed. My own stomach growled. When had I last eaten? "Speaking of which—"

"I'm fine. You?"

"I'm okay. I was just wondering whether it made sense to try to make up time while he's stopped, or take advantage of his stopping to do it too."

"Let's just keep going."

We drove on. The traffic was still slow. I pressed my fingernails of my free hand into my palm, until white half-moons blazed up on my skin.

What was his plan?

I couldn't light on any one idea, and that only added to my anxiety.

What would Paul do if he caught up to Neil? The confrontation that would result was frightening, no matter what scenario I considered. What if they were all chummy, if Neil denied taking my things, Paul's father's letter to his mother, if Neil denied slipping me something and then stealing my work with Genevieve... and then Paul chose to believe him? Or alternately, what if they argued, if Paul attempted to stop Neil from going to Genevieve, if in fact that was Neil's plan? Paul was tall, young—but Neil was wiry and solid, and had the most to lose. If the confrontation became physical, the odds were probably even. There was no way to know who would win.

Would Neil hurt Paul?

I couldn't bear to think about that possibility, and yet my

thoughts kept circling back to it, as though I were probing an infected wound.

Would Paul hurt Neil?

I put a hand to my mouth, to stop the moan I knew wanted to come out. We were in a foreign country. How would the police deal with a foreign national committing a crime—assault—here in the U.K.? How did one hire a lawyer, get bailed out of jail, all those things that came so easily to those of us raised on U.S. cop shows?

What was I going to do?

I had promised my sister I would keep an eye on him, to try to help him. And look what I'd let happen. Everything—*everything*—I held dear was in peril.

Perhaps I did make a noise, because now Lance lifted a hand from the gearshift and touched my arm, gently.

"We'll find him, Aventurine," he said.

North of Oxford somewhere, some time later, we stopped to fill up the tank. I dodged into the services building to use the facilities, and then met up with Lance in the M & S Simply Food. I ordered the largest coffee they had, black, caffeine undiluted. Lance did the same. From the display of sandwiches, all looking a little tired in their packages, I chose a chicken and bacon, while Lance went for the limited vegetarian options. It was growing late, and fortunately, the traffic was beginning to thin; while we would be able to make better time, that also meant that both Paul and Neil would be making better time as well.

"He still won't answer," Lance said in frustration, clicking back through to the Find Friends screen and handing me the phone as we approached the car. He pressed his lips together, frowning.

"He won't answer me, either—he must suspect I've got a new phone." I climbed into the car and slammed the door behind me with more vigor than I had intended. My ears popped. The coffee was still too hot to drink, so I set it in the cup holder between the seats. "How far are we from York?"

Lance, too, set his coffee in the holder, then clicked his seatbelt into place. "In miles? Around 200. In hours?" He snorted as he eased the car out of the parking space and headed toward the motorway. "Maybe three. Maybe five. Who really knows, with this traffic?"

He put on the lights, more of a precaution yet than anything.

The only consolation I had, as I looked at the cell phone screen on my knee, was being able to see the distance between our blue dot and Paul's. Which was no consolation at all. Because if he was, as we thought, chasing Neil, then Neil had a hell of a head start on us. We'd never catch Paul. And by the time he caught up to Neil, if he ever did, then it might just be too late for Genevieve.

I set my sandwich packet on the seat beside me, took up my phone, and dialed Genevieve's number again. The phone rang and rang against my ear. Genevieve did not answer.

Part VI:

Spies

Thirty-seven

We were approaching York. It appeared on the horizon at first as a glow in the night.

Somewhere among those lights was my nephew. And, more than likely, Neil.

I had programmed Genevieve's address into the Sat-Nav. In my sweaty palms, which I took turns wiping on my jeans leg, the glow of the cell phone screen told me that Paul's blue dot was at Genevieve's house. But staring at it unremittingly also told me that it hadn't moved since it had come to a stop there more than an hour ago.

We could be too late. Far too late. We could walk in on disaster.

Unless we were both dead wrong. It was possible, wasn't it? Yet I couldn't bring myself to be that optimistic. And looking over at Lance's set profile, I knew he couldn't bring himself to be that optimistic, either.

In the glow from the dashboard lights, I thought Lance's face had grown more angular, his cheekbones more sharply shadowed, his eyes glinting. His hands gripped the steering wheel tightly, his knuckles showing like tiny light knobs beneath his skin. We hadn't spoken in quite some time, exhausted, tense as we both were. Frightened. At least, I was. Terribly frightened.

I had tried my sister's phone, then Genevieve's, then Micheline's again. Neither woman had answered. One of them was winging her way across the Atlantic to us. The other one was God knew where.

I prayed I wouldn't fail Micheline.

I prayed Genevieve was safe.

I wondered what Lance was praying for, and, examining his rigid jawline, I rather thought I knew, even after this short a time.

The streetlight at the end of the road was out.

Had it been out the last time we were here? I wracked my brains and couldn't remember. Then I shook myself. I was seeing danger at every turn.

Of course I was.

Wipers slapping, Lance inched down the rainy street, made narrow by cars parked at the edge of the pavement. Across the way and two houses down from Genevieve's familiar door, I spotted the rental car. I couldn't remember what the make and model of Neil's car was, couldn't tell if he was here. There was a single light on inside Genevieve's house, shining through the transom over the front door. The outside light was not on, and that, I was certain, was definitely strange. I craned my neck, trying to make out any further clue to the tangled mess we were in. A cat, little more than a lithe shadow with a tail, darted along the wet pavement. Other than that, there was no movement. The street was deserted.

Lance threaded the car into a tiny spot on the next road over. There was a sign, probably warning us away from leaving a car without being a resident, without having some sort of permit, but he ignored it, so I did, too. We got out, and the lights flashed as he locked the doors with the fob. With a glance back at him, I led the way over to Genevieve's street.

Still deserted. Even the cat was gone. We pressed ourselves into the shadows at the end of the pavement. I eyed the doorway, the feeble light from the hallway showing through the transom.

"Stay here," I whispered.

Lance seemed about to protest, but I hushed him with a quick squeeze of the arm. Then, keeping to the shadows, I moved down the street, grateful for the rubber soles of my sandals. Someone well-trained, such as Genevieve, would no doubt have sussed me out, but for the most part I was silent. I bit my lip, praying that she would hear me, that she'd open the door, drag me inside the house with that ironic look. *What the hell is your problem, Aventurine?* But I made it all the way to the stoop without those prayers being answered.

I rang the bell, and I could hear it echoing inside the house.

No one came.

I leaned out over the wrought-iron railing, trying to see through the front window, but it was too far, and to lean any further would unbalance me and send me crashing to the ground, probably with a broken neck. The curtain was drawn anyway, as it normally was.

I rang the bell again, holding it this time.

Still no answer.

I looked back down the street to where Lance remained hidden in shadow: I couldn't see him at first, but then the shadow shifted slightly. I was sweating, along my hairline, under my arms; the rain trailed along my cheekbones, the shoulders of my shirt clinging to my skin. Where was she? Where was Paul? I could feel my panicked breath quickening.

Without hope, I put my hand on the knob. It turned. The door was unlocked.

Genevieve never left the door open. She had several lock sets on the door, and, over the days I'd been to the house, the door had never once been left open. She unlocked it to allow me entrance, and then she re-locked it carefully behind us, double- and triple-checking, each time we'd gone out to walk the wall. When I left in the late afternoon, I had always listened to the bolts sliding into place behind me as Genevieve had secured herself inside her castle once again.

She was an agent, still, after all. Had been for nearly all her life. She 'worked for the government.' She took precautions.

Something was definitely wrong.

I stepped down to the street and beckoned to Lance. He jogged swiftly over.

"Something's happened," I whispered.

He followed me up the three steps, and when I opened the door into the hallway, only the overhead light was on, casting awkward shadows upward along the stairway to the right. I shut the door behind us and peered toward the kitchen, then up the stairs.

"Hello?" I called. My voice sounded shaky and uncertain to my own ears. "Genevieve?"

I strained to listen. No voice replied, ironic or otherwise. The silence pulsed around us, wary, unfriendly.

Lance still at my heels, I hurried down the hall and peered into the parlor, flailing at wall switches. Then the kitchen, the toilet under the stairs. Empty. Back to the stairs and upward.

"Genevieve?" I called again. "It's me. Aventurine. Are you here?"

Looking into bedrooms: the one I had never seen, Genevieve's, spare and undisturbed, bed tightly made. The extra bedrooms, including the one in which the wardrobe was where she hung her uniform, were deserted as well.

"Is there a cellar?" Lance asked. He did not wait for an answer, but dashed back down the stairs ahead of me. I heard him pound his way down the hall into the kitchen; then his footsteps receded further. "Mrs. Smithson?" His voice was muffled, far away. "Genevieve?"

He returned to the hallway after a few moments and met me. "No one down there."

"She's not here," I moaned. "No one's here." I slumped against the newell post. "Oh, God, Lance, where are they?"

From the longcase clock came the chimes for the hour. One a.m. *Where were they?*

"There has to be some logical explanation," Lance protested. He sounded as though he were trying to convince himself, and failing.

"Not in the middle of the night," I shot back. "She's an old woman. She should be in bed. Paul left the car here. The house is unlocked. Lance, *something is terribly wrong.*"

I ran my hands up into my wet hair and pulled. Then, finding that did nothing for me, I kicked the umbrella stand, which tipped over, dumping its collection of walking sticks and umbrellas onto the floor like pick-up sticks.

Walking sticks. I stared at them, trying to make sense of what I was seeing. It took me a long moment before it clicked.

The blackthorn stick Genevieve always took with her was missing. And so, I realized, was the one she always handed me. As well as the ring of keys she kept on the hook above the umbrella stand.

"Lance," I choked out, "she's on the wall."

Thirty-eight

I heard Lance slam the door after us, heard his pounding footsteps behind me as I ran in the direction of the wall. I had walked it so many times with Genevieve that I was fairly certain of the way, though once or twice the darkness threw me, and I had to pause at a street corner and think for a moment.

"Aventurine!" he called after me. "She can't be—they lock the walls at night. Don't they?"

But again I heard her sardonic voice in my ear. *Don't be silly. There are ways.*

Genevieve, for whatever reason, had gone up on the wall: I knew that as surely as I knew my own name.

What would have made her climb up there in the middle of the night? Genevieve, I knew after this time, was not one for taking unnecessary risks, and walking the city walls at night would constitute a risk. Or would it? Genevieve knew the wall so well, having walked it every day since the death of her husband. She had, she said, walked out that first time in the night. Still, she was older now, twenty years older, and presumably, twenty years wiser. And she liked her sleep—she'd said that, too. Things didn't keep her awake anymore: she was too old to let regrets get in the way of the remainder of her life. So what could have made her go up there?

Unless she had been forced.

By Neil?

Again I tried to imagine what Neil would be willing to do to get back on top of the game, to have another prize-winning success. Surely—theft of my story, my notes, my pictures—that was one thing. But… assault? My mind skittered away from that idea, away from my waking—yesterday now—naked and sick and sore, then came smack up against the next logical step. Would he be willing to commit murder? Would he be willing to get rid of the only person who could definitively say she had never worked with him on the story, nor allowed him access to her information or her life?

I hurried on, Lance close behind. Because if Neil and Genevieve were up there atop the wall, there was no doubt in my mind that Paul had followed them up there, too.

We'd always gone to Skeldergate Bridge, and climbed up at Baile Hill. I realized as we approached the mound at the Ouse that I had no idea where she might have climbed up, no idea where she might be, or in which direction she might have gone. If Neil was prodding her forward, there was no telling what he would want.

Except that he had little real knowledge of the wall. He had never had a head for heights, and it was unlikely that he'd have gone up there to explore for himself. To follow us, of course, but even though I'd never seen him in our circuits, I could still imagine him walking that fine middle ground between the crenellations and the rail, or the edge. He would not have been one to look over at the scenery. He would have been hanging back, watching us, keeping out of sight among the crowds of people. The wall was not Neil's territory. The wall belonged to Genevieve.

Which meant that, if she went up with him, she probably had a plan.

I had to think like her. To get into her mind. I squeezed my head between my hands, my hair wet and tangled from the drizzle. So of course she would mount the wall at Baile Hill. And because she was left-handed, she would go in a clockwise direction. The way she always did. The way she had in my company.

There are ways to get up there. The arch of the eyebrow, as though she couldn't believe I'd be so obtuse as to think mere locked gates would hold her back. Her keys were gone from the front hallway. On that chain, no doubt, were the *ways*.

Of course I had no keys. Lance caught up as I crossed the deserted street to the Baile Hill entrance. I caught a sob in my throat, looking up the dark steps to the small tower.

"The gate," I gasped out.

He clicked on the flashlight of his phone, held it close to his body, and jogged up the steps.

"It's open."

Genevieve—or someone—had left it unlocked for us. Just in case.

The way was uneven and treacherous, puddles glimmering darkly here and there. Once we'd stepped out onto the top of the walls, Lance flicked off the flash on his phone, and we moved carefully along the rain-slicked stone, our eyes growing accustomed to the ambient light of the city at night. A slight wind whispered in the trees around the motte as we left it behind and felt our way along toward Bitchdaughter Tower. Somewhere an owl hooted, and further away, a dog barked once and fell silent. There was no one ahead of us yet, but we were as quiet as possible, communicating by a touch of the hand, not wanting to be seen. If we could sneak up on them, all the better.

I counted the steps. I was still sweating, and my breathing was shallow. *Please.* I no longer knew to whom I was praying, but the word echoed endlessly in my head, punctuated by the pounding of

the blood in my ears. *Please.* What would we do if we found them?
What would we do if we were too late?
Please.

Victoria Tower. Micklegate would be next, but there was that blasted
museum in the tower, and there were gates at that passageway, as
well as at the foot of the stairs. I wanted to scream in frustration,
call out Genevieve's name, Paul's. Instead I felt my way along,
staying close to the parapets. Whatever Neil's plan, this would not
be the place to carry it out—on one side, a grassy knoll leading
down to a street of row houses; on the other, a road over which an
occasional car or late night lorry rumbled. No, whatever he was
thinking of doing, he would be looking for someplace where there
was no way to be seen. But where could that be? The older sections
of York criss-crossed to our right; the newer parts grew outward
and away to our left. The walls, instead of being the final bastions
as they had been in the Medieval period, now were only decorative
pauses in the sprawl of the city.

Micklegate loomed, the anonymous saints keeping watch atop
the corners of the guardhouse. I pressed closely to the wall, hiding
in the deeper shadows, as we approached.

"This looks like trouble," Lance whispered. "Probably security
cameras. Probably locked."

I shook his words off impatiently. Then I kicked something in
the darkness, something that skittered with a dry rasp across the
stones.

"What the hell?"

Lance flicked his flashlight on, holding it low, cupping a hand
around it.

A hat lay upturned before us, the crown dented where my foot
had sent it spinning.

Genevieve's broad-brimmed pith helmet, spattered with rain.

I caught my breath.

If there had been any doubt before, there was none now. She was up here, had come this way. Had dropped this hat in the hopes that someone would find it, would read it as the clue it was meant to be.

Without thinking, I bent to grab it. Lance had moved ahead to check the first gate into the passageway.

"Unlocked," he whispered.

I let him lead the way through to the other side. If there were security cameras, and alarms, we'd just have to risk it. The far gate was not only unlocked, but not even fully closed. It squealed as Lance pushed it, and I winced. I squeezed through after him and pushed it closed; it swung open an inch or two, stubbornly.

Somewhere in the city, a church bell rang. Two? Was it two in the morning? I checked the time on my Fitbit.

She was here. They were here. But where?

"Put the light out," I hissed.

"What? Oh—"

We kept on. The inside of the wall now faced flat-roofed industrial buildings, a construction site. We were close to the place where the wall had been breached for the railway lines, before the newer train station had been built. And that's when I heard her voice.

Thirty-nine

S he stood, as always, with her spine straight, her shoulders
thrown back. She held both her hands before her, loosely
clasped, but not on the knob of the blackthorn. Without her
hat, the rain had matted her hair; the stones on which she stood
glittered darkly.

Neil held the walking stick.

He had his back to us, had not heard our steps. I stopped abruptly,
put a quick hand out to keep Lance from moving forward.

I couldn't see Paul.

That meant nothing. Genevieve and Neil stood under the shadow
of overhanging branches from the trees growing to the left side of
the wall. The lights from the parking lot below them on the inside
of the wall cast upwards, and I could make out the sharpness of
Genevieve's cheekbones, and a bit of the angry glitter in her eyes.
She *was* angry, I could tell, from the tautness of her angular body;
but it was a cold anger, a calculated anger—I could almost feel the
waves of iciness flowing away from her, and wondered fleetingly
how Neil could not sense it.

Then again, Neil had made a blind mistake. I could see it
now, the way his mind was working. He thought he was forcing
Genevieve up here, in darkness, in the middle of the night, to
stage an accident. After all, hadn't she said that her doctor had

251

wanted her to move into assisted living, for her own safety, because she was an old woman? Who was to say she hadn't become confused, she who was known to walk the circuit of the wall every single day, and hadn't come up here at night to do the same thing? Who was to say she hadn't met with an unfortunate fall in the rain? Who would notice that she was missing from her home, from her daily constitutional, for a while, perhaps several days? How long would it take for her body to be found, should she fall from the wall, especially here? *Did she fall or was she pushed?* In my near hysteria, I had to press my hand to my mouth to keep from giggling. Because Neil, though—he thought he had brought an old woman up onto the wall, but what he didn't think about carefully enough was that he'd brought a *spy*. And she was far more intelligent—wily—than he gave her credit for. Still. Far more intelligent than any of us.

"Ever killed anyone before?" she was asking now. Genially. Her voice that of a barely interested bystander. She made a curious motion with her fingers, and I realized that she had seen us. That she was directing us. As she had been directing us all along, leaving her clues, unlocking her gates.

Neil shifted the walking stick to his other hand. "It can't be that hard."

"No?"

"And it's not killing someone. It's an accident. You are going to be having an unfortunate accident."

"Unfortunate for me, you mean. Perhaps unfortunate for Aventurine."

A bark of a laugh. "She doesn't enter into it anymore."

Lance's hand on my arm, squeezing. I bit my lip, trying to still my breathing. I *didn't enter into it*? I needed to kill Neil, and *I* had surely never killed anyone before. I inched forward.

The gesture again, from Genevieve's long fingers. *Don't.*

"She'll fight you, you know," Genevieve observed amiably. "This isn't twenty-five years ago. She's changed. She's far stronger than you give her credit for being."

"My word against hers."

The tilt of the head, the ironic lift of the lips, obvious even in the strange lighting. "Her word? Perhaps you should say *her words.*"

"Enough."

Neil's timbre changed. She was getting under his skin. She was provoking him.

There was a slight sound, a shuffle, like wind brushing dried leaves along the ground—then gone. I thought I saw the shadows around Genevieve rearrange themselves slightly.

"Aventurine's famous now, you know. That first theft? A mere bump in the road for her."

"Ancient history."

"She's left you behind in the proverbial dust. She's got a loyal following now, an audience who eagerly awaits her next book." I could still feel the icy anger wafting from Genevieve, and I was amazed at how detached her voice remained. *Training*, she would have said dismissively. *Years of practice.*

"They'll have to wait. This is the book that's going to make *me.* It's going to make *my* career."

Genevieve kept on, as though he had not spoken. "Her readers, and her editors—they all recognize her voice. They all recognize her style. They'll know that you did not write this book." Her voice was suddenly hard. "They'll know it isn't yours."

"I said *enough*—"

"They'll know you for the liar and the thief you are—"

It was the sharpened arrow that did it. Neil hefted the blackthorn stick, knob end out, and swung at the old woman with all his might. I wrested my arm away from Lance and rushed forward, but everything in front of me seemed to play out in single frames, an old movie slowed down.

Genevieve's duck.

The force of the swing staggering Neil to one side.

Paul, separating himself from the shadows, swinging the other walking stick over Genevieve's crouching form, and connecting, with a hollow, sickening sound, with the side of Neil's head.

Forty

There were definitely parts of the next several minutes I wanted desperately to forget.

Not much blood. For that I was grateful. The rain was becoming steadier, and, even now, was diluting it, washing it away.

Lance leapt to Paul's side as my nephew dropped the blackthorn stick and cupped his hands over his mouth. The walking stick rattled as it rolled atop the stones, perilously close to the edge.

"Get that," Genevieve directed me in a hiss. "Don't let it fall."

I did as I was told, even as she stripped off her jacket and wrapped it around Neil's head.

"Is he—"

She threw a quick glance over her shoulder at the boys. "Don't you be sick, Paul," she instructed. "Not here. Not now." She bent to go through his pockets. She was, I saw now, wearing gloves. His keys she kept. The battered envelope she handed to me.

"His wallet?" I asked.

"Amateur," she shot back. "That makes it look more suspicious."

A dead person on the wall *not* suspicious? With blunt trauma to the head?

The gaping mouth, the wide surprised eyes—they would haunt me, I knew. Neil alive had been the thing of my nightmares. This would be even worse.

"Hurry," she said. "Help me get him up."

"Should we call someone?" Lance asked.

Genevieve ignored the question. "Get his shoulders," she said to me. She indicated his legs, crossed at a ridiculous angles. "Come on, you two. I need you to pull yourselves together."

We lifted Neil's body. Awkward, heavy: this was what people meant by *dead weight*. Genevieve still held the jacket around his head, raised above the level of the parapet.

"What—"

Quickly she whipped the coat away, then grabbed his thighs and pushed upward. The weight shifted. I lost my grip. Neil tumbled over the wall head first, and I heard another ugly thud, hollow and rather wet this time, before there was a crashing of leaves and branches as his body plunged into the blackness below.

I heard Paul gasping for breath behind me.

"*Don't* be sick," Genevieve said again. She turned to me. "Have you got the stick there? And the hat? Let's go."

We closed and locked each gate behind us, all the way back to Baile Hill. Before we descended the steps to the street, Genevieve leaned toward Lance.

"You two turn right and get back to my house as quickly as you can, but *don't run*. Don't give anyone a reason to look at you twice. Get inside and don't turn on any lights. Wait for us."

In a few moments the boys had disappeared into the street.

"Hush," Genevieve said, when I moved to speak. I shut my mouth. She was counting under her breath; I heard a muffled clink of keys. When she reached two hundred, she beckoned me to follow. We waited for a car to pass with a hiss of tires, then left the shadow of the little tower, crossed the road, and stepped out onto Skeldergate Bridge. We did not stop, but with a quick flick of her hand, Genevieve tossed something over the rail. I heard the slightest of *plops*. We kept walking. I said nothing.

We let ourselves in—Lance and Paul had locked the door behind them—and set our burdens down in the front hallway. Genevieve waited while I went through the two bags we'd retrieved from Neil's car: my computer, my phone, my thumb drives—it was all there. The two boys were in the kitchen, perched atop stools at the island in the center, shrouded in darkness. As directed, they had not turned on any lights. Genevieve flicked a switch, and a glow appeared over the sink.

"I made tea," Lance offered.

Wordlessly, Paul moved to a cupboard and withdrew two more mugs.

Genevieve patted Lance on the shoulder. "You're a good boy," she said. "Who are you?"

"This is Lance," Paul said. "He's a friend."

Genevieve looked at them both sharply. "I hope you're a really good friend, Lance," she said, tilting her head. "Because now you two are inextricably bound together. You're an accessory after the fact."

Paul raised his head to meet Lance's eyes. He still looked frightened, his face pale, his throat working.

"I killed him, didn't I?" he ground.

Genevieve poured herself a cup of tea, fixing it as she liked; then, looking at my shaking hands, she shook her head and filled my cup for me. Black. Steaming. I lifted the mug with two hands and took a scalding, bracing sip.

"He was dead when he went over the wall," she said. She lifted her cup to her lips, gazing at him over the brim.

Paul put his face in his hands.

"Have you been sick already?" she asked, and there was a note of concern in her voice. Just a small one, but it still surprised me. She did not give much away.

Without lifting his face, Paul shook his head.

"Go do it now. We'll wait."

Without looking at any of us, Paul shoved his stool away from the table. He stumbled on his way out into the hallway, and we heard the door to the toilet slam. Lance half-stood, but Genevieve put her hand on his arm once again.

"Leave him alone," she said quietly. "Drink your tea. Then I need you to make a fire in the wood burner, please." She turned to me. "Message your sister. She's landing in a few hours. Have her take the first possible train from King's Cross. I think we need her up here. And have her pay cash for the ticket."

Wheels within wheels. I didn't understand the reasoning behind half her planning; but she was the spy, and I would simply have to trust her. She had done all this since she was little more than a child. I drained my mug and set it down on the island. "What will happen?"

The words fell between us, the worry we all had.

Paul returned, his face white, his hair wet where he had sluiced himself. He sat, dragging his stool closer to Lance.

Genevieve topped off her tea before speaking. "We've bought some time—I'm not certain how much."

"By—disposing—of Neil?"

Her eyebrows lifted and fell. "By disposing of him *there*. It's just about the only place on the entire circuit of that wall where there is tree growth, undergrowth, all the way up to the base. Because of the hill, there won't be dog-walkers there. It's going to take a while for the body to be found. By then, you all will be away, our incriminating bits of evidence will have been destroyed, and if anyone thinks that an old woman could possibly be involved, well, they'll find that she had no way to get up on the wall in the middle of the night anyway."

"Your keys?" Lance asked.

I closed my eyes, heard again the *plop*. "In the river," I told him.

"Wait," Paul said, his voice strained, as he held up an uncertain hand. "*When* he's found, he'll have his wallet. His ID. He'll be easily identified."

Genevieve shrugged. "That's fine. He'll have his money and his credit cards, too, so it'll look less like a robbery. All we want is that he not be connected to us."

"*His* keys, though?" Lance asked.

"With his rental car, which we found several streets over." Genevieve had pushed the unlock button on the key fob as we made our way back to the house, peering down every side street until we saw the tell-tale flash from the lights. "They're under the gas cap cover." She stood to take her tea mug to the sink. "And now, Lance and I are going to burn my jacket and the walking stick, and tomorrow I'll clean out the ashes and scatter them somewhere conveniently far away from here. You two need to go to sleep. Choose any of the rooms upstairs—they're all ready should I have unexpected guests."

I collected Paul's half-empty cup with my own and brought it to the sink. He seemed incapable of movement suddenly.

"You're so calculating," he said to Genevieve, his voice low, and there was awe, and possibly a tinge of horror there. "You've thought of everything."

She stopped, resting one veined hand on the countertop, and looked into his face with something akin to pity. "I've been doing this a long time, Paul," she said gently, echoing my thoughts. "You forget: I was younger than you are when I killed my first man."

He met her eyes, and for the longest moment, they just stared at one another. Then, finally, Paul nodded, as though coming to a realization, or an agreement. Then he stood and followed me into the hall to the stairs.

Forty-one

I awoke to the pleasantly domestic and frighteningly incongruous scent of breakfast: coffee, bacon, something with cinnamon in it. When I opened my eyes, I was confused. The windows were in the wrong place for this to be my bedroom in my own house; they were too low and wide to be the ones in the guest house in Southampton. The curtains moved gently, and sunlight forced its way around them. I pressed the button on the side of my Fitbit to see the time, but the battery had died.

Then I remembered. Horrified, I closed my eyes tightly, then opened them again. The room, a guest room on the first floor of Genevieve Smithson's house, formed itself. The events of the night before did, too. The rain, the fear, Neil's open eyes and white, still face. The sound as we dropped him over the edge of the wall.

I was an accessory to murder.

The murder of my former lover.

Then I berated myself. I might be an accessory, but I could still see Paul's stricken face, hear his strangled voice. *I killed him, didn't I?* If he hadn't, I would have. With my bare hands, if I'd had to.

I wondered, as I dragged myself out of the bed and searched around for my clothes, how Paul would ever learn to live with that knowledge.

But then, I supposed again, Genevieve had done it, as barely

260

more than a child. *I killed my first man at sixteen.* How casually she spoke those words. Perhaps she could teach Paul how to deal with what he had done. Though something told me that they were vastly different personalities, and those personalities would make all the difference in their abilities to assimilate the weight of their actions.

Dressed except for shoes, I stopped at the head of the stairs and listened. Noises from the kitchen: clinks, a scrape of spatula against pan, the groan of the oven door closing. Then voices. Genevieve's, and yes, my sister's. Micheline's. Tears sprang to my eyes at the sound I had known from preconsciousness. I turned back to knock on the door of the room Paul had chosen.

"Are you awake?" I called. "Your mother's here."

It was Lance who opened the door, brushing his dark hair from his eyes with a shaking hand. His glance darted to the stairs and back. "He's in the shower," he said. "We'll be down in a minute."

I hadn't seen Micheline since we'd left her house for Logan Airport. Yet that hadn't been that long ago, only a couple of weeks. When I met her eyes over the countertop in Genevieve's kitchen, I felt the familiar relief: *everything would be all right.* Somehow seeing my sister had always made me know I was home and safe.

Wordlessly she pushed her stool away from the island and stood; she held her arms out and we moved into each other's embrace. My other half, my mirror image.

"Are you okay?" she murmured into my hair.

"Are you?"

When we drew back, she had tears on her lashes. My own eyes were wet.

"I'm sorry, Mick," I said, still holding onto her. My voice felt thick in my throat.

"Me, too."

We were sorry for different things, but we knew that. One of the greatest joys of being a twin was how well we understood one another.

Then, "He's coming down." I knew that's what she needed to hear, where her heart moved next. "He and Lance. Once he gets out of the shower."

Genevieve clucked, flipping crumpets on the griddle. She tested them, then used her spatula to remove the rings. "He'd better hurry. We need to get everyone straight with the plan, and get you all away."

"Away?" I hadn't thought that far ahead.

She threw an impatient look over her shoulder. "You all need to leave York until the body is discovered, and have little or nothing to do with me or this place until I tell you the proverbial coast is clear."

"But—the book—"

"Can wait. Unless you want to be around for the investigation into Neil's death? Unless you want those boys—" she waved the spatula at the ceiling— "to be caught up in it?"

Micheline's grip on my arm tightened. She sucked in a sharp breath.

"Genevieve told you?"

But it was Genevieve who answered. "I met her at the station, brought her back here while all of you were sleeping it off."

I spun back to Genevieve. "Did you even go to bed last night?"

"I slept a little." She checked the undersides of the crumpets, adjusted the heat beneath them. In another pan, bacon sizzled away, and she prodded each piece, frowning.

Thumping echoed from the front stairs. The boys entered. Immediately Micheline turned, but she left her hand on my arm.

Paul hung back at the door into the hallway. I saw Lance's frown, saw him prod Paul slightly.

The atmosphere was suddenly thick with expectation and longing, with tension, with words unspoken. Electric. Uncomfortable.

"Paul," Micheline whispered.

He licked his lips.

Her hand was trembling on my arm.

And that's when I broke. I loved that boy like no other. But I loved my sister more.

"Goddamn it, Paul," I exclaimed impatiently. "Hug your mother."

He lifted his eyes to mine, his look half frightened, half accusatory. I lifted my chin, and shoved Micheline forward.

"*Hug your mother,*" I repeated, and turned away.

Genevieve set a plate of bacon and crumpets on the island in front of me. A teacup on its saucer already stood there, next to the familiar pot.

"By the time the 'Find Friends' signal disappeared, when the battery in Avi's cell phone died, we were already most of the way to York. It was easy to figure out where Neil was going. I didn't have to follow him; I just had to park somewhere near." Paul gulped, then took a sip from his coffee. It was too hot, and he winced, then took another sip, as though trying to punish himself. "I left the car, found Genevieve's door unlocked and the keys missing. It wasn't difficult to figure out what was going on after that." He set the cup down, put a crumpet on his plate.

Genevieve passed him the jar of marmalade, and Paul held it for a moment as though having forgotten what to do with it. "So you took a weapon and came after me," she said.

"Don't you say it," I broke in. "That you didn't need his help. That you had been looking out for yourself for all these years. Don't you say it."

Genevieve sipped her own tea. We had moved into the parlor, had scraped chairs across the Oriental carpets to huddle before the fireplace, in which the wood burner still gave off a bit of heat, having devoured the evidence Genevieve and Lance had fed it in the night.

"It's done, Aventurine. Paul came. And he was useful."

Paul's slight jerk did not go unnoticed. Lance put a hand to his arm on one side, Micheline on the other.

"But where were you?" Lance demanded. "You were up there. We never saw you."

"On the far side of Micklegate Bar. In the shadows. I was following their path, just as you were doing. I heard you."

I refrained from asking why he hadn't waited for us.

It's done. I felt again the rush of air, saw the swing, the duck, the counterswing. Paul had done what he had done. For Genevieve, that was enough. Perhaps it should be for me as well. And if it wasn't, I could always ask later.

Some of it still made no sense.

"He was ahead of you, Paul. Neil. He'd left hours before."

It was Genevieve who answered. "Traffic. The car transporters out of the port of Southampton. Neil got stuck in a tailback, he told me, for hours, or he 'would have been here sooner.'"

I thought of our own cursing at the slow traffic coming out of Southampton, and now was grateful for it. At least ours had not been stand-still traffic.

Paul nodded. "I met some of it, but it was thinning out down there by the time I took off. I was able to make up some time."

"And then, of course, Neil didn't want to go out on the wall until well after dark." Genevieve drank more tea. She had not, I noticed, eaten any of the breakfast she had prepared for us all. Breakfast at two in the afternoon. Brunch? Lunch? No matter. She simply drank tea, holding her cup above her saucer, her eyes flitting from one to another of us over the brim. Considering. Analyzing.

Her words took a moment to sink in. Micheline got there first.

"How long," she said, her voice low, "was he here?"

The china clicked gently as Genevieve lowered her cup to the saucer. "A few hours." Her eyes were steady.

A few hours.

"What the hell, Genevieve?" I demanded.

She turned to me.

"I had a counterplan, Aventurine," she said calmly. "I let him go through things. I let him look at the box upstairs. I answered all his questions." There was her slight ironic smile, quickly bitten back.

I was having difficulty understand all of this. Any of this. "You answered his questions."

She shrugged. "Perhaps not entirely truthfully. After all, I *have* been interrogated before, by people with far more—how shall we put it?—panache?"

I looked at her closely. *Interrogated.* I had listened to her stories. I knew how many layers that word had. But she was giving nothing away.

Paul's breath, though, was a hiss. "Did he hurt you, Genevieve?"

The question fell, a stone into water, ripples moving outward. Everyone stilled, the question an obscenity. Neil hurt people. Neil had hurt me. It turned out that he would not have hesitated at hurting an old woman, should that have enabled him to get what he wanted.

When she turned to look at him, her expression softened, almost to kindness. She looked, for a fleeting moment, as though she might have been someone's kindly old grandmother, had things been different. "That's something, my dear boy, that you should never worry about. Unless—" and her voice was surprisingly gentle— "it lessens the guilt."

Paul bit his lip, but held her gaze. After a moment, he nodded. Just once.

For a while no one spoke. The enormity of what we were all now a party to: it was as though Neil, in death, had joined us at the low table, head still wrapped in Genevieve's jacket. We busied ourselves with the remains of our brunch, but I realized after a moment that

I was only pushing the last bit of bacon, the last bite of crumpet, around on my plate; and when I looked up, it was obvious that the others had also lost their appetites. Except Genevieve, who had never had one; even now, she leaned back in her chair, sipping at her tea, watching each of us in turn.

"One last thing." *For now.* My reporter's brain was sluggishly turning over, an engine that had long ago run out of fuel. "The place on the wall. That place."

Genevieve nodded in approval. "Very good. Yes. I chose it. To make my last stand, as it were."

It had been difficult to see in the dark, but I had walked that route with her repeatedly, had her point out landmarks, explain the brass markers embedded in the stone underfoot. I closed my eyes, and I could make out the gleaming dark circle partially obscured by Neil's leg. I could see the trees growing up to the side of the wall, the old engine shed off to the side, the road down at the foot of the overgrown hill.

"I led him there." She was, as usual, following my thoughts even before I'd fully realized them.

"If—things—had gone the other way—"

Again the shrug. "Then my gamble wouldn't have paid off. As it is, it did, and I bought us all time. He won't be found for a while, Aventurine, and that means it's time for you all to gather your things and be off together. Might I suggest another music festival? There's another one coming up this week in East Anglia. I believe Mobius is on Friday night, and again Sunday afternoon. They're friends of yours, aren't they?"

After I'd helped Genevieve carry the dishes into the kitchen and load the washer, I found Micheline in the front hallway, leaning against the newel post, looking upwards after Paul and Lance, her expression pensive.

"Is he a good boy?" she asked, keeping her voice low. "This Lance?"

"I think so."

She looked so worried, so grief-stricken, lines etched between her brows, at the corners of her mouth. All the heartbreak she had withstood for the past year: it was hard for me to think about her in that pain, because that pain became mine, lodged tightly under my breastbone. I stood behind her, and leaned my forehead into her shoulder. It had been our way, for all our lives, the way we connected to one another. I wondered, sometimes, whether we had established that pattern in the womb, whether that was even possible.

Now, slowly, she turned around. We leaned our foreheads together. With my eyes closed, I groped for and found her hands.

"And you," she whispered. "Did he hurt you?"

She didn't have to say his name. She didn't even have to define *hurt*. I was grateful for that. It was better not to hear it from her lips.

"I don't know," I said. Because I still didn't. It worried me, not being able to remember; but at the same time, I wondered if perhaps that wasn't best. Because if I didn't know, I could make up my own mind. And I knew that I would decide that it never happened.

"If he wasn't dead," Micheline said, "I'd kill him."

"I know."

It was then that I remembered Shep's letter, the one Neil had stolen, the one Genevieve had taken from his pocket. It was in the duffle bag Genevieve and I had brought back from Neil's rental car, and that duffle bag, ratty-looking in the morning light, lay on the chair at the foot of the stairs to my left. I would have to get it out for her, but to do that would mean letting go, and I didn't want to do that. Standing here, foreheads pressed together, hands clasped with my sister's: this was home, wherever we were. After the past couple of weeks, I desperately needed that home.

But my sister needed her husband, and I had the only piece of him she could have now.

I took a deep breath, stepped away, and opened the bag. The letter, now damp, smudged, and with a corner crushed, lay atop the rest of my things.

"We got it back," I said, holding it out. "He didn't get a chance— it isn't opened."

Micheline stared down at the envelope in my palms for a minute, her hands crushed to her lips. Shep's spiky handwriting, spelling out her name, stared back up at her.

"I'm afraid of what he wanted to tell you, Mick." I wanted to protect her from what I'd worked out. I needed to. Still I held the envelope out.

Her gaze flicked upward and dropped again. She squeezed her eyes shut for a moment, and then nodded almost imperceptibly. At last she put out a shaking hand to take it.

"I'll go up and get my things," I said, and left her alone in the front hall with her husband's last words to her.

Forty-two

We took both rental cars, neither of which, surprisingly, had a ticket from a parking warden.

"Can't we turn one in?" Paul asked. He yawned, shrugged his way into his sweatshirt. "We can all ride together."

"Not up here, you can't," Genevieve reminded him. "These cars were never in York last night."

Lance frowned. "Traffic cameras. Surveillance cameras."

"Not that one," Micheline said, jerking her chin in the direction of the one at the corner. The lens hung from the front of the cameral by some frayed wiring.

I looked at Genevieve. She was looking at the ground, tapping her foot impatiently, both hands on the knob of the one remaining blackthorn stick, the other having met its fiery end in the wood burner early this morning.

"The powers that be won't know to look for you unless we make a mistake," she said. "So take the cars, turn one in in Norfolk if you have to. But go."

Micheline indicated the car I'd rented. "I'll ride with you, Paul."

"No," I said. "They won't know to look for us unless we make a mistake. And Paul's not on the contract for this car. I need to drive. Lance has to drive the one he rented."

"But—"

269

"We can't afford to make mistakes."

Paul went with Lance to the other car with much better grace than his mother practiced, as she climbed into my Renault.

I turned back to Genevieve. "When will I see you again?"

She adjusted her hat with one hand. Today she wore a jacket similar to the one which had disappeared in the night, though in a sporting—and somewhat carefree—raspberry color. "We'll play it by ear, Aventurine. I'll be in touch. But not—" and she cocked her head and looked at me sharply— "for a while. Let's see how things settle out."

"But surely—your contacts—"

Genevieve shook her head. "My contacts *might* be willing to take care of me, and I say that with expedience in mind. But their willingness does not extend to you, nor to the boy." She glanced after him, and her expression momentarily softened. Then she returned to her brisk self. "Get in the car, Aventurine. Go to the festival. See your Mobius friends. It might be wise to sleep with your old boyfriend Gio, if you can find him, to throw up smoke should that be necessary. Then go home, work on your article draft, figure out what else you need, and *do nothing until I let you know.*"

I desperately wanted to hug her, but knew she would not welcome the demonstration of affection. Anyway, she had turned and was now making her way along the pavement, away from us, her back straight as ever, her carriage resolute, her blackthorn stick clicking punctuation as she headed for her daily circuit of the city walls.

By the time I had climbed into the driver's seat and clicked the seatbelt, then looked up in the rearview, Genevieve was gone.

Acknowledgments

I had a lot of help on this one. Any errors are entirely my own. I've also taken some liberties, for which I hope I'll be forgiven; for example, you'll just have to accept that Genevieve Smithson has her *ways*, having been an agent for most of her life, and has managed to acquire keys to the gates on the York walls. She's not like us, or like Aventurine—we couldn't do it.

I'd like to thank the following:

Beryl Escott, for her endlessly fascinating *The Heroines of the SOE: Britain's Secret Women in France;* and Russell Braddon for the more specific *Nancy Wake: SOE's Greatest Heroine.* I can only hope Genevieve does these women justice—and perhaps leads readers to find out more about the real women who fought the secret war in France.

Thanks are also necessary for my travel and research companions:

First, Lynne Doble, who put up with my heavy-handed dictation of destinations in Southampton and York. I hope you had fun, even while you had to deal with my getting carried away, because I love research so much.

Second, to Steve Allen and Lesley Collett, of the Reluctant Ramblers, the Commoners Choir, and the collection of loyal followers of Oysterband, who first encouraged me—I don't know how long ago—to walk the York city walls; it took me years, but I finally got there to do it in Lesley's company. Thanks for helping me plan a murder! The looks we got were interesting, to say the least. Thanks to Lesley, too, for not only going back to check on gates and things when my memory and photos failed; and for the traffic information out of Southampton, including the bit about the car transporter lorries. And thanks for the Monk Bar chocolates!

Third, to the Wickham Music Festival, Folk East, and the New Forest Folk Festival. Without going to see John Jones and the Reluctant Ramblers, Oysterband, Ray Cooper, Bellowhead, Merry Hell, Benji Kirkpatrick and the Excess, Rachael McShane and the Cartographers, the Urban Folk Quartet, Gigspanner Big Band, Three Daft Monkeys, and so many others, I would not have been able to give Aventurine and Paul the experience. Thanks—I'll be back. Perhaps Aventurine and Paul will be, too.

Thanks to PlumHall, whom I met after their set at the New Forest Folk Festival, for their song "Mary," which was so synchronous that I recognized it immediately as the theme song for *Aventurine*.

Thanks to Rosalie S. C. Bowman, who gave me the lowdown on the Find Friends feature for iPhone: when one is in doubt about cell phones, one should always consult one's youngest child. Aventurine thanks you, Sweetheart.

Thanks to my favorite wild swimmer, Nick Cant.

Thanks to the stall attendant at Tools for Self-Reliance at the New Forest Music Festival, for trying to sell me a scythe. I had to pass on that bargain, because we couldn't figure out how I'd get it on the plane.

Thanks to Ruth Foley, not just for the crumpet rings, but for volunteering to be the manager of Mobius. Really, they aren't an easy bunch. Drive carefully!

Thanks to Ian Blake, for the convoluted and painful history of The Little Crumps: the Bognor Regis combo, not the group from Penzance. Definitely *not* the Bore of Britain, thanks also for the urban exploration, including Southwark Cathedral and the

Refectory tea room; and for the Fox and Anchor in Farringdon: the pub where I learned just how much copious note-taking fits on the back of a British Rail ticket.

Thanks to Fran Berge, for the *Queen of Sass* picture, which hangs now over my desk. Also, for the new Oysterband/June Tabor CD, for listening while I work. And for the ride from Southampton to Oxford in the middle of the night.

Thanks to Julia Hawkes-Moore and Roger O'Neill, for the compass in case I get lost (which I frequently do), and for the aventurine necklace, which I wore to channel good fortune while writing.

Thanks to the Lord Camden Inn for taking such great care of us when Aventurine and I holed up on the fourth floor for several days in a January snowstorm for revisions. You guys are the best!

And as always, more thanks than I can say to Brenda Sparks Prescott and Rebecca Bearden Welsh, for whom Simply Not Done lives on every February.

About the Author

A nne Britting Oleson lives and writes from the mountains of Central Maine. A frequent traveler to the U.K., she has ublished four previous novels, and four poetry chapbooks. She as three children, five grandchildren, and two cats.

If you enjoyed reading this book,
please consider writing your honest review
and sharing it with other readers.

Many of our Authors are happy to participate in
Book Club and Reader Group discussions.
For more information, contact us at info@encirclepub.com.

Thank you,
Encircle Publications

For news about more exciting new fiction, join us at:

Facebook: www.facebook.com/encirclepub

Twitter: twitter.com/encirclepub

Instagram: www.instagram.com/encirclepublications

Sign up for Encircle Publications newsletter and specials:
eepurl.com/cs8taP

9 781645 993131